ISBN-9798360253969

Cover design by the author

Library of Congress Control Number: 2022948946
Printed in the United States of America

War is hell.
-General William Tecumseh Sherman

* * *

If you're going through hell, keep going.
-Sir Winston Churchill

CONTENTS

VESTIBULE :

a passage, hall, or room
between the outer door and the
interior of a building:
a lobby or antechamber

Midway on our life's journey,
I found myself
In dark woods,
the right road lost.

-Dante, Inferno Canto I

J ohn Allmen, having knocked off the first task on his to-do list that day, went about the second and quit his job with a famous Swiss-based investment bank. It was a rainy Thursday in April. He worked up his courage, along with his blood alcohol content, over two steins of heavy caramel colored German bock at a beer hall called Schroeder's. The bar managed to stay just shy of Epcot Center kitschy, except when the tourists were in. And that day the tourists were in, wearing shorts because it was California and getting drunk because it was raining. Not for the first time, he wondered how much money was made selling sweatshirts to people from the Midwest who froze their usually ample asses off on the Golden Gate. Only because they were unaware that it was always foggy and frigid when crossing the Bay and the gateway to the Pacific.

He paid his bill, and left a generous tip for Sara, his bartender. In less busy times she tended to tell him way too much about her somewhat kinky sex life, but today ball gags and leather were lacking. A curt nod, a brief smile and a "Hullo John" were all she could muster. Beers needed pouring and he watched her hourglass form recede to the other side of the bar as he hunched into his suit coat for the two-block walk to the looming tower on California Street.

On the thirtieth floor he waived at the grandmother manning the reception desk. She looked up briefly and returned the waive, glancing at her calendar to make sure she hadn't missed an appointment or something for him. Reassured, she returned to the cat videos she'd downloaded onto her phone.

"Isn't technology something Mr. Allmen?" She'd once asked. "Should I own more tech stocks in my 401k?"

Sure thing Agnes, though if you'd been getting good tips from the folks on the thirtieth floor all these years you shouldn't still be working in your late seventies.

He took the back way and stepped into the Gnome Garden, a collection of desks in various states of condemnation. They lined the walls leaving an open common area in the middle that had comfortable chairs from the Ford administration and was strewn with financial newspapers and pizza boxes. A dry erase board hung crookedly on the far wall and someone had long ago written in permanent marker:

Abandon all hope all ye who enter here!

The room had the smell of desperation reserved for hospitals, sales meetings, and Star Trek conventions. Amidst it all stood a three-foot tall garden gnome that someone had installed as a joke or as an homage to a home they rarely saw. No one remembered when, and no one took credit for the mascot, probably meaning that he or she was long ago chewed up by the machinery of selling hope and fear on Main Street USA. Regardless, the legacy lived on as the junior financial advisors inhabiting this jungle were nicknamed gnomes. Anonymous faces that came and went, usually without comment from the inhabitants of the plush offices on the other side of the building. Over there, Vice Presidents of Finance lunched with crystal service and demonstrated buy and sell strategies on multimedia projection units in the conference rooms.

Careful not to touch anything, Allmen slipped through unnoticed as gnomes hammered at their phones, and pitched stocks, bonds and mutual funds to angry dinner eaters pulled away from the most recent episode of America's Got Talent. This was where the grunt work happened, and it was rarely pretty. It was also where a young business school dropout named John Allmen had cut his teeth and nearly his wrists until he'd made himself into someone by short selling his way through the 2008 financial crisis. But that was nearly a decade ago. And it was time to give it all up.

He forced a smile and walked into Bob Strong's office unannounced.

"Something has to change here," Strong was saying to the ceiling. "And it isn't us. Work harder. Make more calls, it's a numbers game." Robert Strong had been a source of disappointment to those who judged him by his name before meeting him since his first chess camp. His thick glasses and balding head did nothing to take attention from his weak chin or expanding paunch. His entire life was apparently a misnomer. "Got a minute Bob?"

"Yeah sure. Listen," he turned back to the sweating twenty something in front of him, "be more like this guy and you'll be just fine. Now beat it gnome, go make us some money."

John stopped the kid with an outstretched hand. "Wait. I've seen you before. What is your name?"

"Gary."

"Gary, hang on for a second, okay? I promise, it will be worth your time."

Stepping around the confused inhabitant of the gnome jungle, he got to the point. "Bob, I'm done. I'm quitting the business. And I want Greg here to take over my clients, run my book."

"My name is Gary," the gnome half whined.

"Shut up," Bob growled.

"Bob, that is no way to speak to a future Vice President of Investments," John chided. He pulled his best "tsk-tsk" face.

"You shut up too," Strong countered. "This shit isn't funny. We've all got work to do."

"Nope, sorry Bob. *You* have work to do. I'm serious. I quit. And I've had my eye on, uh, Gary here for quite some time. I think he will be a worthy successor."

Strong arched an eyebrow. It gave Allmen the feeling he was being chided by a Muppet in an expensive suit. "What school did Gary go to?"

"Fuck, I don't know...Davis?"

"I went to Cal," sighed the gnome. "Sorry Mr. Allmen."

"Cal? Jesus, was Google not hiring the week you signed on? Bob, clearly this kid is overqualified to be peddling tax free bonds to the merchants in China Town. His ship has come in." He gave an expansive wave toward the other side of the building. "The future is calling."

Strong was unconvinced, his dome of a forehead creased in frustration. Allmen stared out the window past his bald pate. It was coming down in buckets and he suddenly craved a drink, something stronger than beer. He needed a change of clothes and a martini.

"You are a President's Club Producer, a rainmaker!" Strong practically whined.

"Well, mission accomplished," Allmen drawled pointing out the window with a sly grin. Fat raindrops were beginning to pool on the windowpanes. "Time for the next adventure."

"Listen, I know things haven't been easy for you these last few years. But this is no way to cope." Strong put on his best Dr. Phil face and almost succeeded at looking like he truly cared.

Allmen felt a pang, fought the familiar urge to feel something. He pressed it down, conquered it, but did not kill it. Then he said quietly, "Free will, Bob."

"Huh? You mean the song…by Rush?"

"Sort of, yeah. But I was more thinking along the lines of William James." The lines on his forehead had disappeared and Strong looked genuinely perplexed. 'My first act of free will shall be to believe in free will.' Well, for a long time I haven't believed, haven't taken a side." He pointed at the company logo behind Strong's desk which featured an outline of the home country. "I've been Switzerland. And I didn't set out to be Switzerland, Bob. I don't want to be Switzerland, Bob. Here is my security card and my company phone. I've got some things to do. Gary, congratulations." He patted the younger man on the head and made for the door.

At a loss for words, Strong blurted out the only thing he could think of: "Don't forget you have a non-compete agreement."

Allmen paused with a Neil Peart drum solo substituting for his heartbeat. The rest of his life was in front of him. *Free will.* He extended the middle finger of his right hand as he headed back toward the elevator. The next day was Good Friday, and the US Stock markets would take a break, a respite from the madness on the street of dreams. But for Gary the gnome, born to working class Vietnamese immigrants and a proud Cal Bear, it was an Easter fucking miracle.

✳ ✳ ✳

Allmen caught a cable car because, for once, there were no tourists snapping photos from the back of it. He was feeling a bit nostalgic anyway and what is more wistful that the clickity clack of a cable car going up the hill and unfolding the wonders of San Francisco Bay? At least, that was what he was thinking as he trundled up toward Russian Hill. In reality, the storm clouds had moved in over Oakland, and he couldn't see shit past Treasure Island. It was a doleful and damp city, but he didn't notice.

What he did notice was the woman looking him up and down from across the car. Heavy makeup, more bust than was appropriate or even warranted by the weather. She was wearing leopard print yoga pants and he felt like he was being undressed by her overly made-up eyes. She caught his eye and licked her heavily painted lips leaving a momentary bright red smear on her front incisors. He felt like he was being stalked, hunted. *Russian*, he thought? *Escaped mental patient? Raiders fan?* Regardless, it was time to find other transportation. At California and Larkin, he dropped with a splash onto the street, lengthened his stride and didn't look back.

He reached for his personal phone to pull up Uber. In three minutes a small, but shiny new vehicle appeared at the curb. He noticed the iconic lion emblem, standing on his hind legs moving forward in a zombie pose and commenced the identifying ritual.

"Hey, are you Manny?"

"Yeah, you John?"

"You bet, Thanks for the ride," he said sliding into the back seat. "Is this a Peugot? Never seen one in the States."

The man grinned, clearly proud of his European anomaly. "That's right, the king of the jungle is back. They just started importing them again this year after, like, two decades. I think the new logo looks more like a drunk guy in a lion suit stumbling out of a costume party, but that is just me."

Allmen gave a nervous laugh and waited for the car to take him home. He felt in desperate need of a shower. Like most newer European cars, this one had turned itself off, the transmission powering down automatically when at idle. And usually, once put in gear or the clutch engaged, it would spring to life. But this lion of the 415 area code didn't wake. Didn't come to life. It just sat in the rain while Manny tried various automotive versions of CTRL-ALT-DEL.

"Son of a bitch!"

Allmen sighed. "The lion sleeps tonight, eh my friend?"

Manny slapped the wheel and again tried the ignition without so much a purr in response. "Never happened before, man. Sorry about this, I will cancel you out of the system."

Allmen was back on his phone looking for another ride share, but suddenly it seemed as if every car in town were on the other side of the Golden Gate, leaving him with a twelve-to-fifteen-minute wait.

He knew the cab was a mistake as soon as he hailed it, but necessity is a mother fucker. The cab swerved erratically in response to his outstretched hand, but as soon as John opened the door the driver's heavily accented English brought him to a halt in a half crouch with one foot still on the wet curb.

"I can't take you nowhere man."

"You're shitting me."

"No, man. My wife." He pointed to the pulsing blue light in his ear, a headset. "My wife," he explained. "Crazy woman. She says she sees a wolf, what am I to do?"

Allmen, living in the outer reaches of Pacific Heights had heard stories of wolves in places like Golden Gate Park and the

Presidio. There had even been a YouTube video going around the office a while back. So, he was way more annoyed than surprised. "Scared shitless," the driver continued. "Sorry man. I go. You stay. Please."

Allmen took a half step back as the cab swerved back into traffic, the door closing on its own. *Okay, I see that I am not meant to go home.* Bereft of transportation options, he decided on a stroll through Nob Hill, past the karaoke lounge, thrift store, sushi restaurant and coffee bar to what he considered the real deal. A place fit for a celebration where no one would care much about his accouterments. Along with the German bar, it was a place where he could feel authentically San Franciscan, though he was originally from a couple of hours west of Pittsburgh and didn't truly know the difference. He'd been too busy working, then trying to save a failing marriage to really bother figuring it out. But now...

Head down against the blowing rain, he narrowly avoided smacking into the oyster guy delivering twenty-pound perforated plastic sacks of saltwater mollusks. They would be delicious. He followed the smell of brine and dropped into a stool at Swan Oyster Depot, beneath the fish posters and celebrity photos. He was ready for an Anchor Steam draught and a feedbag of fish and sourdough bread. His first half dozen oysters went down in more or less record time, oozing and salty and accompanied by the vague sensation of Russian Roulette due to food borne illness. *Killed by an oyster. Ah, but what a way to go. A man should be so lucky.* He chased them with a couple of pints and was feeling good when he smelled... her. Literally become aware of her scent, which was saying something during the olfactory assault that was a raw seafood dinner. But lilac and an ocean breeze wafted in as the door opened and she leaned in and he was awash in her. Backlight by the lamps outside, he thought in a slightly tipsy internal monologue, that she was surely angelic, heaven sent. She was dressed in white, a long sweater with a high neck against the cold and her blonde hair fell in soft ringlets around it.

"I'm sorry, but did anyone ever tell you that you look like George Clooney?"

Oyster juice rocketed from his nostrils, and he pulled a napkin over his face just in time to cover the gaffe. He choked, gasped, and willed himself under control. She wore a smile like a cat and the way she slipped into the stool next to him, took her drink and sipped it without looking away, that too had a vague feline quality to it.

"Why, no. No one has ever said that to me." He sipped at his beer. "Tell the truth, I get a lot of Gregory Peck, but that is only because I work with a clientele of, shall we say, a certain vintage?"

"Ah," she sighed, "you hustle old ladies. Male escort?"

This time it was the beer that made an effort to exit via his sinuses, but he mastered the impulse. "Finance," he managed with a barely audible snort.

"How shockingly... mundane." She'd probably heard it at least a score of times if she frequented the area around the financial district.

"Tell me about it. But here is the exciting part. Actually, I'm unemployed as of an hour ago."

"Well, then, this is a celebration." She hailed the bartender and suddenly, there was champagne. Not sparkling wine or a Euro substitute, but real, fine, French Champagne that lit up his palette like Bastille Day and made the next half dozen oysters, which they shared, taste like the last meal of a condemned man. Fatty, sloppy and juicy oysters paired with neat, compact and effervescent wine. If he thought the day couldn't get any better than telling Bob Strong to shove off, he was wrong. Now, here he was sharing delicious food and a beautiful wine with a woman he knew to be beautiful, and he imagined delicious as well.

"Well," she practically purred, "If we are going to share such a decadent appetizer, I feel that it is only proper I should know your name. Before we get on to the main course, anyway."

"John." It was her turn to snort, this time fine bubbly, a napkin judiciously raised. "Sorry," she said wiping a dainty,

French manicured hand across her face, "John the john. Escort to the elderly? It struck me as funny."

"Obviously," he grinned, feeling cool. *Cool like Clooney in Ocean's Twelve. No, not a good movie, but close enough.*

"And you are?" He asked, raising an eyebrow.

"Hungry. What's for dinner?"

There was a tender, oily and unctuous octopus salad once the oysters were dispatched. And one with saucy steaming crab meat that they decided went better with a shared glass of Chardonnay. Then they moved on to that quintessential San Franciscan delicacy, lobsters flown in from Maine. They ate side by side at the counter as would be patrons queued up outside wishing horrible maladies on them to free up two more seats. The huddled masses were yearning to breathe fish.

She leaned in and asked coyly, "So, what is next for an out of work John?"

"I'm taking a trip. A series of them actually. Going to see the world and spend the money I've been hoarding like a miser for a day that might never come. I'm going to chase the eternal summer, drink too much, eat too much and then...well, I'll just see what else happens."

"Sounds like an extended bender."

"Something like that, perhaps. But first class and with a periodic change in scenery."

"So, where to first, sport?"

"No idea. Had decided to do away with details and that one has escaped me. But I know I need to get out of the rain for a while."

She reached into an expensive handbag, Kate Spade, the real kind, not a China town knockoff and handed him a business card. Heavy stock, cream colored with bold type. "My friend Virgil is exactly what you need. High end travel agent. Takes care of all the details so you don't have to. Tracks your journey start to finish and cleans up any details you need taken care of on the fly. You should call him."

Allmen pocketed the card and smiled. "I'll do that. Thanks."

She touched him then. A slight pressure with the fingers of her non-drinking hand. He felt something like an electric current pass through him. Or perhaps it was just gas bubbles from the champagne. "No, seriously John. Go call him. I'll wait. Carpe diem, seize the day, strike while the iron is hot…"

"Choose free will," he said a bit dreamily.

She cocked an eyebrow. "Sure. Cheers to free will." They clinked glasses for about the tenth time since dinner had commenced, and he stood just a tad woozily. The rain had diminished to a mere hard drizzle when he stepped outside under the bright blue awning, took the card he'd been given from his coat pocket and turned it over in his hand.

Circle Nine Travel
3005 Ninth Circle
Sausalito, CA 94965

Clever. Travel, adventure, some time to get away. It all beckoned. He reached into his other pocket and pulled out his phone and dialed.

"Circle Nine Travel, Virgil Speaking, Can I help you?"

"Yeah, Hello Virgil, my name is John Allmen."

"Yes Mr. Allmen, I was told you might be calling."

"You were?" He pegged this as a canned response, a cheap sales gimmick. "What can you do for me?"

Virgil started a chatty dialogue, giving him the medium hard sell, on and on about the value they added and how he'd personally be available for his travel concierge needs.

"Fabulous Virgil, this is the beginning of a beautiful friendship, I'm sure."

"Yes sir. And what kind of work do you need from me?"

Allmen told him. They agreed on a price and a test run of the service. Then Allmen hung up, anxious to get back to dinner.

*　*　*

The phone was ringing. No, not ringing, not really. It was some ridiculous sing song melody. And he immediately knew something was wrong. *Not scary wrong, just not right. Off. Out of sorts. Weird.*

"Mr. Allmen?" The voice was tinny and far away. He had to focus.

"Yeah?" Something shifted in the bed next to him. Blonde hair splayed across the pillows and onto the comforter. He was not in his home.

"Ah, this is Virgil. From Circle Nine Travel Services. We spoke last night?"

"We did?"

"Yes, sir. You wanted to book a trip someplace, departing as soon as you could."

"Right, sure. And?" He slid from the overstuffed bedding and padded toward a room of tile and stainless steel.

"I have something for you leaving this afternoon from SFO."

"No shit. Listen, Virgil, I'm not sure how to ask this" he muttered, closing the bathroom door, "So I'll just say it. Did I book this trip for one or two?" He cracked the door and peeked out at the bed again.

"For one sir." Allmen sighed gratefully. "But it was close, sir. She didn't let you off the hook easily."

"That a fact?"

"Yes, well, you know women."

"That I do Virgil. So, where am I headed?"

"The one o'clock flight out of SFO direct to Miami, first class of course. Rent a car and drive down US 1. Then a few days in Key West to unwind. Fishing, pool, nightlife. Be sure to catch a sunset at Mallory Square."

"You know this much about every trip you book?"

"Yes sir. It is my job."

"Great Virgil, then I know who to call if I get in any trouble"

"I'll be here."

She was half dressed when he emerged wiping cold water from his face. She looked up with dreamy eyes and slipped on a shoe, a gray high heel that matched the capri pants she wore. "I guess oysters really are an aphrodisiac, huh?"

"I never got your name." Her sweater slipped over her shoulders and she had lost none of her feline grace despite whatever had gone on the night before.

"No," she said, "no you didn't." She smiled an almost matronly smile. "Take care of yourself out there in the big blue world, John." She glided to the door and it clanged shut behind her echoing up the hallway of what looked to be a pretty nice hotel. He heard the elevator ding a second later. And that was that. It was time to get to the airport.

"Jesus, what a woman," he said to the empty hotel room.

LIMBO:

a place or state of oblivion to which persons or things are regarded as being relegated when cast aside, forgotten, past, or out of date

For these defects, and for no other evil,
we now are lost and punished just with this:
We have no hope and yet we live in longing.

-Dante, Inferno, Canto IV

"**S**ir?" Allmen turned a bleary eye from the dark landscape of Middle America hurtling past thirty-six thousand feet below. A miserable, foggy hangover had dogged him for the entire flight eastward into the darkness. "Sir? Can I refill that drink for you?"

An attempt to chase it away with the airlines half assed Bloody Mary, a mixture of watery V8 juice and vodka, had failed miserably. It left him dehydrated, debilitated, and dejected. *I'd rather you kick me in the crotch. It would at least take my mind off this hangover.*

"No thanks," he managed to croak and watched the flight attendant amble back toward the galley. Sleep, along with relief, had proven elusive, even in the relatively comfy confines of a first-class seat. She...her....the mystery woman and her splay of blonde hair kept appearing as he closed his eyes. For a moment, the stale smell of an airliner cabin sealed from the outside world like a levitating Ziploc bag, was replaced by the wafting scent of her he remembered from the Oyster Depot. He opened bloodshot eyes to the middle aged and morbidly obese management consultant in the next seat. He was sweating through his dress shirt and emitting a wheezy laugh while watching reruns of 'Friends' on the inflight entertainment system. Allmen thought for a minute he might cry.

An excruciating hour or so later, the jetliner settled dutifully onto the runway in Miami. As soon as the plane was "safely at the gate" Allmen pulled out and powered up his phone. He silenced it after a moment of it pinging and gonging like a possessed pinball game. Messages and voicemails were coming in fast and furious, led by one that caught his attention. The screen read: Missed Call- Mack Mason. Ah, Allmen wasn't the only one just landing, so too was the fallout from yesterday's fun. Mason was his largest, best and now former client, once known as Marine

15

Major Mack Mason. *Try saying that three times fast with a mouth full of MRE, the dehydrated-food-like- substances they'd shared in combat.* Mason had done what all jar headed, knuckle dragging, devil dog infantrymen do and founded a Silicon Valley start-up. *Sometimes truth is stranger than fiction.* As Allmen had joked to him on more than one occasion over port and cigars, you just couldn't make that kind of shit up. Barrel chested, brick jawed and profane to the extreme, Mason was straight out of central casting for a Marine, if not a venture capitalist. And Allmen was sure he was royally pissed.

It was just now after nine-thirty on the east coast when he finally shuffled off the plane, feeling vaguely like the dirty mat in the back seat of a San Francisco Yellow Cab. He felt the vibration as yet another text message came through and glanced down to see it was Mack again:

Mason: What the FUCK...OVER?

Simple, profane and with proper combat radio etiquette, it was a classic example of Mason's muse at work. As he strode through the airport, Allmen composed a reply, one-handed while dodging two luggage carts and what he could only assume was a ferret with a 'comfort animal' vest. *When did airplane travel turn into a ride on Noah's Ark?*

Allmen: Explain later. Retired. Fishing—Key West. OUT.

With that he turned off the phone again and slipped it into his pocket.

Leaving the departure area and turning the corner toward baggage, he saw a young Hispanic looking man holding a sign with 'Mr. Allmen' in neat block letters. John was confused. Virgil had said he'd have a rental car, not a chauffeur. He was looking forward to a drive down US-1 and began to feel a bit let down by the unannounced turn of events. He'd have to shake this interloper and straighten Virgil out when he found time.

"You looking for me?" He practically growled the question, and the man took an involuntary step backwards.

"Mr. Allmen?"

"That's me."

The man extended his hand, he took it. "My name is Caesar, and I will be your concierge."

"My what?"

"Your concierge, sir. I am to retrieve your baggage." he checked his phone, "One leather travel suitcase, jeez that won't be hard to pick out from all the other black suitcases," he smiled sarcastically at Allmen "and an Orvis fishing rod case. Yes?"

"Yes. That's right. I do have a luggage tag at least."

"Excellent. I will show you to your rental car. There is bottled water and a variety of sandwiches while you wait. Is there anything else you might like?" He saw the confusion on Allmen's face and paused. "You didn't know I was coming to greet you? Virgil didn't let you know?"

Allmen shrugged. "Might have...I turned off my phone."

Caesar feigned astonishment "You turned off your phone? Man, that's like....un-American or something."

Allmen chuckled. "Doing my bit to combat the zombie apocalypse. That is what I call it when I see someone looking at their phone while walking down the street. It's an epidemic."

Caesar was nodding. "Yeah, man, my cousin did that. Sending a text and got hit by a city bus. Splattered him all over the curb."

Allmen stood slack jawed for a second. He had a vague mental image of a mangled human body tumbling through the air. He pushed the image down and muttered "Oh, shit, I'm sorry, I didn't know...I mean, I didn't mean to..."

Caesar held up a hand to check him. "No problem Mr. Allmen. He was an idiot. Total bottom feeder, man. I think God was just, you know, reaching down with one of those plastic skimmer nets to clean out the gene pool." Allmen smiled. *I like this guy.*

Led to a sporty red convertible and somewhat rehydrated, the vague stirrings of his humanity returned, although grudgingly. While Caesar retrieved his bags, he sat with the top down and breathed in the Southern Florida night. Heavy and humid, a shower had passed through late in the afternoon, it seemed to coat and soothe him from the inside. After the recycled atmosphere of the aluminum airborne cattle car, this was like breathing for the first time. Caesar returned with the bags, shook hands warmly with Allmen and bid him a safe journey. It was time to hit the open road. His estimated 1:30 AM EST arrival time in Key West was no problem. Hell, he might even have time for a beer before closing.

He was feeling positively human as the lights of Homestead faded in the rear-view mirror and the Everglades loomed dark and sinister to his right. The air became even more humid, if that were possible, and a bit dank with the smells of the jungle. *Imagine the rot and decay there, side by side with the teeming life of awful, sometimes nightmarish creatures.* The Glades were still one of the foreboding places left on earth that were better not experienced at night. To that list he added the Amazon River basin and the front row of a Justin Bieber concert. He was happy to continue cruising south.

He was across Manatee Bay and into Key Largo when the ocean took over, bathing him in salt, the smells of fish, the call of birds in the night. John Allmen left mainland America behind and crawled through the 35 MPH zones of the Upper Keys feeling cleansed, though the day was wearing on him, and fatigue began to wrap around him as the night wore on. His circadian rhythms were off, and they didn't really give a damn about the three-hour time change that was supposedly in his favor. The previous evening, lack of sleep and airline travel pummeled him with waves of exhaustion and as his adrenaline ebbed like the tide. He needed coffee. He pulled to a squat brick building with a hand painted sign dimly illuminated by a fading spotlight at the side of the road. Castle Convenience and Liquors, announced a blinking neon sign, was open. The smell of industrial cleaner and burned coffee greeted him like smelling salts.

Allmen knew of the website FloridaMan.com, a collection of stories about the ubiquitous Floridian, usually in an inappropriate state of dress. And usually committing larcenous activities throughout the state, more often than not in the company of an exotic animal. Florida Man Found Naked with Gator in WalMart Parking Lot, Florida Man Found Shirtless

Wrestling Giant Python, that sort of thing. So, he was not terribly surprised by the figure that greeted him behind the counter. Standing barefoot and bare-chested next to the countertop sign that clearly read No Shirt, No Shoes, No Service, was a man of his mid-sixties, balding and with only a distant memory of what his abdominal muscles looked like. His forearm was tattooed in a faded green that probably used to be black and next to him on the other side of the counter was a four-foot iguana. The man, his discarded button-down shirt on the counter said his name was Hector, was singing along with the music piped in-store, belting out ACDC for his audience of one. Two if you counted the iguana.

"*Highway to hell*...Hey, man." The last, dropping into a normal human octave, was delivered with a nod to Allmen as he headed for the coffee and filled up a 20 oz cup.

The man's hand drummed the glass on the counter and his head bobbed with the drumbeat. He bent the song's title to the beat, ignoring lyrics that he didn't know "*...Hiiiighwayyyyy tooo hell, don't you know...the highway toooo hellll...*that's a buck seventy-nine amigo."Allmen pulled out a twenty. "Sorry man, no change." Without breaking rhythm with his drumming hand, he pointed to a hand printed sign on the cash register in awkward cursive letters and red magic marker:

Sorry Man, No Change.

Undaunted, Allmen walked back to the cooler, selected a six pack of Corona, and put it on the counter.

"*High....way....High way ey ayyy.... to hell!*"

"Tell you what. Here is a twenty for the coffee and beer and you can keep the change. I noticed your tattoo."

The man stopped singing in mid screech and the drums likewise fell silent. The iguana looked up, relieved or perturbed, Allmen couldn't tell.

"Vietnam," the old man said simply, getting a familiar vacant look in his eyes that made Allmen flinch.

To relieve the knot in his stomach, he took a sip from the coffee. "I know," he said after a long swallow. He offered him a closed fist and the man bumped it. A fist bump was preferable because God only knows where Florida Man's hands have been. Coffee in the cup holder and beer on the floor of the back seat, John Allmen rolled back onto the highway.

Plantation Key and Islamorada drifted by. He saw lights and smelled grease from the few fast-food joints that dotted the Overseas Highway. The coffee was a dud. It bought him perhaps another hour of mental clarity, but as he rolled past the Dolphin Research Center and through Marathon, he knew he was fighting a losing battle.

In the looming shadow of the Seven Mile Bridge, he pulled to the side of the road where it met the old bridge, now a pedestrian way and fishing pier, put up the car top and killed the motor. He sat for a while listening to waves gently lapping at the bridge and the breeze gently pushing through the palm trees overhead. In the distance he heard an aircraft, probably a Coast Guard Search and Rescue helo heading north back to Miami. It was the last thing he heard before he slipped beneath the waves of fatigue and slept.

* * *

"Lieutenant! Sir! Lieutenant! This way...we gotta move!" No one had called John Allmen Lieutenant in a dozen years, so he knew he was dreaming. But for some reason knowing it didn't change much. He still felt the fear of combat, smelled the stale sweat of a uniform worn in the desert and not washed, and tasted gunpowder.

"El-Tee! Sir! We need to get on that chopper!"

Faceless men, kids he sensed, were pulling at him, trying to get him to move, to cross the sandy wash in front of him and get to the landing zone. But, in that way dreams have of examining everything, but explaining nothing, he couldn't move. He stood still and watched as bullets began to whine in the air around them. Men, boys, were falling. And now, as if freed from a leash by enemy fire, he was running. Lights on the chopper flared in front of him. *That's not right, why do you have fucking lights on in a combat zone?* But he forgot that as he reached the landing skid and vaulted himself toward the open crew door. It should have been teeming with weapons pointed at the enemy engaging them. Instead, he saw that the entire interior was dark, formless, a void.

You are dreaming John. Stop this and take control.

But the bullets kept flying and in the turmoil the darkness was closing in around him. And then he heard them. Three shots that rang out above the din. *High powered sniper rounds.* And he knew with a certainty reserved for dreamers and drunks that the three shots were coming for him. ONE. TWO. THREE.

He was awake, eyes wide and looking into a pink and purple, misty dawn that would have stretched from over his left shoulder down across Bahia Honda Key if a giant shadow weren't blotting out the rising sun. A flashlight swept the interior of the car and the three taps came again, this time rattling the car window near his head, where a voice said in a clam, but authoritative manner: "Can you roll down the window please, sir? Slowly?"

Allmen did as he was instructed, careful to keep his hands in sight as the glass slid down. He turned slightly, squinting, to see a sheriff's SUV pulled in behind him with the lights flashing and a middle-aged man with a badge holding a flashlight that he mercifully extinguished.

"What do we have here?"

"Ah, sorry Sherriff, I got a little tired and pulled over for a nap. Guess I was out longer than I figured."

"Uh-huh. Have you been drinking friend?"

"Not since yesterday on my flight to Miami. And only if you count the airline's version of a Bloody Mary."

The Sherriff guffawed. "Hell no. If that is drinking, I don't know the meaning of the word. And I suppose that six pack in the back seat didn't used to be a twelve pack?"

"No sir. Picked it up a few miles back and planned to celebrate my arrival in Key West."

"What are you doing in the lower keys?"

"Drinking that beer to start. And getting in some fishing." The man crouched now to look Allmen in the face, and to smell the car and his breath. Satisfied, he softened, even grinned a lopsided 'aw shucks' sort of smirk.

"Well, I didn't mean to startle you, I got a call that something may have happened to a tourist out here. Guess the only thing that happened to you was a visit from the Sandman."

"Yes, sir. Sorry for bothering you."

"No bother mister. My job is to keep these seven miles and flowing waters safe for travelers. You get down there and want to slay bonefish on the flats or fight a few tarpon, give my cousin Horace a call. He's got a charter boat out on Stock Island and is the bane of all things with flippers and fins."

"Huh, sounds great."

"Yep, boat's called Divine Revenge. Tell him his cousin Homer said hello and he should get his ass up here from time to time for Sunday supper."

"Will do." Allmen cranked the ignition and noted the time as the radio powered up. It was 6:15AM and he'd be in Key West for breakfast. Not bad, all things considered, though only the fishing crews and Navy guys ate breakfast. No one else there would be awake at such an ungodly hour.

"The Lower Keys classic rock station," droned the radio, "here is a classic from AC/DC. It's Highway to Hell." Gooseflesh rippled across Allmen's neck. Or was that the chill of an early morning in the Keys as the top came down on his convertible?

He checked his phone before pulling out, purely out of a long habit. It was off, and he remembered he'd stopped the madness the prior evening. Curiosity forced him to turn it on now. Fifty-seven text messages, fifty-eight if you counted the one of an emoji middle finger that Mack Mason had sent. Twenty-eight voice mails, most from former clients, though quite a few had come from Circle Nine Travel between the hours of 1Am and 6AM. Allmen punched the call back button.

"Mr. Allmen?"

"Hello Virgil. What's up? Other than you at 3AM on the west coast? Help me out here Virgil, are you some kind of stalker? Or just overworked and losing touch with reality?"

"Well sir, I assume you mean the missed calls and voicemails? We were worried about you. *I* was worried about you. With the phone turned off we don't get tracking data on you. When you didn't check in to your hotel, I tried you several times and then called local law enforcement."

"Wait, *you* called Sheriff Homer? And wait…you are *tracking* me?" Allmen felt vaguely violated and yet protected, like a girl with an abusive boyfriend he'd had a crush on in college. He'd watched her get pushed down a flight of steps in his dorm and then stepped forward and knocked the guy flat on his ass.

"Yes. And yes. Hopefully there wasn't any unpleasantness with the local law enforcement?"

"None whatsoever. I learned long ago how to use proper deference to avoid most complications. Can we get back to the part where you are tracking me when my phone is on?"

"Of course. Through our app that you downloaded. We track you so that we can tailor your experience, sometimes down to the minute. You did agree to the terms of service."

"I did?" Allmen was just as guilty as every other American of freely giving up his rights by scrolling through pages of legalese and hitting ACCEPT without thought.

"Mr. Allmen," Virgil chided, "you should really read the fine print."

"Virgil, you have no idea."

"What's that?"

"I'll keep that in mind. Gotta go. The highway calls, man."

He disconnected and though he left the phone on, he turned off the ringer. And then, for good measure, with a wary look, he put it in the glove compartment for the remaining hour he was on the road.

The Conch Republic of Key West rose out of the shallow waters of the Gulf of Mexico like a hurricane resistant, concrete Atlantis. For years, this had been a different world where the marginalized of society, or those merely too lazy to participate to the fullest, drifted like human flotsam and jetsam. Sure, there was money here, rich southerners whose bank accounts could reasonably be assessed by the size of their outboard engines. And there were tourists, usually divorced ladies from Fort Lauderdale looking to go somewhere to let loose where they wouldn't be recognized. But the raw nerves of Key West were intact. This was a place where one could fit in no matter what. Gay, straight, black, white, let out of prison for good behavior or escaped in the middle of the night, Key West didn't judge. These were virtuous people in their own way, living their best lives without hope or desire to associate much with the mainland.

Allmen rolled through town as kids were going to school and golfers were teeing off at the club on Stock Island, continuing to follow the signs for the "Southernmost Point." Just short of mile marker 0 on the Overseas Highway, he turned left on Southard Street, following the tourist signs for Truman's Little White House. He went through a security gate, gave his name and unit number, then continued through a maze of condominiums to his reservation, a 2-bedroom unit with plenty of space for a fisherman on a mission. He parked the car in front of a canary yellow, two story building across from the community pool and lugged his bags and beer onto the small wooden porch. The door swung open, and he was hit by hues of the Caribbean, blues, greens and more yellows. Color blind had multiple meanings here in the Keys.

Allmen opened a beer and set about laying out his gear and unpacking his clothes. He had the windows open in the cool of the morning and the wafting scent of orange blossom mixed with frangipani let him know he was in the tropics. The ever-present salty heaviness of the sea air reminded him he was on an island. And the guilt-free morning beer reminded him he was on the right island, at least for him. *For now.* After a few reverent minutes, he completed his unpacking mission, sat down on the couch to assess a whirlwind day or so, and promptly fell asleep.

He awoke after noon on his own accord. No dreams disturbed him this time and he slipped on the Key West uniform of a tee shirt, baggy shorts and his "dress' flip-flops, retracing his path up Southard Street while sipping at another beer. Where Whitehead street intersected, he stopped and bought a Cuban Sandwich. The ham was salty, the bread crusty and the pickles perfectly tart. In his depleted state, the food lasted about half a block and necessitated yet another beer. The Green Parrot, a local's bar, beckoned on the horizon. Allmen slipped amiably through the cowboy style double doors and grabbed an open stool next to the cash register at the main bar. He was rewarded with a quick Corona with ice chips still clinging to the neck like translucent barnacles on a freighter for the tropics. He was also rewarded with a pleasant smile from the pretty, petite bartender, whose name, so the tag on her ample chest noted, was Maggie.

Content, Allmen drank two more in peace and began to think about his next move when a booming voice called out from the door.

"Well crikey! Check out this tosser fresh in from the mainland! Hey, college boy, you know you are on the wrong side of the clock tower?" It was well known in Key West that most of the straight bars fell west of the town clock and the gay ones to the east. The burly man with the Australian accent who darkened the entrance of the Green Parrot was clearly a local and was clearly making a jest at Allmen's sexuality. "Your boyfriend know you are about?"

Allmen sighed. So much for a peaceful afternoon. "No, but I let your mother know I was going out... right after I put my pants back on." Predictably, the big man stepped forward. John rose from his barstool and pretty little Maggie winced behind the bar and then seemed ready to say something. The big man moved like a footballer, graceful for all the raw muscle. Quickly Allmen felt himself overcome, crushed against the bar in a muscled holding maneuver. Slowly, it turned into a hug with the big Aussie slapping his back.

"God almighty Johnny, you could have told somebody you were coming back to town."

"I would have told you if I'd known myself. I'll explain later."

"Right-oh. First things first. Maggie, my love? Will you pull me a Fosters out from the bottom of the ice chest?"

"Sure thing Rusty." Allmen noted the gleam in her eye as she responded and he knew her lovely face had probably been done up after awaking in Russel's bed that morning. "How about one for the college boy?"

Allmen smiled, "Please and thank you. My name is John." They shook hands and she poured beers. There would be no peaceful afternoon, no lazy nap by the pool now that word was out that he was in town. He was in for a long day and would need to be properly hydrated. With this in mind, when his Corona came to an end, he ordered another.

While Maggie was off taking orders from the end of the bar, where the crowd was beginning to trickle in from the fishing charters, Allmen nudged Russel and nodded at her. "Nice upgrade for this place. And yours, I'm assuming." The big man just smiled. "But what happened to the old crew? Rachel, David, are they still around?"

"You've been gone a while Johnny. Not often, but occasionally things do change down here. You remember the bar-back who worked over at Sloppy Joes? The little Cuban guy, Jesus, with big dreams and lots of charisma?"

"Sure. I liked that guy."

"Everyone liked that guy. Well, he started a club up in Miami. Came down one day and scooped up a bunch of staff from Sloppy Joe's and the Parrot. Took Rachel and David from here. Abe from over there. And some bartender named Noah who worked at Margaritaville. Didn't know that dude."

"Huh. What's the name of the club?"

"He calls it Havana Heaven. Funny, Jesus taking people to heaven, right?"

"I guess. Folks down here think it was funny?"

"Not terribly. Conch's can be a territorial lot, as you know. But I suspect it was mostly just jealousy. He came for some and not for others. It's not fun to know the chosen people but not be one of them."

"No, I suppose not. But hey, free will, right?"

"Sure. Besides, this little piece," he pointed a chin toward Maggie, bent over the bar and now demonstrating her other assets, "came down on holiday around the same time. She decided not to go back to Alabama. I think she's an improvement."

"You'd clearly know better than I would." Allmen fell silent for a moment. Friends had gone, and change had come to the last place on earth he expected it. Even here the world kept turning.

As the silence stretched, Allmen felt his companion grow fidgety. "Johnny..." he began haltingly "...we all heard about what happened. I'm sorry. It must have been rough for you."

Allmen felt sweat beading at his forehead and his tee shirt grew sticky.

"Thanks Russ. I appreciate it. Maybe someday I can talk about it all. But not any time soon."

Rusty nodded, stood up and stifled a belch. "Come on. Let's go see what's shaking at Sloppy Joe's. We need to find a boat for tomorrow."

"We do?"

"We do. Unless you are planning on spending the day at the Hemingway Museum petting fuzzy little six toed kitties?" He said the last in a cooing baby voice.

"Nope, fishing sounds great. Early night so we can hit 'em hard?"

Rusty barked a short laugh. "Fuck that, mate." He leaned in for a peck from Maggie, they said their goodbyes and walked into the fading light of the afternoon toward Duval Street.

❋ ❋ ❋

Allmen plunged into consciousness sweating and choking like a newborn baby wrapped in its own umbilical cord. From a deep, dark sleep he felt rather than heard the incessant pounding on his door. He would have run to the door to stop the noise, but there was no way his limbs would move in anything like athletic coordination. He had passed out, he knew instantly, fully clothed on the couch in his condo. At what time he could not say, except that it had been late then, and it was still early now. The pleasant smells of the day before were now replaced by the artificial air getting pumped out of the air conditioner and his own bodily emissions, pickled from a night of heavy drinking. The pounding on the door stopped as he opened it, transferring immediately to a pounding throb around his temples. Rusty, all six feet two of him stood smiling while hurriedly gesturing toward his battered pick-up truck.

"'Morning mate! Oh crikey, but you look like hammered shit. Out drinking late last night, were you? Tsk tsk...the fish won't wait! The boat won't either Johnny, so move your ass."

Allmen gaped. One might have thought Rusty had been at home and asleep by eight after drinking Evian spritzers all afternoon, instead of drinking a case of beer and a handle of rum between one o'clock and whatever time they had terminated the evening.

"What time did we call it a night? Never mind, I don't want the details. Let me brush my teeth and grab my rods."

"Yes, clean yourself lad. But don't worry about the rods. Won't need those today." Allmen had brought two fly fishing rods, reels and associated tackle and he was halfway toward his bedroom when the comment registered. He groaned and shuffled back to the door.

"Please, you bastard, tell me we are going flats fishing today," he whispered.

"Nah mate. Captain Sal is taking us offshore for tuna." He slapped him on the back and Allmen felt bile rising, "No sport fish for us. Tonight, we feast!"

✻ ✻ ✻

Sal, it turned out, was short for Saladin, a wiry Persian with long black hair whose bare chest looked like he'd acquired a bear costume for the island's annual Fantasy Fest. And decided to keep it. He had piercing green eyes, a sing-song voice and an easy laugh which he demonstrated as soon as they came aboard his boat. Ayyubid was written in cursive blue script across the transom on the starboard side of three Mercury 350 horsepower outboard motors. She was a spotless Boston Whaler 350, with a center console, fish tower and bristling with rods and serious slaying gear.

"Sally, John here spent some time a while back in your old neighborhood." Rusty announced as he heaved a cooler on board.

White teeth flashed and Sal's dark eyebrows rose questioningly. "Iraq or Afghanistan? Rusty is geographically challenged when it comes to the Middle East."

"Rusty is a knuckle dragging moron about many things. But to answer your question, Iraq."

Sal nodded. "My parents left Iran when I was a boy. After the Shah. I don't remember much. But I know there are no Tarpon in the Persian Gulf."

"Ah… but the women," Rusty said, kissing his fingers like a French aristocrat, "so much bloody mystery beneath that burqa."

"How'd you end up here?" Allmen asked, abruptly changing the subject.

"How does anyone end up here? Happy accident, no compelling reason to go elsewhere." He shrugged. "Family bounced around, lived in Paris, then came to Michigan of all places. I hate snow."

To continue to drill down would be rude in Key West social circles, so Allmen let it go, instead focusing all of his energies on not throwing up all over the gleaming deck of Sal's boat.

There was one more passenger aboard, a wiry, thin-lipped man with slick backed hair. He wore khaki shorts and a polo shirt like he was going to the yacht club for a wine tasting. He also wore what appeared to be a perpetual expression somewhere between haughty disinterest and 'oh dear, I've just ingested bad mussels.'

Rusty made introductions. "Johnny, you and Wallace here are more or less in the same business."

"Yeah? He retired too?" It came out gruff and unfriendly, due partially to his two-day extended hangover, and partially out of a desire to see all of his uppity former colleagues burn. It seemed to settle things. They would not be friendly and would not converse. *Much better that way.*

Rusty and Sal continued to banter as the lines were taken in, fenders removed, and the vessel slid out of her slip destined for open water. Mr. New York Finance Guy looked on passively. An hour later and the boat was wallowing over giant blue swells somewhere between Key West and Cuba and all pretense of John Allmen keeping his shit together had been left far astern.

"Good God lad...I've never seen a Navy boy turn so green at sea." Rusty laughed between hearty swigs of Fosters.

"I'm a Marine you dick."

"Aren't the Marines part of the Navy Department? I've heard that from the Squids here.""I'm sure you ha..." The last syllable disintegrated into a heave of his internal organs and another fine slick of chum appeared behind the boat.

"I'm surprised the sharks aren't circling, your barf must be toxic."

Allmen just moaned. Mercifully the starboard outrigger began humming and everyone who wasn't a hungover basket case announced, "Fish on!" in unison. The Australian settled in to battle what turned out to be a decent sized tuna while Sal maneuvered the boat with skill, one might even say grace.

Allmen appreciated his deft handling of the vessel, no movement was wasted, no hair ruffled on his finely coiffured head. He was a model of efficiency and seamanship. And given

Allmen's shaky hold on reality and an upright posture, he appreciated the smooth ride. The New Yorker sat looking bored until he too hooked on to a fish a few minutes later. Suddenly the cockpit was all action and motion, reels spinning and quiet words exchanged between guide and the guided. Time ebbed and flowed in a practiced ballet and soon each victor had his vanquished along-side the boat.

Just as two tuna were going on ice and the boat returned to normal, the port side outrigger bent with a whine as line peeled off into the deep. "Fish on!" came the announcement and Allmen, who was closest now, turned, grabbed rod and reel and set the hook with practiced aplomb despite his miserable state of being. He was rewarded with another run as the fish took more line and headed deeper, annoyed that someone had punched a hole in his lip.

John moved toward the bow, trying to stay with the fish and avoid the line crossing under the boat and potentially breaking off on the hull or getting caught in the prop. He should have gone the other way, but the cockpit was crowded, and he was still avoiding The New York Fucking Money Guy. He recognized his mistake as he moved a foot around the outrigger pole, felt the boat lurch the opposite way and stepped into space. For a moment he hung there like an animated character walking the plank of a cartoon pirate ship. Then he was falling. And then he was flailing in the salty warm waters of the Gulf. *I can't be in the water.* He spat. *Not the water.* His brain convulsed and he screamed. It was animalistic, reptilian. It was something born of equal parts frustration and fear. And though he was treading and his head was well above the surface, he thought about what it was like to drown. The darkness zeroing in from your periphery, tunnel vision, the white light at the end. *Stop it!*

I can't be in the fucking water! He realized the rod and reel were still in his right hand. He decided not to drop them, lest he add to the tally of breaking the outrigger. That gave him something else to think about, so he concentrated solely on kicking, paddling one-handed and keeping his grip with the other. The good news was his wrecked body was responding quite well.

What pissed him off was that the boat didn't turn. Not for a while at least. They knew he'd gone overboard. His final futile act before going in the drink had been to reach out and grab the flimsy aluminum outrigger which had snapped loudly enough for everyone to hear over the droning of the engines. And the outboards cut off as he watched the vessel coast downrange, but it did not come back for him. Finally, the Ayyubid began a slow turn and chugged back toward him. And he understood why it had taken so long, why Sal's seamanship had suddenly gone to shit. Every single man aboard was bent over, hands on their knees hooting with laughter. Even Mr. Goldman Sachs placid façade had cracked. Captain Sal had managed to get one hand on the wheel while wheezing and gasping for breath like a lifelong smoker after a 5k fun run. Red faced, Rusty managed to shimmy down to the dive platform and haul Allmen, soaking wet, onto it.

"Oh, Jesus Johnny that was the funniest thing I've ever…." He stopped when he saw Allmen's face. He read something primal there and it made him take an involuntary step backward.

Then the reel spun again. It whined as line ran out and the rod began to bend. Rusty's face turned from anxious to astonished and then to unrestrained delight. "Fish still on!"

The anger and anxiety in Allmen drained from him like Mexican beer on a hot day. Blood pumping, muscles groaning as he reeled, he forgot his hangover and it forgot him. He forgot the water, forgot drowning, forgot about death. Except, of course, for the impending death of whatever was at the other end of the line, pulling for all it was worth. The salt forming on his skin as the water evaporated felt like some sort of detoxifying spa treatment. And the smell of coconut in his sunscreen made him feel like a Māori warrior, now standing his ground and wearing the fish down. In a few minutes it was all over. The line was rolling in next to the boat and Allmen looked down and saw his tormentor lolling in the wake.

"You have got to be kidding me." A small, exhausted grouper gaped up at Allmen as he brought him the last few feet into the boat.

Rusty barked a laugh. "Shit mate, not sure if he is going to make the twenty-four-inch limit. Guess I can pull down my pants and measure him up."

Wallace, of the House of J.P. Morgan or whatever, visibly flinched, probably figuring that Rusty would actually do it. Allmen sighed. What did he expect on a fishing boat other than beer and dick jokes? "No Russ, he'll be dead before you can line him up ten times to measure him."

Sal was frowning. "I was afraid of that. These little guys get spooked and head for the bottom and try to get lost in the coral. They make for a bigger fight than their size, that is for sure. Want to keep him? Good eating if he's above the limit."

Allmen squinted at the creature, dark gray with irregular black marks on him. He felt old feelings come back, a vague gnawing hate, a dark desire for revenge. He pushed them down out of his consciousness. "Nah, the little guy fought valiantly. Let's get him back in the water."

After that small act of kindness, they were merciless the rest of the day, despite fishing with a depleted stock of outriggers. Allmen apologized profusely and assured Sal he'd make it right for him. Captain Sal just smiled and nodded. "No worries." It was easy to be magnanimous when you were pulling in fish for wealthy customers at a clip that, if sustained, would put you on PETA's Ten Most Wanted list.

Rejuvenated, Allmen even made peace with the stiff from New York, engaging in small talk about fishing here and there, but scrupulously avoiding talk of investments or banking. They returned to the dock a happy and successful crew. They selected two meaty tuna and hauled them across the road to be cleaned and prepared at a local favorite of a restaurant. Dante's was a clubby hangout with a cascading waterfall emptying into a swimming pool and a chef who knew how to cook a fish, by getting out of the way and not screwing it up. Dante's also had one of the better Tiki bars south of Daytona according to their menu. Which was odd given that no one associated Daytona with Tiki bars.

Victory toasts were made, and tuna steaks consumed. But first was a tangy, acidic tomato-based conch chowder that they washed down with a local ale. Fresh oysters were all over the table being slurped at irregular intervals, and you could smell the mignonette sauce of shallots and vinegar. Allmen felt as if he'd been brought back from the dead, a vague sense of anticipation creeping into his previously moribund corpse. After dinner they made their way down to Duval Street and a familiar pattern established itself: fish, dinner, drinks, pass out and do it all over again. He found himself on island time and surrendered to it without much fight.

✻ ✻ ✻

It was a few days later, after an uncharacteristically crappy run after Tarpon in a flats boat captained by a surly old cracker from Louisiana. Rusty had excused himself after dinner to tend to hurt female feelings, though he promised to be back before Duval Street really got rocking. John took up a stool at the outdoor bar at the Hogs Breath. There were several old timers with sagging bellies and long gray hair at and around the bar. They were gesticulating and occasionally shouting one another down.

"Marcus, you are so full of shit!" said a man of about sixty, though he could have been plus or minus a decade depending on the lighting, wearing a tee shirt that read in bold block red letters, One Tequila, Two Tequila, Three Tequila, FLOOR!

"Piss off Ari, you wouldn't know a proper drink if you swam in it."

Allmen caught the eye of the bartender, a young gym rat with barbed wire tattoos around his bulging biceps. Though he didn't know the kids name, his face was familiar enough after a week or so of the Duval Crawl. He was rewarded by a smile

34

of recognition. Allmen nodded toward the locals. "What are the philosophers arguing about today?"

The kid smiled, showing newfangled braces. "The best drink after a day of fishing. The local intelligentsia takes this kind of thing very seriously. As I think you know by now."

Allmen nodded gravely. "Well, I know my opinion." The kid arched an eyebrow. "I'll have a mojito please."

The bartender, Dave, his nametag said in sloppy cursive, nodded approvingly and Allmen wondered briefly if he ought to wade into the pissing match amongst his elders. But the argument seemed to end as an enormous man in board shorts and a Miami Dolphins jersey with the sleeves cut off bent to expose his ample buttocks to the crowd.

"Kiss my ass you sack of shit," he told someone in the assembled crowd.

They were the town philosophers, the same in any town, except that here they met in an outdoor bar instead of a Starbucks. That made them a little more crass and infinitely more fun than the coffee shop crowd. Usually the loudest, most affronting of them would end up buying a round for the group, and sometimes the bar.

The fresh mint, fragrant, sweet and earthy was suddenly in his nostrils as it was muddled. Then came the faint smell of citrus. The taste was similar, sweet on his palate until the syrupy lime came over the top to hit him with a one two punch. Sweet, sour, syrupy, effervescent. It was a trap, John knew. Your taste buds were so confused by the extreme combinations, they never even registered the rum sliding coolly down your gullet. And there, occasionally, was the problem. One was never enough, but a few quickly got out of hand. True to form he got the first one for free when the massive Dolphins fan picked up a round for the bar.

Allmen was well into his second concoction when he felt a hulking presence settle into the stool beside him. He smelled Old Spice aftershave and knew who was there well before a gravelly voice muttered "Hoo...rah, Marine...been looking all over town for you."

"Hello Mack." John waved to the bartender. "Can I have another mojito and a Budweiser for the man who can't take no for an answer?" Mack held up a hand.

"Make it a hundred." The kid stopped and instinctively flexed an arm making barbed wire expand like a free-range cow's nightmare. "One-hundred bottles of Budweiser... for the bar." Mack flashed a few hundred-dollar bills and in no time the bar in front of him was filled with brown bottles and fellow patrons, including the philosophers were partaking and saying thanks to their closely cropped benefactor. Allmen had seen this before. It was a power move, a wealthy man marking his territory.

Mack turned from his admirers to Allmen. "Damn right I don't take no for an answer. But don't assume this is all about you. Maybe I needed a vacation too?"

"Your last vacation was a sandy spot in Afghanistan."

"True statement." He took a long pull from one of his beers.

"Then why come all this way?"

"Look you made me a lot of money. And you made my friends a lot of money."

"You're welcome."

"Yeah, well, it puts me in a bit of an awkward position when they call me and ask what the hell is going on with you. You know, the guy that I convinced them to give most of their life's savings to? Since you wouldn't take my calls, I came down here to investigate myself."

"I can't say I am surprised."

They were quiet for minute. Then Mack broke the stretching silence. "So, how's the fishing?"

"Good offshore but the flats have been a bust. Tarpon aren't running and nothing will hit a fly."

"Didn't understand a word of that."

"I know. Mack, do you remember the last time you pulled the, hey I have a big dick and am going to buy one hundred beers for the bar, thing?" He was feeling the rum and becoming a bit nostalgic.

"You mean the last time I pulled it when you were around? Sure. Louisville for the Derby." A few years back, Mack had called him out of the blue the first week of May and more or less ordered him to accompany his entourage to Kentucky for a weekend of horse racing and mint juleps. Allmen had come home with a few new clients and a fat wallet courtesy of a trifecta in race number three.

"Trisha hit the roof when I told her I was going. And again when I got home."

"Why? It was business."

Allmen sighed. "It was always business."

"I called her, you know. To find out what was going on. Make sure you aren't cracking up."

"Jesus Mack, you called my ex-wife to check on me?"

"I did."

"Well?"

"She was noncommittal about whether or not you've gone off the deep end. Which is why I am here."

"Super. Both of my former commanding officers are working together to prove that I'm nuts."

Mason turned serious. He laid a meaty paw on Allmen's shoulder with....what? *Tenderness? Was that the word? Could that possibly be the description for anything Mack Mason, Captain of industry and Major of Marines, all six feet two of American bravado and bullshit, did?*

"John, buddy..." he said measuredly, "I was worried about you."

Allmen's throat caught. "People keep saying that. Thanks. I'm fine. I just need some time off." The lie was rehearsed, and unconvincing without the aid of alcohol. Thankfully they were in Key West and not Salt Lake City. Mason accepted it as fact, or at least a current data point and allowed the conversation to move on.

"Hey, are these beers taken?" Rusty had appeared visibly drooling at dozens of free beers and trailing Wally the New York finance guy, like a pet poodle. Allmen nodded in recognition,

Wally tried to smile but it came off awkward as he grabbed a Budweiser and seemed to be contemplating an exit strategy. Allmen decided to twist the knife and torture him a bit, socially at least.

"Rusty, Wally, meet my friend Mack." Rusty shook hands grinning and then the intended mortar round backfired. Recognition dawned like a tequila sunrise on the New Yorker's shrewish face, which turned suddenly animated.

"Are you Mack Mason, the Venture Capitalist? I saw you speak at a conference last year in Boston."

"Why, yeah, I am." He extended a meaty hand and Wallace winced visibly as he endured the ham-fisted handshake of a former Division-1 linebacker with pro prospects. Allmen watched amazed as Mason turned professional and Wally vaguely human discussing this deal and that tranche of financing, It was as if they were in some waspy country club in Connecticut having a martini before the lobster thermidor was plated.

Allmen tried to refocus on their conversation through the Bacardi. "Amazing Mack," Wally was saying shaking his head, "and you did all that after getting out of the Marines what twenty years ago?"

"Ten, actually. I've had an amazing run Wally, what can I say. And I got into it at the right time. Missed a lot of the unpleasant stuff... doing other unpleasant stuff."

"Yeah, I see what you mean. Different story for me obviously. I've been doing this forever. Different firms, some good, others bad. Heck, I was working for Lehman Brothers in '08. That was a financial and personal disaster for me."

"No kidding? John Allmen here made me a lot of money shorting them around that time." Wallace's face went dark.

"I see." Détente was over. He polished off the warm remains of a Budweiser and disappeared into the night. Allmen allowed a fantasy to play out in his mind, picturing Wally shirtless and running wild through the strip clubs spending his kid's college savings fund. But the truth was he was probably in bed before

John, Mack and Rusty stumbled down the block.

Back on Duval, Rusty stopped to talk to everything in a skirt and the two old soldiers told stories and relived what parts of the past they could without a licensed therapist on hand.

"Where to boys?" Mack asked.

"The Parrot?" Allmen thought he was glad there were no S's in the sentence because he was well past the time for slurring.

"Sure mate. But I have to warn you about little ol' Maggie."

* * *

In the morning, Allmen stumbled out to his living room and saw through the open door to the guest room that Mason had already collected himself and gone. No note, of course, but John could expect a text message, probably when Mack woke up aboard his chartered jet somewhere over Iowa.

The night had ended early, at least on Key West Standard Time. It turned out Rusty and Maggie had hit the rocks, mostly due to the former's complete inability to avoid having one-night stands with tourists in from the mainland. It was hard for him to understand why it was wrong of him, since, after all, it was how Maggie had met him. "But who could understand women anyway, right mate?"

After her shift behind the bar, Maggie had countered Rusty's studied indifference with a classic move, one Allmen remembered from his college days.

"He's an idiot. I was so stupid to get involved, not my type at all," she'd confided to him leaning in closer than required in the space near the restrooms, next to the digital juke box. Then, with an appraising look. "Want to get out of here and go back to my place?"

"Tempting," Allmen had said, "but I can't." God, it really was tempting. She was a lovely girl, all curves and easy grace, with a fine innocence to her that not even a clumsy proposition could spoil. At least not permanently. And in truth it had nothing to do with loyalty, but more with John Allmen's inability to even contemplate sexual intimacy given his current blood alcohol content. The clock might have said it was early, but his liver didn't tell time very well.

Regardless, she had taken it badly and tossed a half full glass of Captain Morgan and Coke in his face before stomping out, throwing the cowboy doors wide in her wake. Allmen had seen Rusty talking to her out in the street a few minutes later. Then she was crying on his chest. And then they were walking toward his restored craftsman on Caroline Street.

John still felt the sickly-sweet stickiness of the rum and coke he'd inadvertently bathed in and noted that his hair smelled like lime. He knew he'd have to do something about that. Later, as the locals were known to say. But as he made coffee and contemplated another day in paradise, it occurred to Allmen that things were starting to go sideways in Key West. Island fever was taking hold. It always did, eventually. He picked up his phone from the kitchen counter and dialed.

"Virgil, can you book me out of Miami tomorrow? It's time to get back and see my kid."

LUST:

an intense longing, usually intense or unbridled sexual desire

T here is no hope that ever comforts them –
no hope for rest and none for lesser pain.
And just as cranes in flight will chant their lays,
arraying their long file across the air,
so did the shades I saw approaching, borne
by that assailing wind, lament and moan.

-Dante, Inferno Canto V

Sad to say, the reality of time spent with his daughter was usually a letdown, though thinking that made Allmen feel like more of a shit than usual. It was just a fact that the long silences and the yawning gap between them wore on him as time went on. He was happy enough after seeing old friends in Key West. He hoped she could understand he needed time away. Soon enough he'd be with her, a full-time father at last. Just not yet. There was so much more to do. Sitting in the rare San Francisco sun in June, dewy grass beginning to soak his chinos and quietly watching over her, he felt a certain uneasy contentment settle in. She'd grown into a good kid, despite his psychological and physical distance. *And that was something, wasn't it?*

He looked up, heard sea birds calling to each other overhead, buffeted by the inshore breeze. They seemed to float, never making way against the ever-present wind. Allmen thought he knew the feeling of facing an incessant headwind. His thoughts began to turn darker, and he knew it was time to go.

Alone again, he was walking slowly toward his car and pondering the plight of the birds when a text came in from Virgil:

"Please call when able."

Allmen got to the car and dialed, driving out toward the beach and found out that he was ready to book him on a flight to Rome.

"Wonderful Virgil. Rome sounds like the perfect antidote."

"Antidote to what Mr. Allmen?"

"To deep thoughts about birds."

"I see, I mean...I have no idea what you are talking about... but you are one of my best clients...maybe I should stop talking now."

It didn't matter. Allmen had stopped listening. As he'd come to a halt at an intersection on Great Highway, the blonde woman, he was sure it was her, had crossed in front of his car in black leggings and a Stanford sweatshirt. Moving up Fulton Street and into Golden Gate Park, she was jogging past the old Dutch Windmill. He watched agape as blonde curls bounced down the pavement and into the fog, the June gloom, that was moving in from Ocean Beach.

"Son of a bitch."

Allmen swung his BMW into the left lane, cutting off a Prius that was distressed enough to give him the finger through his rolled down window. The number of Prius drivers on the planet who could give Allmen physical trouble in an altercation was exactly zero. So, he ignored the gesture. Allmen also ignored the profuse apologies now streaming from Virgil on the other end of the phone.

"I wasn't calling you a son of a bitch Virgil. Text me the flight details. Allmen out." He swore he could smell her, that same scent even though he was in his car and she was a couple hundred yards away. There was a convenient illegal parking spot in a fire lane, and he lurched to it, leaping out like Dirty Harry chasing some Seventies lowlife perp. Allmen, a natural athlete, felt the adrenaline kick in and was soon racing through Golden Gate in his designer chinos, and Gucci leather moccasins. *Both from Barney's of New York.* He knew his inner monologue was rambling, but he was...what? *Nervous?* Three combat tours in Iraq and he was nervous about what would happen when he found this woman? Well, unless he had swallowed a butterfly on this little jaunt, it was the only explanation for the feeling rippling through him from chin to chest.

He came to a stop a half mile into the park scanning left and right to see if she had turned on Chain of Lake Drive. Nothing. He continued another few minutes toward the Polo fields and the smell of her was gone, replaced by the earthy scent of the Bison Paddock to his left. Had he actually smelled her? Was he really 'on the scent' like a hound dog? He walked up to Spreckels Lake and stood for a few minutes looking at his reflection in the water.

"Idiot," he said to himself. *I lost her again.*

⁕ ⁕ ⁕

A flight to Italy is a wonderful thing. The women aboard are usually smart and pretty, the men dressed impeccably like Gregory Peck in Roman Holiday. At least in the tony capsule of first class. *Impeccable. Gregory Peck.* Allmen smiled, amused by the slight alliteration. The flight attendant, a dusky woman with sharp Greek features and striking long black hair smiled back. Allmen thought there might be something there. Perhaps his own Roman romp with the anti-blonde woman? *The Yin to her Yang, the Mary Anne to her Ginger?* And then the champagne she had served him on boarding hit him like an out of control Vespa and he fell into a deep, long sleep.

For the first time since his nap on the Keys, he dreamt something memorable. The birds were back, floating, fighting what was now a hurricane force gale. They were white forms in a darkening sky. A storm rolling in on the horizon. After a minute of hearing their screeching, agonizing cries of anguish and frustration another sound came from behind him. He realized it was a helicopter. It was no hurricane; the birds were stuck in the rotor wash of that goddamn helicopter.

Now the birds were screaming in English. And with a shiver, he recognized a voice.

"Lieutenant!" This was Gomez, his favorite kid in the squad.

The bird with Gomez's voice called again "Lieutenant! El-tee, help me!"

And then the rotor wash pulled him in shredding him into a cloud of blood and feathers that swept aft of the dark looming shape of the helo.

The flock of birds called as one: "Lieutenant! LT, help me!"

Allmen knew with a dreamer's certainty that they were all

going to die. They were all to be sucked in, shredded by the machinery of war.

"Noooooo!" It was a long, futile scream that merely blew back in his face on the wind. And mercifully, he awoke. Sweating, breathless, he looked around. This time, no one returned his gaze from around the darkened cabin.

❊ ❊ ❊

Rome, Fiumicino International Airport or Leonardo da Vinci field to be exact, came as a surprise. He had fallen back to sleep, and the pilot must have been seeking to loosen some dental work or momentarily forgotten the laws of gravity. They say any landing you can walk away from is a good one. But *they* say a lot of stupid shit. And the controlled crash into the runway had scared him almost as badly as the dream. He was jolted awake, pockets of drool forming at the corners of the mouth. And then came a bunch of fast, loud Italian. It might have been a call to run like hell, the plane was on fire. But once translated to blessed English, it turned out to be the normal stuff about cell phones and lap belts. *Because, dear passenger, if you thought that bone jarring landing was frightening, just imagine the terrors that might await while parked at the gate if you prematurely release that belt. So, buckle up buttercup.*

"Ladies and gentlemen, we apologize for your late arrival given the headwinds we encountered and being unable to get past that infernal storm over the Mediterranean. Sorry for any inconvenience, we hope you fly us again." His well scripted mea culpa complete, the captain entered the galley where passengers were deplaning and stood there mutely. No pleasantries. No banter. He wasn't sorry for any of it, he had just read the script.

Allmen couldn't resist. He quickly grabbed his phone and had Google translate smart ass English into smart ass Italian. "Grazie," he said "Bel atterragio." *Thank you, nice landing.*

The pilot, his name tag just said Minos, just stared. He had a watch on a chain, an old-fashioned timepiece that looked worn and battered. Maybe it was from one of the World Wars in which Italy had fared so poorly and changed sides so often. He had it in his front pant pocket and was absently wrapping it around his wrist. One wrap, two, uncoil. Repeat. The Captain stared. One wrap, two, uncoil. Allmen felt a chill. He shrugged and walked off the plane, heading for the bar to await his baggage and ride into town. *Pilots always took themselves too seriously.*

Allmen met his driver and they set off up the Italian coast in a Mercedes convertible with the top up and the air conditioner on full blast. It was a hot, steamy summer in southern Italy. They stopped for a brief dinner in Grossetto. The driver, not very chatty to begin with, had insisted in monosyllabic English that he knew a place, the best meal on the way to Tuscany. Allmen ate alone in the square in front of the town's cathedral, it was a typical Renaissance church with stained glass and statues lining the frails and recesses of the upper floors. He felt a sense of vague unease with so many Saints peering over his shoulder.

"Vino bianco per favore." *That would do the trick.*

His waiter, who doubled as the sole proprietor brought him a glass, sized him up with a furrowed brow and a slight frown, and came back with the bottle. It was a light bubbly and dry white wine and Allmen found that it quite hit the spot. To be fair, the spot was wide and large, and could not have been missed by an ocean freighter, no less than most things that came in 750ml bottles.

Dinner began with succulent and juicy squid in tomato sauce that positively sang on his taste buds when paired with a slightly 'frizzante' wine. Spaghetti with radicchio and Parmesan followed, and Allmen was introduced to a red wine called Monte Cucco, a bustling, half Chianti and half Pinot Noir, which he'd never heard of in all his travels or wine binges. He raised the glass to the saints over his shoulder and toasted himself. *To old dogs and new tricks.*

Last was a beef dish with truffle sauce as he polished off the last of the red wine. Allmen lingered. Every Italian town is like a fashion runway after darkness descends. He drank some chianti and watched pretty Italian women stroll through the square, some leaving the shops and heading home. Others heading out for night on the town. Lovely women with the dark olive complexion of the south and dark eyes like pools of jet. Long, lean legs bared against the summer heat. High heels clicking on the cobblestones. He felt the saints behind him looked on stonily as he leered. It was time to go.

An hour later his driver deposited him on the ferry for the short ride over to Elba. He was drowsy but not enough to sleep. He uncorked the rest of the chianti and drank it from a Styrofoam cup he'd pilfered from the coffee service inside. He drank in plastic outdoor chair as the sea breeze cooled him. He felt full, yet hungry. Satiated but not satisfied.

There was music playing over the din of the engines, tinny pop music from a speaker welded to the roof. It was in Italian and after the fiftieth repetition of the chorus, Allmen looked it up on the translator:

Stare con te, stare con te.
Be with you, be with you.

Allmen went back to ignoring it. Italian and other European pop was of little interest to him. When it came to literature and music, he usually preferred the classics. Instead, he shifted his thoughts from blonde women in San Francisco to Italian fashion models. *To be with someone. That would be nice.* The music got louder as the engines went to idle and the lines went out at the dock. Then it ended and the DJ switched to English to announce a song by the artist Dido. Allmen smiled. He had a vague recollection of the name Dido from history, a Queen of Carthage. Something tragic had happened to her, he thought. But his head was too muddled to remember much. He gave up and shuffled off the boat and into the van taking him to the hotel.

It was a shabby chic relic from the 1920s with a shaded pool, a good bar and an excellent restaurant. He checked in and found that they had graciously saved him a plate from dinner, though he had missed service by being on the late ferry. Amazingly, he was hungry again and dined on his balcony eating fish crudités, and a succulent oily Veal Satimbocca, a cutlet stuffed with prosciutto and fresh, aromatic sage. The Italian wine list, he decided, would take a few days to get through. *I will read this like it is a John Grisham best seller. Deliberately poring over it, dispassionately looking for the next surprise.* The bottle of Tuscan red wine which he chose wasn't that memorable. But he blamed himself for that more than the wine. He didn't come close to finishing it before falling into a deep, dark, dreamless sleep.

* * *

In the morning he woke lazily and took stock of the room. It was moderately sized by European standards, though the shower, he was sure, would be a tight squeeze for some of the more sizable German rear ends that frequented the island. This was a place few Americans tread, preferring the scenic beauty of Cinque Terre or the crowded canals in Venice. But like the Blitzkrieg , the Germans headed here unimpeded and to this island, they came in force. Indeed, in a nod to their Euro brethren, many of the street signs were in both Italian and Deutsche. *The Krauts and the Italians together again. What could possibly go wrong?*

He had a balcony, overlooking the Tyrrhenian Sea, the lighthouse and the smudge on the horizon that was the mainland. He threw open the doors and felt the breeze on his face, smelled salt air and blinked in the sunshine. Then he took to putting his clothes into the massive bureau that stood across from the bed. He noticed the artwork. There were always reproductions of great works in a place like this, and on the wall next to the bureau was a dark-haired woman in a blue cloak that had fallen to her knees, baring her breasts. *You wouldn't see that at the Holiday Inn in Topeka.* On her lap was a young child, blonde curls and pudgy appendages who held an arrow. The fallen cloak suggested a struggle, the woman fending off Cupid with both arms outstretched. Allmen looked closer and saw she was smiling. *Love conquers all.*

He went for a stroll around the grounds before the heat of the afternoon. He heard the game of tennis before he rounded the hedge, solid groundstrokes on a hard court. Thwock. Shuffle. Thwock. Shuffle Thwock. Shuffle. The rhythm of the shots told him it was a serious game with good players. The length of the rally said it was evenly matched. And he knew that someone on the court was British from the cry of "Well played!" when the shots subsided.

The path through the hedge had sunlight slanting in from all angles between the branches and led him through a little garden where the far fence enclosed the court. There were a few benches and tables, but there didn't seem to be anyone bringing drinks, and he desperately wanted a beer. So, he took in the game at a stroll, heading for one of the outdoor bars.

On court were three men and a goddess. One tall, thin, and Germanic looking right hander with a full head of graying hair. He was paired with a portly, dark-haired left-handed man who was the Brit and also the weak player of the four. Something about the others told him it was father and daughter. They had the same moves and effortlessly played positional doubles tennis without exchanging more than an occasional word. They had been doing it for years, Daddy and his little girl. Well, the little girl was now in her thirties and a bona fide *bellisima*. Dark hair fell to her shoulders and framed one of those classically Mediterranean faces you saw on statues. Angular, yet softly feminine. And her coloring was sun darkened with taut muscles set in bronze. All this he took in at a stroll, along with the wives and mothers watching with bored expressions that seemed to say: "Do we have to make our Holiday about serves and volleys when the club at home would do just fine?"

A right turn after the tennis court brought him past the wide front patio of the hotel where they were setting up for evening cocktails. But they weren't yet ready, so he continued on toward the pool bar, giving that body of water a wide berth. The bartender was a swarthy southern Italian with long hair pulled back at his neck and a scruff of black beard.

"Signore! Buono Sera." Perched on his cash register was a long-tailed bird with bright green feathers, a red beak and red shoulders. The bird bobbed its head and cocked an eye at Allmen.

"Buona Sera. A beer please." The bartender drew a large frothing beer from the tap and handed it wordlessly to Allmen.

"Thanks. Do I pay the parrot?" Allmen nodded toward the bird who was eyeing them in turn.

"I will put it on your room, sir. You checked in late last night, correct?"

"I did, thanks." Allmen hefted the glass as the bird began to peck at the register's keyboard. The instrument protested with a series of beeps and whirs.

The bartender sighed and turned to shoo the bird away. "Achilles you naughty thing. I'll serve you for dinner tonight! Ay me, he is a pest. But pretty to look at, no?"

"Most naughty things are." Allmen smiled, took a long pull from the glass, left a generous tip and sauntered back toward the tennis court feeling the odd little parrot watching him until he rounded the hedge.

On court, the Brit was bent over the baseline, wheezing. "That's it for me," he announced. He saw Allmen standing idly nearby and said, "You there, do you speak English?"

"No sir. I speak American."

The Brit barked a laugh that might have been genuine, or it might have been dismissive. "You don't play tennis, do you? I'm a worn-out old man and these three want to keep on at it."

"I play a little."

Well, then…what do you say?"

"I say, my name is John. Can I borrow your racquet?"

"Yes, of course. My name is Tristan," he extended a sweaty hand that Allmen shook.

"Vee vill be partners. Mein name is Maximilian," said the

Teutonic looking man. He turned out to be from Austria and spoke passable, though heavily accented English.

"My name is Alberto. And this is my daughter Francesca." They all shook hands at the net. Her fingers were long and slender and cool to the touch. He didn't pay much attention to the father's handshake.

"I sink she could have been a pro," Max confided as they strode to the baseline. "Hit it to zee father whenever you can."

Max had a thundering forehand, a weak backhand and moved well for his age. Allmen adjusted his positioning after the first game to protect that backhand, poaching the net frequently and putting away a few easy winners. The Brit, Tristan, cheered them on, peering over a gin and tonic while his wife still looked on, bored, but not enough to do something else. The goddess glowered as they traded games on serve. Allmen held his at "love" after acing the father and serving and volleying the next three points.

His next service game came at 4 games all in the set. The old man finally got a racquet on the ball and popped a weak, angling backhand that barely cleared the net. Max was out of position and couldn't cover it. Charging forward on the drop volley, Allmen had two choices, a risky shot down the line that had to carry over the highest part of the net or the safer play. Safe for him at least. He heard his college tennis coach preaching his mantra: some shots look better than others but winning looks best of all. Sometime, in closed practices without prying ears he would add:

"And winning is what gets you laid." *Still tough to argue with after two decades.*

On the dead run he swung hard and hit the high percentage shot right up the T formed by the service lines. And he drilled the goddess. The sound of tennis ball on bare, beautifully bronzed flesh echoed between the garden wall and the hulk of the old hotel. Francesca grunted and screamed six words, three of which he recognized as filthy curse words in English, French and Italian. *My god, a woman who can swear like that, with those*

51

legs and that beautiful backhand.... That combination of talents should be illegal.

Allmen hurtled the net, apologies already forming on his lips. "My god, I am sorry." She waved him away, walking silently to the baseline. Allmen noticed the Brit's wife shaking her round, matronly head.

"Honestly, it wasn't intentional. I haven't played enough to control a shot like that."

"Or you just aren't good enough." She muttered.

The father looked on and then said. "Francesca, the man says he is sorry."

She turned and accepted the apology by nodding stonily.

"More?" She asked. But afterward, she was not the same player and her net game became erratic. John and Max took the set 6-4.

❋ ❋ ❋

As evening came, Allmen sat and watched the sun descend over Portoferraio, the old stone buildings turning pink and then orange. He vaguely wondered if he shouldn't venture into town and see the sights. But the thought of tourists fawning over Napoleon's commode made him vaguely nauseous. The tourists, not the toilet. *A man, even an Emperor, had to do what he had to do, after all.*

Instead, he went down to the dinner service to enjoy a good meal and wash it down with a healthy amount of wonderfully expensive Tuscan wine. He found his table prepared in a corner so that no one would bother him. He sat alone and sipped at a Negroni while he perused the menu. The gin warmed his stomach and the smell of orange slice awakened his nostrils and the sweet vermouth softened his palate. The Negroni was a drink to enhance the senses and make life a little better. *If only it lasted.*

Francesca appeared after about half an hour. She wore a

baby blue sleeveless blouse, dark pink skirt and beige heels with an elegant strap around her slim ankle. Her hair, dark and luxurious, fell in loose curls around her squared shoulders. She had a vaguely avian look, a hawk coolly surveying the hunting grounds and regarding the possibilities over a glass of Chianti. Occasionally, she laughed, showing white teeth to her parents. She briefly met Allmen's eye and frowned, shifting uncomfortably in her seat. He'd certainly made an impression. *Right around her left buttock.*

Her father was all smiles, the same teeth as darling daughter. And when he caught Allmen's eye, the old man gave a friendly wave. The waiter approached. "That table of three," he gestured in the direction of Francesca, "would be honored if you would join them for dinner." He detected a slight note of envy, a crack in the habitual professionalism.

John smiled. "Tell them I accept, and please bring us a bottle of the 2000 Gaja Sori San Lorenzo."

"A good choice sir. A very good choice."

Allmen strode to the table and the old man stood and spread his arms. "My friend John, you play great tennis. Smart tennis. Where did you learn it?" Italians really were about the friendliest people in the world. *Even when the German and then the American tanks had rolled through back in WWII they probably waived and said Ciao.*

"I played doubles in college, ah at university. I haven't played regularly in some time, though, and I appreciate you allowing me to join in and get some exercise."

He waived the comment away. "It was our pleasure. Well, maybe not Francesca's!"

She didn't laugh.

"Yes, about that. I do want to apologize again to you." John turned to look at her, held her gaze and felt some of the frost begin to thaw.

After a moment, she said haltingly, "It was the right play. You'd have never made the shot down the line. Too difficult. And I should have seen it coming. But enough. Let's drink wine and forget tennis."

Her father seemed slightly stung by the idea of forgetting tennis, her mother delighted. Allmen sensed something there, a tension. Francesca's tennis was mechanical. Technically perfect, to be sure, but she certainly didn't seem to get the joy out of it her father did. *And when Italians do anything without joy, take notice.*

"Do you drink wine?" The mother asked in halting English.

"Only to excess." Everyone laughed and soon they were all chatting away like old friends who desperately needed a few hours to catch up after a long separation. The wine worked wonders on Francesca. She became animated, even chatty as dinner passed pleasantly by in a succession of fast arriving and disappearing dishes. Like a spring released from tension or a tennis racquet with a broken string, she seemed to stretch out and unwind. Her motions became languid and her speech laconic. Somewhere during dinner, she had taken to calling Allmen, 'my American friend.'

"So, my American friend, what brought you to our little island paradise?"

"Sunshine, tennis and Italian wine. Is there more I need?"

"Oh, there is always more." She said this in a low voice, then glanced to see that her parents were well engaged in their own conversation. She moved to pat his hand as she said, "I hope we get a chance to play again. Tennis, that is." The hand stayed a fraction of an instant longer than necessary to convey the verbal point, but the non-verbal cues might as well have been in skywriting with fireworks erupting around them. Briefly, her hawkish look came back. Seeking a historical comparison, Allmen settled on Cleopatra, stunningly gorgeous, just a little bit crazy and thoroughly manipulative. There was certainly something about her that indicated a degree of damage. *Perhaps it was a single woman her age traveling with her parents? Or the crack in her demeanor on the tennis court.*

Dinner was winding down. It was time to make his move. "Can I interest you in a nightcap?"

She smiled and looked slyly at her parents, still chatting away, but now in slow motion. Fatigue, like death, came for everyone eventually. "No, thank you. Perhaps another time?" She gave him a lingering kiss on both cheeks, a friendly European goodbye and then hustled her parents away toward their rooms.

Denied, but hardly discouraged, Allmen finished the wine on the table. *Waste not want not.* Then he trod slowly back to his room. He heaved himself into bed, feeling his phone jab him from the front pocket. He extracted it and briefly glanced at his messages. There was but one, from Mack: "Hey, your wonder kid replacement isn't half bad, decent quarter but we all know it's not what you make it's what you keep. I don't have to tell a genius like you...Do I?"

Allmen frowned, annoyed to be interrupted with financial considerations, then stifled a yawn as he put down the phone and turned on the television.

* * *

The knock on his door came at around 1:30 AM by the bedside clock. He'd been dozing, fading in and out of a movie with English subtitles. He'd left it on because it starred Sean Connery. But the story didn't hold him, and he had drifted off. It had something to do with being well exercised, lubricated with olive oil, full on red meat, and high on amazing red wine.

Francesca breezed into the room and was on him before he had the door closed. It slammed shut as her lips met his, hands clawing at his shorts, soft murmurs of approval as he responded in kind. Suddenly she pulled back and brought his face to hers.

"Just don't touch my ass."

Allmen arched an eyebrow. "Have I missed something in translation?"

She put a hand on a hip. "So much wine you forget how you

bruised me here?"

"Shall I kiss it and make it better?" She laughed, and he liked the sound of it. And she didn't say no.

He bent as if to give the healing kiss and she pulled him upright, back to her face. "Kiss me here instead. Kiss me anywhere but there." This time it was Allmen who didn't say no. And though he enjoyed it all immensely, he couldn't help feeling like he was now in a movie. That her moves were scripted. That it was mechanical. Regardless, it was a pleasure to have this woman of incredible beauty.

After lying in bed for a while, she went to her clothes, her body moving lithely in the moonlight and extracted a cigarette from her handbag and lit it in Allmen's bed.

"My parents would kill me." She said flatly.

"For which part?"

"This." She held the cigarette high in front of her. "And before. Both, really."

"Well, you are a grown woman. You can take care of yourself, that it for certain."

"How do you know?"

Allmen shrugged. "Call it an educated guess." She considered this for a moment, pursing her lips and inhaling slowly.

"You've come so far to be with me. All the way from America." It was a strange comment, as if her destiny was all and his was nothing. He let the comment pass.

"What was that movie you had on when I came in?"

Allmen pretended to think. Her style of speech was a bit like an interrogator, considered pauses and rapid changes of topic. *Probing for weakness or inconsistency? Or hunting for it?*

"Not sure, but I think it was some sort of Camelot remake. Sean Connery as King Arthur. Richard Gere as the backstabbing Lancelot. We have a saying in the states. The book is usually better."

She swatted at her own smoke cloud, dismissing the comment. "I know someone who would have said the same thing. He was very... literary, is the word?"

"It is the word. So, who was this genius of a man?"

She rose briefly to put the cigarette out in the sink. "My ex-husband." She sighed sliding back into bed. "I am very tired. We can just lay here for a while?" It was no surprise, a woman in her mid-thirties who looked like her was either married or had been.

"We can." Allmen sat for a few minutes and heard her breathing grow heavy. He fell asleep, waking to streaming early morning light in the still open balcony door. The lovely Francesca was gone.

* * *

Breakfast was served on the pool deck and, though a more modest affair than dinner, it was still replete with meats, cheeses, eggs, sausage, cold cuts, various dairy items and, to Allmen's chagrin, breakfast cereal straight from a factory in Battle Creek, Michigan. *Some things probably ought to stay in the American Heartland.* Corn flakes were one thing he could do without in Europe.

It amazed him how good he could feel the morning after drinking so much wine, as long as it was quality stuff. Then again, the afterglow of a night with Francesca probably didn't hurt his mental or physical state one bit. He found himself sipping coffee and indulging in long, extended thoughts about her body, its angles and edges. And he shivered, but not from pleasure. A great gray billowing cloud had rolled overhead blotting out the sun. Allmen gazed out at the horizon and saw more building up behind it. Then he felt the first drop of rain.

That day there was no tennis. No one visited the pool or the beach. Instead, clouds blew in off the sea in great black masses and hard rain splattered the windowpanes. Allmen spent the day reading magazines and watching poorly dubbed Italian movies. In the evening a thunderstorm made dinner, usually in a great open air grotto, impractical except for room service. He ate and drank in a tense stupor, wishing for a knock at the door. He waited and drifted into an uneasy sleep.

For once, the wine didn't chase a dream away. He was walking through a wide, recently plowed field in the middle of summer, where seeds lay bare in mounded furrows. Great embankments of wild red roses and blooming orange trees formed looming hedges around him. In them were cut triangular alcoves where a menagerie of animals- parrots, monkeys, a coiled snake- all sat in repose. Rabbits darted about as he strode, legs thrusting and arms pumping with a rhythmic effort. The sun was on his face and the breeze blowing through the hedge brought the smell of lilacs in the air. In the distance he saw bare mountains curving smoothly skyward, rams and goats running through fields while a falcon circled above him, riding the currents and calling out mournfully into the wind.

He came to an end of the field, now facing a white meadow of carnations in bloom. He paused, wondering where he was going and the bird swooped low, called out and banked nimbly off to the left, then rose high and repeated the maneuver. The falcon was guiding him, urging him onward across the field. He walked gingerly now, feeling his way forward as the day wore on and shadows lengthened around him. He looked back often and saw that no matter how careful he had stepped, a wide swath of white flowers lay trampled behind him, broken and instantly decaying. The falcon swooped low again, calling him on, hurrying him forward and he warily resumed, finally angling off of the flower path and into a labyrinth in the hedge row.

He lost sight of the bird, the hedge too high to see over and found himself stumbling and shuffling feeling lost and alone. He turned a corner in a hedge and there, sitting on a stone wall was a blonde-haired woman. *The* blonde-haired woman, straw colored curls streaming over bare breasts, a blue cloak at her feet.

He watched her for some time. She seemed to be waiting for someone. Then she noticed him and beckoned. He walked toward her, but when he went to touch her, she extended a soft hand that checked him. He tried to say something, but he was strangely mute. He wanted to tell her of his, what? Love? That wasn't really the word that came to mind, his thoughts a more carnal mix of desire and ownership. He wanted this woman, her body sure, but it was more. He wanted possession of her. And he had waited long enough.

He tried again to reach her, the warmness of desire radiating through him as a shaft of sunlight poked over the hedge row casting a spotlight on them. She shook her head, extended her other arm and pushed him away.

She spoke then, a single word. "No." Her soft voice had a hard, steely edge and the word echoed off the hills in the distance, filling his ears. Anger and frustration rose in him. She didn't understand, he had to have her. He needed to have her.

"No," she said again.

And suddenly she was gone, the hedge and the faraway hills gone too. There was just the bird, a solemn black spot circling high overhead in an azure sky. And soon it too disappeared over the horizon. He waited for it to come back, to show him the way out of wherever he was. Instead, a different shape loomed up out of the horizon and he heard the mechanical sounds of flight. Rotors whirling and gears engaging, a black helicopter flew into view and hovered over him.

"Oh shit," he moaned, and woke to the sound of the air conditioner whirring in the bedroom.

❊ ❊ ❊

He rose at first light and went to breakfast. She hadn't shown up at his room. He played a singles match with Max, allowing the older man to save some face by winning 6-2 when it could have been much worse. And he had dinner alone, never seeing Francesca or her family. He thought, perhaps, they had gone.

Around midnight, he awoke to the knocking. Again, she

breezed in and took charge. And again, sweaty and breathless, they lay for some time on the bed before she got up and lit a cigarette.

"I thought you had gone," he said.

"We did. Shopping in Portoferraio. I told them I had to get back and make love to you. That you were going to marry me and take me back to America." It was quiet for a moment and then she tittered, turning into a full giggle and heaving laughs.

"Funny. I never thought I would hear you laugh, especially after our tennis match."

"Well, things change, don't they?"

"They certainly do." They lay for a while stretched out against each other. And then Allmen asked, "How long were you married?"

"For a while. Until I fell in love again." He was quiet. Beyond the stony façade, he got the feeling there was real pain there. This woman was beat-up and it was about more than just tennis and her father. He felt the strange stirrings of pity.

"It wasn't my fault. Love happens and people...they do bad things to each other."

Allmen just nodded. There was nothing untrue there. *Understatement of the century.* She had been flicking ash onto a towel by the bed and got up when her cigarette was finished and tossed all of it over the balcony. She came back and curled next to him.

"Were you married?" She asked.

"For a while."

"Until you fell in love again?"

"I fell in love with my work," he said. "That was enough." It was true, but like most truths, not the whole truth. He was absently stroking her hair. She took his hand away and sat up to face him.

"The man I fell in love with was named Paolo." Her eyes grew weary, sad. The look was foreign on her. "I was married to his brother."

Allmen was quiet for a long time. "You neglected to mention

60

that last time. I bet your parents didn't approve of that either."

She barked a laugh. "Of course not. They thought I had gone mad, leaving the great intellectual man to run off with his idiot brother. They thought he was a no good, lazy fool. But they didn't know Paolo. Not like I did. They didn't know how he could make me feel. Maybe they were right, maybe I was mad. But my life was out of control. Things happened. When I was with Paolo, it was more than man and wife. We were like god and goddess."

"Or like king and queen." Allmen noted, thinking of Guinevere and Arthur. *And Lancelot.*

"Sure. Whatever you like. Nothing could touch us. I loved his body. I loved his soul. I would have done anything for him and he for me. They thought he was stupid, but he would read to me, mostly poems." She sighed. "Such poems."

"And then..."

She elbowed him playfully. "We stopped reading." Allmen smiled in the dark. "When my husband found out, I thought he would kill Paolo. And me too. He was in such a rage, I thought he would send us both to he..." She stopped. *Was she going to finish with the word heaven or hell?* Instead, she said flatly, "I thought he would kill us. Instead, the police came and hauled them both off. I haven't seen either one of them since. My parents have seen to that." Allmen realized she had begun to cry softly, the kind of tears you wouldn't know were there in the dark, but he could feel her body moving in little silent sobs.

"Wow. That is some story." *Camelot falls.* But then he realized that Francesca might not see the moral lesson of Camelot. It was more likely she'd see it as an instruction manual.

"It is. A love story. A tragedy. What could I do? I was in love? My parents brought me on Holiday here, to forget, to move on. But, you see, it is hard."

"So, this is a recent development." She just nodded, still silently sobbing.

"Love came for me and I answered. What choice did I have?" She asked.

Allmen thought for a long time. "Free will. Is there an Italian word for free will?"

"Free will? What does this mean? Are you mocking of me?" She was upset and a little drunk. Neither contributed to speaking perfect English.

"No. Not purposely. I was just curious if there was a translation."

"I don't know." She murmured, curling onto him and resting her head onto his chest. "I don't know," she said again and fell asleep, breathing softly into his ear. He realized that it wasn't that she didn't know what the translation of free will was, she didn't know what it meant in any language. She was, in her own mind, a plaything for fate. Free will was a foreign concept to her. She wanted his reassurance that she wasn't wrong, that it had been okay. He couldn't give it. John Allmen was not in the reassurance business.

In the morning, she was gone again, the bed leaving a cast of her body in rumpled sheets like a form for a master sculptor. He snapped some photos out the window of the sun rising slowly over the sea.

While he had the phone handy, he dialed Virgil.

"Mr. Allmen, everything okay?"

"I think so Virgil, why?"

"Hadn't heard from you in a few days. I figured that no news was good news, but you never know."

"I met a woman, Virgil. I don't know what else to tell you."

"That seems to be a common theme with you. Congratulations."

"Save it Virgil. I think I need an extraction plan. I don't like the vibe if you know what I mean."

"Of course, Mr. Allmen. I think I can get you into the hotel in Florence I had picked out. Maybe some art and culture? Exercise your intellect where the Renaissance began?"

"Sounds like the perfect change of pace. Give the other parts of my body a rest."

* * *

David, Michelangelo's larger than life masterpiece, lurked in a capacious room under a giant rotunda in the Galleria dell 'Accademia. Light streamed down on him from above. From tangling the bed sheets on an island with Francesca, to staring at the world's most famous giant naked warrior in the span of a day.

People forgot that David was a soldier, a killer. In the bible, he engaged Goliath in single combat. *And won when the latter brought a knife to a projectile fight.* Brains and technology won out over brawn, in the Old Testament and in Allmen's own combat experience. Though it was nearly always a close contest.

He walked away from the giant nude warrior and began to stroll aimlessly. He found himself back near the entrance in the Hall of the Colossus, staring at three winding, serpentine figures carved from a single slab of marble. He stopped and read the sign nearby in English: The Rape of the Sabine Women. A cringing man hid his face, while another had hold of a naked woman who reached skyward toward, what? *The gods? Freedom?* It was an old sculpture, from an old story and a plot as old as time. Man has needs, man makes war, man conquers. But there was more. Two men. One woman. *That was the real reason for war, wasn't it? A scarcity of resources.*

He stared at the woman, her body arching, muscles tensing, her hair falling back from her classically lined face. It was Francesca, grabbed by one man while another watched helplessly. And a third circled on the periphery. He followed the curve of her shapely legs, walked around the pedestal and followed the form up to her hips, her breasts. One arm reached up skyward. The other down. *Heaven and hell. Pain and struggle. But also...ecstasy?* Or was he imaging that? It was hard to tell.

Allmen felt the shadows lengthening and a presence beside him. He felt a moment of panic. Was some feminist listening to his decidedly impure thoughts and about to attack him? Then a decidedly male Italian voice whispered: "Signore, the Galleria is closing."

He checked his watch. He felt his stomach rumble. And he

realized he'd spent several hours here gazing at a naked woman and her male captors.

"Grazzie," he mumbled and headed for the exit. He needed to clear his head. He ate a sandwich of mozzarella and tomatoes at the café across from the Duomo washing it down with a bottle of red wine. He didn't know what kind and he didn't much care. The Duomo, the great cathedral loomed over him with its towering arches and Renaissance dome. Allmen thought it looked like a woman's breast. *Like Francesca's. Jesus man, what are you? Twelve years old?*

Trying to recover himself and his dignity, he shuffled over to the Baptistry to have a look at another of the masterpieces of the Renaissance. The squat octagonal basilica in the middle of the square is one of the oldest buildings in Florence, and the Medici family and Dante Alighieri were said to have been baptized there. The doors on the east side were reputed to be some of the most amazing art in the world. Allmen stared at ten panels in gilded bronze depicting the old testament from the time of Adam and Eve to King Solomon. Adam and Eve. Man and woman.

Stare con te, stare con te.
Be with you, be with you.

His mind was in Elba, in a bed with a woman who should be cast in marble and who was trying to break free. His head started to pound and Allmen turned his back on the Gates of Paradise and headed for the hotel. There he turned off his phone and stuck it in his pocket. Then he arranged through the front desk to rent his own car. They dropped it off and went through the necessaries with him and in an hour, he was out of the city and heading west.

He caught the afternoon ferry, hailed a cab in the port and arrived back at his Elba hotel as a late afternoon game of tennis was wrapping up. These were new guests, no amiable Brit, no solid Austrian and no Francesca.

He walked briskly around the building toward the bar and found the same bartender polishing glasses, a bored expression on his usually happy face. His parrot cocked one eye and then the other at each glass as he pulled it from a steaming wash basin and went to work with a dry cloth.

The gravel crunched under Allmen's leather loafers. "Ah, Signore! A beer today?"

"Sure. Thank you." Allmen paused for a moment unsure of how to proceed. He went straight ahead. "There was a woman staying here. Tall, athletic, Italian." He accepted the beer and took a tentative sip, his mind churning.

"Si, I know the one. My God, what a woman. But she checked out with her family yesterday."

Allmen nodded. *What did you expect?* And what had he wanted of her if she were here? "Idiot," he muttered to himself.

"Signore, she left this for you in case you came back." The bartender looked at him conspiratorially. The parrot bobbed and stared . It was hotel stationary, folded once and in the middle, written in her lipstick were two Italian words:

libero arbitrio

"Can you translate this for me?"

The bartender arched an eyebrow, then smiled ruefully: "I can, but I don't understand. It says…free …will?"

John Allmen took the ferry back to the mainland and turned the phone on while sitting in his car. No messages. He dialed.

"Look Virgil, I'm not feeling well. I think it is time to call it quits a little early and head home."

* * *

Allmen landed in San Francisco and had the driver let him out downtown while he delivered his bags back to the house. He told himself he needed to stretch his legs, and of course, get a drink. His mind wandered, and came back to women. His wife, Tricia, the good and the bad. The bad hadn't really been her fault, had it? *Nope, totally on me.* Then his thoughts turned again to the blonde woman who could be anywhere in town right now, and then Francesca.

"Beautiful women." A form loomed at his shoulder.

Allmen whirled and gave him a hard look. "What? What did you say?" He was a massive bald man in a muscle tee shirt and black jeans.

"Beautiful women, man. Right this way." Allmen had wandered up near Columbus and Broadway where the sex shops and strip clubs loomed. The man was pointing down a stairway that dove downward into the darkness.

Allmen took a step down to look past the man and asked: "You have a full bar?"

"Sure man. Whatever you want."

Allmen considered. "What the hell." And he took another step downward.

GLUTTONY:

over-indulgence and over-consumption of food, drink, or wealth items, particularly as status symbols

I arrive, of show'rs
Ceaseless, accursed, heavy, and cold, unchanged
For ever, both in kind and in degree.
Large hail, discolour'd water, sleety flaw
Through the dun midnight air stream'd down amain:
Stank all the land whereon that tempest fell.

-Dante, Inferno, Canto VI

Allmen's life in San Francisco had taken on a pattern in the days after his departure from the working world. He lived like a hermit most of the time, spending long stretches reading in a semi-circular kitchen window in his twenty-one hundred square foot home in the Cow Hollow neighborhood. The nook had overstuffed pillows and when the sun shone in, he could relax there surrounded by the great works of history and literature. He loved books. He considered them windows to other worlds, just like good music. And he usually had a few dog eared paperbacks out for easy access. Occasionally throwing them into backpacks when it was time to hit the road or casually thumbing through them while having a coffee or cocktail. The two he had out now were consciously curated to capture his current spirit of adventure. Hemingway's The Sun Also Rises about an extended multi-country bender was an obvious choice. It was also his favorite book from childhood. The other was a newer obsession, Kitchen Confidential, by travel and food guru Anthony Bourdain.

Allmen was no chef and Bourdain's book had put him off of sushi for some time. So he set about cooking his own meals, when he remembered to. And he lived off of leftovers for extended stretches. He'd venture out for coffee most mornings and a few times a week set off on a long rambling hike through the city or into the hills above the Golden Gate Bridge. Occasionally he would accept an invitation to play tennis or golf, but usually regretted the intrusion into his routine. Conversation was forced, no matter who he played with. It was the life of a retired bachelor excepting the expanded time he spent visiting his daughter. The break in the routine came when Virgil reentered the picture, sometimes with questions about this or that preference on an upcoming itinerary.

"Next up is France," Virgil was saying as Allmen sipped at an industrialized cappuccino at the chain on Union Street.

He closed Kitchen Confidential and said with mock sternness: "Virgil, it is almost like you are reading my mind."

"How so?"

"I'm reading a book right now about a young man who learns to love food while traveling through France. This isn't another of your apps, tracking me...listening to my conversations and, you know my thoughts?"

"You didn't read that part of the service agreement?"

"Uh....I uh...well, you know I don't read that stuff."

"I'm kidding Mr. Allmen. Coincidence. You said at some point you wanted to go to Paris and this seems to be the best time. Besides, all great books should have at least a few scenes in Paris. Like The DaVinci Code."

Allmen snorted. He'd come to loathe that book over the years with its stilted dialogue and religious overtones. "Virgil, what wine would you want to drink from the Holy Grail?"

"A red certainly...old world."

"Touché!"

"See, you are speaking the language already. Have a good trip. And don't get into any trouble."

Allmen feigned both innocence and injury: "Moi?"

*　*　*

The flight, direct from SFO seemed interminable at just under eleven hours, and it would have been more so if it weren't an Air France flight complete with real bottles of wine being doled out with an edible meal in First Class. Allmen tried in vain to catch some sleep after a dinner of pasta and chicken and a passable attempt at a baguette. *Washed down, of course, with copious amounts of French merlot.* But he found himself reliving the last few months of his life instead. He had had no recent glimpses of the blonde woman and for a time he had forgotten about

Francesca as well.

But now, bored on a transatlantic flight, headed vaguely in her direction, he thought of the Italian goddess again and wondered how her tentative steps toward free will were coming along. He connected his phone to the inflight internet and began some general Google searches for junior Italian tennis players named Francesca.

Airline internet is like airline food, the same in name only. So, it was slow going. But eventually, after sifting through pages of news on the professional player Francesca Schiae, who was in the downside of her career in her late 30s, he found some promising hits on a player named Francesca Rimini near Ravenna. After a bit, he was able to pull up a picture of her in an off-circuit doubles match. Even in her twenties, she had the same hawk-like features and an even harder muscled body. *Hadn't thought that was possible at times when we were pressed against each other.* He put down the phone and stared out the window as the Atlantic Ocean rolled by underneath him. It was a pleasant image to fall asleep to, which he did somewhere over Greenland.

His dream was brief. Francesca, hard muscle and bronzed skin, wearing a white tennis dress, boarding a helicopter and waving goodbye. Slowly. Sadly. When he woke, the cabin lights were on and the airliner was lumbering downward toward the continent, preparing to land. He barely had time to wonder what, if anything, it had meant.

Paris was a gray smudge on a rain splattered window, wipers working spasmodically to clear away the sludgy precipitation that had been falling since he'd landed. His driver edged his way through traffic occasionally mumbling in complaint, but otherwise saying nothing. Indeed, he had hardly said more than a few monosyllabic words since picking Allmen up at De Gaulle for the hour-long trip skirting the slums north of the city.

"Hey, looks like you'll be driving me today. My name is John. What is yours?"

"Giacomo." He had a massive head and jowls and was

overweight, tending towards slovenly wearing a Paris Saint Germain football jersey, a white neck scarf and khaki pants. Allmen guessed from his craggy hands and jet white hair that he was in his seventies. A layer of fat clearly coated over what used to be muscle. He demonstrated his strength by hefting luggage for a ten day stay as if it were a child's backpack.

"Ah, and where are you from?"

"Corsica." Allmen thought Giacomo perfectly morphed a combination of Winston Churchill and Rocky Balboa's brother-in-law, at least in looks. As for wordiness and wit, it was mostly the latter.

But Giacomo was an adept driver, weaving into and out of tight traffic spots as they inched toward Paris proper. Here in the hinterlands, graffiti was everywhere, usually in French but sometimes in English. Neither the former nor the latter made much sense. Allmen watched as a tent city rolled by, sullen and soggy watchers in the muck and mire. They were keeping the gates to the City of Lights. They seemed unaware of each other, just watching him as he rolled by with the doors locked. Allmen thought for a moment about the crisis of European immigration, strangers in a strange land, living in squalor that made the Tenderloin district in San Francisco look like a yuppie's Kentucky Derby party. Thinking about big problems in the rain was a sure way to darken his mood. Instead, he opened the file box in his mind, a large and ever expanding one, to the folder marked Shit I Don't Worry About. He deposited his darkening thoughts there.

In ten minutes, they had crept into a tonier environment, lit shop fronts that didn't require bars and graffiti of whimsical tags in neon capital letters. The drizzle continued through a line of dark clouds bathing the 20th Arrondissement in depressing fog. Soon they were rolling past Pere Lachaise Cemetery and Allmen was considering all of the marble grave markers. A mist hovered over them and the rain splattered off the asphalt.

"Say, Giacomo, do you mind stopping for a few minutes?"

The reply may have been "Oui, bien sur", or "What a bastard."

Allmen had trouble deciphering the driver's determined mutter. But he assumed the former when the car swerved to the curb and idled. Giacomo handed him back a small umbrella.

"As a Corsican, do you prefer I say merci or grazie? Or thank you?" The driver shrugged as if to say it was all the same to him.

Allmen entered along Avenue Gambetta across from the Metro station and hoofed it up thirty steps to the gate. He wandered around a bit, looking for famous graves, but not bothering to take a map. Without much effort, he spotted Jimmy Hendricks, and then Oscar Wilde and Fredrick Chopin. *Very different people, all similarly dead and gone.*

Just as famous, or perhaps notorious, and certainly just as dead was Jim Morrison and Allmen found himself stopped in front of his slab. Morrison's music and that of The Doors was an acquired taste, one that had mostly eluded Allmen. But he lingered there with a particular song reverberating through his brain: The End.

It was the song used in the extended introduction to the war movie Apocalypse Now, a classic of the genre. And one Allmen hadn't thought of in years. He felt cold and pulled his jacket tight and adjusted the angle of his umbrella against the sleety wind. He tended to avoid those kinds of movies that could trigger what his therapist had called "latent traumatic memories." But now, his mind's eye saw a young Martin Sheen sitting under a rotating fan blade. And that fan blade morphed into the whirling blades of helicopters.

The rain began to come down in a slushy mix, thumping hard into his umbrella, making popping sounds like bullets against metal. For a while he couldn't move, though water had started to drip down the back of his blue Brooks Brothers raincoat.

Only the soft vibration and chime of his phone broke the spell. Allmen walked slowly back to the car and distracted himself by taking out the phone. There was a text from Mason. Doing the math, Allmen figured it was around 5:30 AM his time. Just about right for a hard charging Marine who had probably already hit the gym before paying attention to his social life.

"Dude call me."

Mack Mason didn't often descend into dude/bro speak, opting for the universal noun 'Marine.' And if you weren't a Marine, you were 'hey you'. So, Allmen took this message seriously and dialed as Giacomo was pulling away from the curb.

"Well, well, the prodigal son returns...returns my text anyway. Where are you Marine?

"Outside Paris. In a cemetery."

"Somebody die?"

Allmen sighed. "Lots of people Mack. Every day."

"No shit, asshole. I mean anyone we know?"

"Not this time. Edith Piaf. Jimmy Hendricks. Jim Morrison. There is a cemetery for the tragically famous here."

"Of course there is."

"So, *dude...*tell me what your text was about."

Mason paused, digesting the change in topic. "Okay, I'll cut to the chase. A woman was asking questions about you. I was at the office in San Mateo, checking on my minions. She cornered me downstairs in the basement coffee shop with the whole fawning over Mack Mason act. I fell for it for a bit and next thing I know she mentions you and starts asking how I know you, the last time we talked, that sort of thing."

"You sure you weren't just lost in her cleavage?"

"Jesus Marine, I'm sure that I *was*. She's got the curves of a bay clipper, and apparently the brains to match. Dangerous combo. But eventually, I got suspicious. I hated for her to leave, but I liked watching her go."

"Tell me about it."

"So, you know her?"

"Think so...we've met at least. It's a long story. Or a short one, I'm not sure."

"I don't copy."

"I know. I don't really understand either Mack. Thanks for the intel. Can I call you later?"

"Sure thing. Take care of yourself."

"Of course. It's Paris, what could go wrong?"

73

"The French. That's what."

"Mack," Allmen sighed, "you should learn to appreciate the French. You know, there were more French soldiers at the Battle of Yorktown than there were Colonials? We wouldn't be around if it weren't for them. And likewise, as we all know."

Mason was quiet for a minute. Allmen could hear him typing with two index fingers. "Huh, you are right. At least according to Wikipedia."

"Well, it's on the Internet Mack, it has to be true."

"Okay, enjoy your frogs' legs and Chablis." He pronounced it Cha-bliss. "Call me when you can talk."

"Rodger that." Allmen hung up and sighed. So, she was looking for him... and he was half a world away. And Francesca was somewhere in Italy, likely still seeking comfort from whomever she could find it. Despite being in the City of Light, he felt dark and brooding. But Mack had a point. Food and booze would certainly help.

"Giacomo, I need a beer. Is it possible?"

"Oui." Allmen wasn't sure if he meant yes, or that they both needed a beer. But it hardly mattered. In twenty minutes, they had crossed the 11th arrondissement, and passed the Centre Pompidou, a modern art holding pen that looked like the architect had accidentally put all the sewage pipes on the outside of the walls. They pulled to the side of Avenue Victoria, a typical Parisian side street with a wide sidewalk shaded by trees. The trees were dripping rain from a line of café awnings set back from the street. Allmen took note of a dark awning with white letters: *Dernier Bar Avant la Fin du Monde.* The Last Bar Before the End of the World.

"Perfect."

"Oui. Si. Yes." Giacomo said three words, smiled. *Actually smiled.*

"You coming?"

Giacomo held up one of his hands with fingers like andouille sausages to beg off. "No, but my grandson is waiting for you. Be careful." He laughed, maybe cackled. Allmen couldn't be sure, so surprised was he to have gotten two full sentences out of the big man. He neglected to ask what he should be careful of.

Allmen was greeted at the door and after offering the password, "Giacomo", another heavy-set young man a few decades junior to his driver showed him to a café table in front of a huge bookcase.

Allmen had had an apocalyptic vision of the Last Bar Before the End of the World, with fire and brimstone and beholding a white horse a la the Book of Revelations. In this, he was disappointed. Instead, displayed in the bookcase were various knick-knacks from the sci-fi universe and dungeons and dragons. Clearly, this place really was meant to be the last way stop before another dimension. A nerdier one. A chilled pint glass and a bottle of beer appeared on a silver platter before Allmen had a chance to bolt out the side door.

Little Giacomo smiled. *"Bon chance mon amie."*

Good luck with what? This ain't my first beer junior. He poured a glass and glanced at the label. It was a place in Paris called the Brewery of Being, Brasserie de l'être.

He downed half of the beer bottle in a long, grateful swallow. *Nectar.* He practically moaned with delight, the finish lingering with spice and a touch of bitterness to remind you that you were drinking beer. Then he looked at the other side of the label and saw a three headed hound from hell. Cerberus was the name. A Belgian style Tripel hop, it featured a creamy head of fine bubbles, a malty nose, and a black and white drawing of a snarling, snapping three headed dog. This was good beer, real beer. And Allmen polished off his first bottle with another long pull. Little Giacomo appeared again with a large plate of charcuterie including sliced sausages, ham and a spicy Spanish chorizo.

*"Gloo*tony." He said as only a Frenchman pronouncing an English word could. Allmen cocked his head and furrowed his brow. Little Giacomo pointed to the menu, which looked like a middle school project to reproduce someone's favorite comic book. Under various appetizers options was the plate of cured

meats. Which they had named 'Gluttony'.

"Ah," he said, "wonderful. Merci." Allmen dove in with a fork and knife, eventually devolving into a frenzy of fingers as the beer and the time difference took hold. The beer, which turned out to be about twice as alcoholic as the king of American crappy lagers, hit hard. He felt himself sagging into the couch a little further as each arrived. And eventually, with a few sips left of his sixth, his world went dark. A last glimpse of the model Millennium Falcon above him on the bookcase, and he was hurling past planets and stars into the blackness.

He had strange, half-conscious dreams. Jabba the Hutt was driving him around in a blue BMW X-5 as they were pursued by tiny helicopters and three headed monsters. His dreamy interlude was then chased away as Big Giacomo put a massive paw around him and lifted him from his seat like a child from a Chuck E Cheese booster seat. Through the haze, Allmen noticed Giacomo passing a 20 Euro note to his grandson. Little Giacomo beamed. Then Allmen reached, picked the remaining beer bottle from his hand, and finished it, the brew and the mirth on Little Giacomo's chubby moon-like face, simultaneously draining away to nothing.

"Ha!" Bellowed the grandfather, now practically bear hugging Allmen. "Six!"

Little Giacomo handed back the twenty, dug into his pockets and produced a like bill that he placed in Big Giacomo's massive hand with a dissatisfied slap.

"What just happened?"

"You went to sleep," chortled the driver, guiding him toward the door.

"I mean with the money." Allmen slithered into the back seat.

"You won me twenty Euros." Giacomo grinned broadly as he adjusted himself in the driver's seat. "My grandson said you couldn't finish six of those monster beers. I sized you up. You are an American, yes, but still there is some backbone in you." Giacomo slapped the steering wheel and chortled.

After a short drive through a foggy night, they pulled up

in front of his apartment in the Marais district of the 3rd arrondissement. Big Giacomo again helped him inside, waving off his half-slurred apologies with a great big smile.

"If you need me again, tell them to ask for Ciaccio. It is my nickname. Call me Ciaccio from now on, okay? If you want to eat, you let me know. I know how to do it." He slapped his great belly for emphasis, the sound like a hammer against a gigantic barrel. Then he drove off leaving Allmen somewhat stupefied by all of the chit chat.

He stumbled toward the bedroom, but never made it. Before the large room with a four-poster bed, he paused to rest on the leather sofa. As the rain drummed down again outside, he lost consciousness for the third and final time that night. Thus, did Cerberus, the snarling dog of ancient literature guard Paris from John Allmen. At least for a while.

❊ ❊ ❊

He was asleep for just over five hours, waking after the day's rain had ended and the night rain began. Lights were up in the city and the dinner hour was ending. It was just after 11 PM. Ciaccio was nowhere to be found and Allmen figured he had done enough to model the 'Ugly American' stereotype for a day. He was ravenous, belly rumbling in confused, time distorted sobs. So, he grabbed a cab and got let off near the Champs Elysees. He knew better than to be gouged by the tourist traps along the main road, but in the side streets he figured he could find a hidden gem. One usually could in Paris, at almost any hour. The first few were full, typical of the City of Lights, even under a deluge. But on the third try, in an alley he'd have a tough time navigating back from, he found a little mom and pop with a yellow awning and one seat still open for dinner.

The meal opened with a small *amuse bouche* of toasted baguette and fish rillette. A split of champagne washed it down. Foreplay finished, the meal began in earnest. A Burgundian white wine, a Montrachet came in a glass, but the proprietor also brought the remainder of an open bottle and added it to the table without asking. Allmen liked the gesture. He loved the wine. It was soft, yet angular. Not like some California chardonnay for a lady's book club. This was real wine and it was perfectly paired with green beans on a square earthenware platter with golden pats of butter and white pearls of shaved garlic. He helped himself to a mound and then another before the roast chicken appeared. The bird had skin alternately charred and bronzed to a perfectly crisp finish that crunched audibly as the *monsieur* plunged a carving knife deep into the flesh, paring off legs and wings. And then slicing off a perfectly shaped breast of white meat still clinging to its golden casing.

They had taken more butter and stuffed the bird's cavity as well as under the flesh, adding herbs and salt. This was a glorious and exalted chicken and Allmen continued to fill his plate until an empty carcass was carted away with a nod of approval from the owner/waiter/bartender. Of course, there was more wine, red now, to accompany his feast. He drank a bottle of deep red Burgundy, an eloquent accompaniment from Nuits Saint George. It was all berries and cedar and fit in with both the chicken and the cheese course that followed.

Allmen stifled a belch, and declined desert, opting instead for a glass of sauternes to end on a sweet note. He felt drowsiness creep in and stole a look at his phone. It was well after two in the morning. He sat for a while happy to be full and more than a little drunk in Paris. Finally, he motioned for the bill, slurred a few thank yous in various languages and found his way back toward the main thoroughfare. A *Tabac* was still open and he selected a Cuban Montecristo cigar.

It was a light tobacco, perfect for after dinner, not some stinking rag weed that he'd wake up choking on in a few hours. He smoked for a few miles, walking off the meal, enjoying the taste and smell of the tobacco and the sights and sounds of Paris. The city was slowly turning in as the middle of the night descended like a dark cloak. When the cigar was spent, he hailed a cab, glad that you could still do so at all hours in a great city and went back to his apartment, dropping into an exhausted sleep just after 4. His last thought before drifting off was that Paris was the perfect place to satiate one's non-sexual appetites. And then he thought of Francesca and then the blonde mystery woman in white. He would have enjoyed sharing that dinner with either one of them. *Or both. A guy can dream.*

He awoke again just after noon local time, showered and dressed, donning a sweater and jeans, plus the Brooks Brothers raincoat against the continued drizzle. Paris was used to this and the café down the street showed no signs of a weather-related business downturn. Allmen found a table with two chairs, one looking out onto the street where the flotsam and jetsam of Paris came to and from the underground. He watched pretty girls in parkas and old bums in garbage bags while he sipped an espresso and tried to wish away his hangover. His father had a saying, "wish in one hand and shit in the other. See which gets you further." Hard to argue with pops.

And so, Allmen opted to take care of said hangover with a time-honored remedy: the hair of the dog, in this case, somewhat literally. He asked if they offered the local brew called Cerberus, but the waiter, whose English wasn't much of a compliment to Allmen's French, assured him they did not. So, he switched his tactic and ordered a carafe of rosé wine from Bandol, in the south. What better way to pretend it was sunny and warm than to drink something from a place where it was probably sunny and warm? Next, he took his phone out of an interior pocket in his coat and called a restaurant that came highly recommended and made a dinner reservation. And then he called Virgil with an idea.

"Yes, Mr. Allmen?"

"Virgil, can I borrow my driver from yesterday, Ciaccio his name is?"

"Ummm....I'm not sure I follow you."

Allmen sighed. "Can we hire my driver for a few days to get out of this rain, or at least go and visit the finest wine and food where it lives and breathes? Some day trips. Maybe overnight? Hell, maybe we'll get all the way to Italy?"

Virgil was quiet and Allmen could hear him typing. "Shouldn't be a problem but let me confirm and get back to you."

"Text, don't call. I am going to be up to my ears in fire and charred flesh."

Robert et Louise wasn't much more than a couple of red doors off of Rue de Temple, about a ten-minute walk in the drizzle from the café where the carafe of rose and a couple of Kir cocktails had kept him occupied until his reservation. Inside they seated him at the bar, the last seat in the house, and one he was lucky to get on late notice. The place was all wood, stone and bric-à-brac, embraced by an ethereal layer of smoke from an actual wood fired stove to his left as he took his post. It was the kind of place you only found in the old world, mostly due to modern fire safety laws. But they had been serving carnivorous feasts here for six decades and hadn't burned the place to the ground. Allmen figured he was on the right side of history. Besides, he was on the top floor. It was the people in the basement who were royally screwed if everything went up in flames. *C'est la vie.*

He asked for the wine list and skipped past anything pink or white. *Been there, done that. Time to get serious.* This was going to be an old school orgy of meat and it demanded hearty red wines. Plural. So, he ordered a bottle of single vineyard Côte-Rôtie, a northern Rhone Syrah that would stand up to the coming assault.

First, an appetizer of boudin noir. Black blood sausage was filled with cream and apples, a hearty opener, soft and savory, tasting like meat but with the texture of a puff pastry filling. It was like what meat would be in a Jetsons cartoon and yet it was an idea probably almost as old as fire. *Kill something and use all of it for food. Even the parts your squeamish offspring in first world countries will recoil at if you bother to explain what they are eating.*

Feeling slightly superior and satisfied, he dove into the terrine de foie gras, a decadent little delivery filled with fatty, pulverized duck liver, white port and herbs. It was cooked and set in a dish that yielded up chubby slabs of self-indulgence to be slathered on rough bread. Illegal in San Francisco for a few years due to the force feeding of the birds to fatten up their livers, Allmen thought briefly about their plight. Then he again opened his mental file cabinet. And...

"Shit," he murmured into his wine glass, promptly forgetting where he wanted to put those thoughts. Such were the effects of the wine and cocktails. *Vive la France.*

No matter, another dish arrived and saved him from the effort of philosophical consideration or file organization. It was a fragrant dish of potted pork. Fatty pork belly was swimming in butter and peppercorns and had been slow cooked to the consistency of a gritty paste. He was winding down on the first bottle of wine and, to address the sin of an empty glass, ordered an angel. *Doesn't everyone need one of those?* This particular one, Château Angélus, was one of the finer producers from Saint-Émilion, a right bank Bordeaux of soft, seductive Merlot. The server gave a nod of approval while arching an eyebrow at the rate of consumption. His expression seemed to say "Anglo-Saxons, can't live with 'em, and after all these centuries, still can't figure out how to kill them all."

For the last act in his one-man extravaganza, Allmen had ordered a seared beef rib. He was promptly warned that it was meant for two, but he didn't care. He wanted it and no one was here to share it, so he ate it. Again, he thought of the blonde woman and how much fun it might be to share a meal like this. *A man sharing a rib with a woman. Like Adam and Eve. Original sinners.*

Finally, for the curtain call, was cheese. This was Allmen's idea of acceptable dessert. He chose a soft unpasteurized Reblochon that one could not get in the States due to food import laws. Yes, you could poison American youth with potatoes cooked in laboratory fluid and call them French fries. But you dare not import a cheese that isn't hit with microwaves for your protection. *What the fuck is that all about? Is our biggest problem as a country the mold on our cheese? I'm quite certain that there are bigger issues at stake in the world.* But it was not a night for epiphanies.

One problem at a time. And he had to feed the beast, the one demanding more food from within. The Reblochon oozed a bit in the smoky warmth of the room. It had a nutty taste that lingered on the tongue well after the runny cheese evaporated and it paired well with his wine, at least for a while. He sat for a long time, savoring the fatty taste on his tongue and eventually staring at another empty wine bottle.

Allmen paid the bill and unsteadily headed for the door. A vague uneasiness kept creeping into his foggy brain about how he might, or might not, sleep. *Helicopter dreams? Thoughts of Francesca? Thoughts of the blonde woman?* He couldn't be sure, so he decided to put sleep on hold. The café, he was coming to think of it as *his* café, was still open. And his seat from earlier in the day was again unoccupied.

He passed out there in the middle of a Scotch, the waiter kind enough to leave him be for thirty minutes before 'accidentally' bumping his chair while bussing an adjacent table to bring him out of his stupor. He left a clump of Euros, more than enough for the bill and stumbled to his apartment through the crosswalk. When he got to the top of the stairs, he fished in his coat for the keys and brought out his phone too. He dialed Mason's number with thick, unresponsive fingers.

"Mack," he whispered for no reason other than he was intoxicated, "it's John."

"I know." It was all Mason said and a more astute listener might have picked up on the tone of annoyance.

"I had to call you."

"Why? It is late there, isn't it? You in the bag?"

"Ye...thir. True statement." In his state his words came out thick and slurry. "You thee, there are a few things bothering me."

"Oh?"

"That beautiful woman. I can't get her out of my head."

"The one that came here digging for info?"

"Sure. That is the one."

"Normal. She's a good-looking woman. Do something about it when you get home. So why drunk dial me?"

"Well, Major..." He almost stopped there. But suddenly the words tumbled out of him. "The fucking helicopter." Suddenly, Allmen found he felt slightly more sober.

"Say again?"

"The chopper Mack, outside of Fallujah. I'm dreaming about it again."

"Oh...shit."

"The good part is that drinking enough and passing out seems to cure it, so...."

Mason was quiet for a long moment. Then, his tone softened, he said, "John, that was not your fault. We've covered this ground. You did your job, did well, did the right thing..."

"And people died."

"Somebody told me not long ago that lots of people die every day."

Allmen barely recognized his own words being used against him. He was curled up in the fetal position on the leather couch that served as a sitting room between the bedroom and the bath and substituted nicely in a pinch for a proper bed. For the second night, the bed remained neatly and tidily made.

"John, maybe it is a signal from your subconscious that it is time to drop this wayward gypsy act and get back to your life here. Stop reliving the past, get on with your future. Maybe come see the therapist again. She helped a few years ago. Until..."

"No...no..." Allmen dropped the phone and fell into a deep, dark, drunk sleep before he even had a thought to pick it up again.

* * *

He'd fallen asleep six or so hours earlier, mid-sentence, and left the phone powered on to drain itself of battery. Which was kind of how Allmen himself felt: dropped on the floor and draining slowly of battery life. When he finally awoke to the sounds of bustling city life on the streets below, he needed recharging and thought he might start with some culture. He showered while leaning against the wall and letting a hot waterfall roll over him for several minutes. Walking home had helped him burn off some of the booze of the previous night, or morning, and the shower now helped finish the job.

Dressed and fresh, he had charged his phone and realized he had missed calls and text messages from Virgil, Ciaccio and Mack. The latter he could do nothing about for hours due to the time change. But Ciaccio and Virgil had teamed up to solve some problems for him and despite a lethargic feeling, he forced himself out into the world.

He walked, striding hard to get a sweat going as he headed toward the Seine at the Pont Neuf. Then he strode along the left bank dodging a press of tourists and scooters. The former had been here for centuries. But the latter were new to Paris, the vision of some hipster genius who envisioned a scooting utopia that replaced cars and zipped pedestrians from the Hotel de Ville to Trocadero in a fun-filled flash. In reality they were a nuisance. Users tended to discard them wherever they damn well pleased including in the middle of the sidewalk. Allmen thought it typical to underestimate the human race's tendency to be selfish and lazy. He had seen it many times with shopping carts strewn about the parking lot of his local Safeway.

He navigated the human minefield to the old train station serving Lyon and points south, the Musée d'Orsay. Picking up his pre-ordered tickets he headed up the stairs to the second floor and took a seat at the restaurant. For fortification before viewing art there was nothing like a bottle of Burgundy and duck foie gras on brioche under gilded ceilings and expansive crystal chandeliers. It was just after noon. He finished and wandered about the mezzanine outside the restaurant with sculptures from the post 1880s. Above and below were some of the finest art in Paris, but Allmen found himself standing for nearly an hour in front of a large slab that was vaguely familiar. It was about twenty feet tall, looming overhead in hulking white plaster. A miniature version of Rodin's famous meditator, known as The Thinker, was three quarters of the way up above what looked like elevator doors. The rest of the figures were foreign to him, though despite being cast in white marble, they looked morbid and foreboding. *Going up? Nope. Probably not.*

"You are at the gates to hell, my friend." It was Ciaccio. The big man wore a lopsided grin and Allmen realized belatedly how bad the man's teeth were, perhaps a reason why he so rarely opened his mouth when he didn't know someone well. And the actual name of Rodin's work was The Gates *of* Hell, not the Gates *to* Hell. *But foreigners were always mixing up their prepositions when speaking a foreign language. Weren't they?*

"Bonjour mon amie. Sorry to bother you. But you rang for me?"

"I did. I wanted to take you up on your offer. I want to eat...and drink...wherever you think is best."

"Okay. I spoke with your friend Virgil. It is all arranged. You know this piece?" He gave a massive nod at Rodin's work.

"Yeah. In fact, I saw the Florentine version a few months ago. The Baptistry across from the Duomo."

"Rodin was inspired by those Gates of Paradise you saw in Florence. You see how good things can be when you combine Italy and France?"

"Like, say, in a Corsican?"

"Ha! You said it, not me. Time for champagne?"

Allmen checked his watch. "Seems like the right time to me."

Ciaccio lingered a moment longer, his eyes taking in the massive structure, clearly appreciating its form and lines.

"You see this one? Sublime." He pointed out the right panel, where a man and a woman embraced on a rock. She seemed to be slipping away from him. "That's called *Fugit Amor*. Ah, in English...Fugitive Love. Timeless beauty is about to be just out of reach," Ciaccio sighed.

Allmen craned his neck to see the man and the woman with

the nearly translucent alabaster skin. She somehow seemed awfully familiar.

"Come my friend. Statues are not the only art in France."

In a few minutes they were rumbling out of Paris in the BMW. He was somewhat disappointed to learn that Ciaccio was referring to the *region* of Champagne and not an immediate afternoon beverage. No bottle of bubbles awaited him. Not yet. Though he only discovered this as they got on the A4 motorway headed out of town towards Reims. He dozed for a while, watching the landscape outside of Paris roll by, mostly billboards and train tracks and then green square tracts of farmland. Several of the smaller billboards were touting 'Frexit' these days, a French exit from the European Union following their good friends the British out the communal trap door.

"Frexit? Isn't breaking up hard to do?"

Ciaccio nodded, staring intently as the multilane highway unraveled before them. Allmen thought that might be all he would get, but the big man surprised him by turning down the radio and looking at him in the rearview mirror. "Big thing here for a few years and the Presidential election. How can you tell a Frenchman how to make cheese? They do that now, from Brussels. You have had the white asparagus from the Loire?"

"I don't think so."

"Sublime. You must try it while you are here, my friend. But from Brussels they now tell the French farmers to grow it in Normandy. Tear out the Norman orchards! You see, there are too many apples and not enough asparagus. White asparagus in Normandy. It is the end of days."

Allmen shrugged. "All for the greater good?" It was a question, not really intended as an answer.

Ciaccio shrugged his massive shoulders. "It's not something I worry about usually. Except for the cheese." He patted his expansive paunch. "My family, my ancestors, were Italian. But we lived on an island that became French when the Genoese needed to pay their debts. Corsica is only famously French because of Napoleon." He shrugged again. "And two or three times, we all came close to being German. So, a master in Paris, Brussels or Berlin...what is the difference? You are still ruled by someone either way."

Allmen sighed, "How can anyone govern a nation that has two hundred and forty-six different kinds of cheese?"

Ciaccio laughed. "You know your history Monsieur. De Gaulle said that, and he is right. And the answer is don't govern us. Don't rule us. Just let us make our cheese and grow our asparagus where it tastes the best. Even the Germans got that right when they rolled through here." He waived a meaty hand toward the horizon.

"Which time?" Allmen grinned, mischievously.

"All of them." Ciaccio deadpanned. "The Germans know what to leave alone. They drank oceans of Champagne when they were here in World War II for two reasons. One because they could... and two because they knew they would lose and perhaps never have the chance again."

"Well, I may never have the chance again, so I will plan to drink a bathtub full... if not an ocean."

"A good plan my friend. I'll pick you up after dinner."

"Ciaccio, you can call me John."

"Okay John. Enjoy the ocean."

Allmen slid out of the car's backseat and ambled through the raindrops toward a yellow brick façade set back from the road in a cobblestone courtyard. Given the weather, he had opted to skip the guided tour up to the vineyards. He'd seen plenty of Chardonnay plants back home. Instead, he descended one hundred feet into vaulted chalk ceilings dug out by the Romans in the time of Cato and Caesar. The massive caves held endless barrels stretching on into the faraway darkness to ferment. His mind kept wandering to bigger issues of the world, like politics and conflict. If you believed the twenty-four-hour news networks and social media, you didn't need to walk through any door or descend into the underworld to find hell. It was available right outside, next to your suburban manicured lawn if you could put down your iPhone long enough to notice. It was all theater, of course. *Poverty is in decline the world over. Violence at multi-generational lows. Life expectancies are longer. No one cares. Everyone is miserable and afraid. Theatre!* Give the masses fear and anxiety and they'd gladly give away their rights, their individuality, to feel safe. They wouldn't even realize what was happening until too late. *Hail Caesar!*

Allmen heard little of the commentary from his guide, a thin man in impossibly skinny jeans, a white shirt, blue blazer and white scarf. He spoke impeccable English and seemed to guess that the American guest, true to stereotypes, didn't care much about the backstory and just wanted to be shown to the tasting room. *Cue the Ugly American.*

Allmen sipped at a straw colored, creamy and brightly acidic brut champagne with a tight cluster of bubbles erupting at the center of the glass. Then he indulged in a vintage demi-sec that tasted of faintly toasted pears covered in honey. Nice, but not really his style. Then the wines got older, the tastes more sublime and as the bubbles rose, so did his spirits. After six tastes, he bought a bottle for the road and headed back out into the rain.

He wanted to stretch his legs before dinner and so walked, bubbles turning over in his stomach, toward the looming cathedral about a mile away. He entered the cathedral courtyard, where generations of French kings had come to receive their crown, the symbolic center of French kingly power. But Allmen didn't go inside. He didn't want a quiet cathedral for his thoughts to echo around today. Instead, he stood in the rain outside and spent long moments staring at the statue of Joan of Arc. A warrior who suffered for her cause, was used up and then thrown away once her usefulness ran its course. Then they burned her at the stake.

The memories, and there were more and more coming to him these days, made him feel empty. And like his usefulness had also run its course. He needed to eat and stop thinking so much. So, he finally crossed the square and launched himself into a late dinner of steak and frites. The meat was smothered in Roquefort cheese and the fries crisped a light brown with a tender middle. He drank a bottle of cabernet, a dusty wine that opened up hesitantly, and really needed food to make it palatable. More cheese arrived. *Problem solved.* This was a beige crusted beauty with a woody flavor and soft center, sourced from cows in the high altitude of Mont d'Or. After that he closed with a half-bottle of champagne, a local label, nothing that was famous and overpriced after being mentioned on some hip-hop album. He felt full in the belly, but the rain and the arc of his thoughts had made him sullen. His stomach was digesting a lot on this trip. And so was his mind.

Ciaccio drove him back to Paris, ignoring the open bottle of twenty-year-old vintage champagne and the souvenir glass Allmen had purchased from a shop across from the restaurant. He didn't want a souvenir, had no need for one, other than to avoid drinking from the bottle on his ride home.

Ciaccio eyed him in the rearview mirror and finally decided to speak.

"What about you my friend? John. You asked me about my politics on the way here. What are yours?"

"Ha, now I know I am in France Ciaccio."

"How do you mean that?"

"I mean in America it is considered poor form to discuss politics, too divisive. Then again, if you had the same hang ups here, you'd have to close all the cafes." Ciaccio gave a short laugh and Allmen continued, "It is also poor form to discuss sex or religion. In truth, as conversationalists, we are a rather boring set of people."

"True." The big man smirked. And waited.

Allmen sighed. "Well, I tend to agree with the Frexiters I guess. I think we have the same problem in America. We keep giving people power over us, giving up our freedoms to a bunch of bureaucrats or career politicians believing that they are somehow better or smarter. And yet, history shows over and over that they aren't. America was a unique experiment, Ciaccio. At the time no government had ever been created from nothing and focused on the rights of the individual. Not classes or guilds. The individual. Amazing, right?" Allmen tossed off half a glass of the champagne and poured carefully as Ciaccio meandered through traffic.

"You said it *was*."

"Huh?"

"You said America was a unique experiment."

"Oh, did I?" Allmen said with mock innocence. "How terribly unpatriotic of me."

The driver was quiet for a while, then asked, "Did you vote for the reality television star?"

Aren't they all reality television stars?" That got a chuckle. "No. I haven't voted in twenty years."

Ciaccio raised bushy gray eyebrows at him in the rearview. "You don't belong to a party?"

"I don't believe in parties. Unless they are serving wine at them." Allmen threw him a mock toast and again refilled his glass. "As far as voting, I took some time off while I was serving in the military. I thought it was wrong to take political sides while the dust and the bullets were flying. And I guess I got out of the habit."

"Iraq." Ciaccio said knowingly. He looked like he wanted to spit, but remembered the windows were closed.

"Yes, not a popular foray over here. Brought about some ugly anti-French stuff for a while. And yet, for all that, we are becoming more and more like Europe Ciaccio. More like France. Not the good parts either, like the food and culture. We are killing the individual to feed the administrative state. We are ruining the cheese."

Ciaccio said mischievously, "Maybe you should join the EU."

"And maybe we should just let it all burn," Allmen said wistfully looking out the window as the darkness rolled past. After that they were both quiet.

"Rain again tomorrow," Ciaccio finally said, stifling a yawn.

"So, what will we do?"

The big man shrugged, something Allmen noticed he did

often. "We can try the coast. Brittany is famous for oysters. You like oysters?"

"Oh god, I love them."

* * *

In the morning, the sound of oversized meat-filled mittens hammering his door brought him to life and they were once again off in the BMW. Allmen certainly did like oysters and Brittany did not disappoint on that account, offering up juicy flat and rock oysters from their nearby beds. He polished off a dozen of them, salty and fresh while drinking a white Muscadet from the Loire at lunch. The weather, however, did continue to disappoint. Great gusts kept blowing in off the sea, driving him indoors to eat, instead of being on the deck.

The oysters, each one of them, made him think of the blonde woman in white and he allowed himself many long listless moments in between bites. The floral notes of the wine brought back the scent of her perfume he had caught that night in the Oyster Depot and again on his chase through the park. She had called oysters an aphrodisiac but try as he might he could not remember what her body was like. Her face he could recall in an instant, but nothing more. He contrasted that with his memories of every inch of Francesca. What a difference it was, between darkness and light.

He walked the oysters and wine off along the ramparts around the town of Saint Malo, gazing out over the storm swept passage at the big houses in Dinard. Then had a dinner of fresh caught pompano and mussels before meeting Ciaccio. The BMW was idling near the port where another great gale was blowing in, making life difficult for a ferry boat coming in from England.

"The weather isn't getting any better, Ciaccio."

"I think you need to head south. Burgundy. Maybe the Rhone. Better food, usually better weather..." Ciaccio grinned, "And plenty of wine."

Allmen felt a flutter in his stomach. A bad oyster? Or the fact that they would be getting closer and closer to Italy? Allmen stifled a belch and asked, "Will you drive me?"

The big man's head nodded once, and they were off toward the soaking hulk of Paris in the distance. Tomorrow they'd head south.

* * *

They set off the next morning after working out all of the arrangements with Virgil, stopping first in Burgundy where Allmen tasted through several vintages at a négociant outside the city of Beaune. He selected six bottles in case he needed some for the voyage. Then they pulled up in front of the entrance to a subterranean restaurant with steps leading down to a large cave-like dining area. Ciaccio had accepted Allmen's offer to join him for lunch, and for a moment John had held his breath wondering if the big man would make it through the small entrance. But he proved nimble enough settling into a two top table where he dominated most of it with his bulk. They each had a soup of mushrooms and local herbs and then a tarte, also featuring the local fungi with onions. Finally, there was a confit of duck and, of course, cheese. Allmen washed it all down with white and red burgundy while Ciaccio declined to imbibe in anything but food, which he did joyously and in massive quantities.

"You know," Ciaccio said between bites, "I went to war too."

Allmen nodded, did some quick math and said quietly "Algeria?"

"Yes. A terrible war, worse in many ways than your Vietnam."

Allmen just nodded again. If Ciaccio wanted to share more he would, but there was no point in digging further with someone who had seen combat and didn't want to talk about it.

"That's why I stopped drinking." Ciaccio indicated the empty white bottle and half empty red on the table in front of them. Allmen raised an eyebrow, detecting the slightest hint of disapproval, or reprimand. But the moment passed quickly and Ciaccio didn't bring it up again, instead expressing his breathless pleasure at the runny Epoisse that appeared on the cheese board to close out lunch.

The weather was still murky and wet as they reached the outskirts of Lyon for dinner. While Paris remained the cultural and political center of France, Lyon was the culinary counterpoint. The historical home of gastronomy. And Virgil had secured a table for them at a Michelin three-star temple to one of the old school masters, Paul Bocuse.

Allmen opted for the Menu Grande Tradition Classique, seven chef-selected courses for a mere 270 Euros, wine not included. Ciaccio, still feeling full of lunch, demurred and ordered the truffle soup and Bresse chicken. Allmen was served foie gras, a strong beginning that he chose to pair with a syrupy sauterne, savoring the interplay of sweet and fat to wake up his palate. Amazingly, his appetite responded to the challenge and he joined Ciaccio in relishing the soup of black truffles that Bocuse had, so said the menu, served to the French President back in the 1970s. A bottle of Condrieu came next to accompany a filet of sole in a buttery sauce of herbs. Then a sorbet. He ordered an aged bottle of Chateauneuf du Pape from the Southern Rhone and awaited the presentation of the Volaille de Bresse en Vessio. The waiter appeared with what looked like a platter with a giant water balloon in the middle, which was in actuality a pig's bladder. He popped it with a knife extracting the chicken basting inside in a pool of butter and truffles. This was a succulent bird, flesh dripping off its bones, with an earthy taste that mixed well with the grenache based wine in his glass. Finally came a cheese plate the size of a wagon wheel and then a desert tray of pastries and local delicacies. Allmen passed on coffee, drained the bottle of Chateauneuf and settled on a port with his desert. Ciaccio eyed him over his coffee.

"My friend, you drink too much."

Allmen imitated the big man's iconic shrug. "I'm on vacation."

Ciaccio nodded unconvinced. "And tomorrow?"

Allmen stifled a belch. "I'll still be on vacation." Ciaccio just shrugged.

* * *

Morning came again. And they followed the river in the rain, curving south toward Avignon where they joined what had once been called the Sun Road. They exited the motorway and climbed the valley for a few minutes until a large stone rampart appeared on the horizon.

Ciaccio turned down the radio and asked, "You remember that beautiful old red wine you drank too much of last night with the chicken?"

"Not particularly."

Ciaccio rolled his eyes.

Allmen laughed. "Okay Ciaccio, I remember it. Chateauneuf du Pape. Late 90s, I think. Yes, 1999. Not *my* greatest year, but the wine didn't know that."

"Well, they make it here. In this village. We'll stop here for lunch."

Allmen shrugged. He'd picked up the habit from his driver. "If I must choke down another delicious French meal and drown it with amazing wine, I guess I will have to live with that."

There was a covered square in the middle of Chateauneuf du Pape. It was tree lined with a fountain gurgling across the one-and-a-half lane road where they sat for lunch. The rain had slowed to a soft trickle and Allmen felt vaguely hopeful that he might actually see the sun once they were back on what was called the Sun Road. Ciaccio knew the proprietor, one of the local old school winemakers, and Allmen sipped his excellent rose after the pretty young waitress seated them and went back to smoking her cigarette. Then he ordered a massive plate of Magret de Canard, a fatty breast of duck, seared rare and served with crispy *frites.* Allmen took a long appreciative swallow of the pink wine and poked at the thin, fried spuds. Then he picked one up and held it out to Ciaccio.

"Behold my friend, the symbol of the Franco-American relationship in all its simplicity and complexity. Hardened by fire, but tender at the core. And brittle."

"Quoi? What? Explain."

"Have you ever heard of Freedom Fries?" Ciaccio stared at him dumbly, his massive mouth trying out the words without sound. In the end, he just shrugged. "They are what some of my countrymen took to calling frites, or French Fries, in a snit over your lack of support for our invasion of Iraq."

Ciaccio rolled his eyes. "Truly?" When Allmen nodded, the big man let out a belly laugh. "Well, we turned out to be right about that, didn't we?"

"Sort of," Allmen said noncommittally. "I mean, you didn't know any better than we did that it was all one big magic show. You just didn't want us beating up on anyone and using your doorstep to do it."

"It is true. We thought you were being very...American."

They were quiet for a while and Allmen sat staring at the waitress and the smoke rising in small circles around her head. "I don't know about you Ciacicio, but I came home from the war pretty disillusioned. Used up."

The big man stopped chewing a piece of bread he had used to mop the bottom of his bowl, raised his eyebrows and sat back with an expression that said 'go on.'

"I mean, there I was supporting and defending a constitution that no one pays much attention to anymore. Fighting for rights that don't seem to exist when they grow inconvenient. We argue over whose idea of right should rule us, no one even thinking to limit the power that we give to politicians in the process. We've fractured into two sides fighting each other, not over freedom or ideals, but to tell the other side what to do. How to live. I'm caught in the middle and I don't know where I fit in...if I ever did."

"Is this why you drink? Because you are disillusioned?"

Allmen lifted his glass in a mock toast then drained it. "It's certainly part of it." The waitress actually noticed, unusual in most of Europe, and came to take the glassware. Allmen ordered a bottle of red local wine, from the rolling vineyards beyond the ruined castle as the bells tolled in the local church just up the hill. Ciaccio waited a while to see if there was more from Allmen. When there wasn't, he heaved a great sigh. "My friend, I am going to get the newspaper."

Allmen watched him heave his bulk out of the chair and stroll leisurely across the street, disappearing around the corner where stairs headed down into one of the many wine caves. Above them was a sign pointing to the local *Tabac* where one could buy newspapers from across Europe and tobacco from wherever you could get it these days.

The driver returned and maneuvered his oversize frame into the bistro chair and ordered a cappuccino while he thumbed through the news in Italian.

"I guess there is one good thing about the EU." Ciaccio thumped the table with his index finger for emphasis. "Italian news in France. And not just in Paris."

"I bet they also have the New York Times," Allmen said, pouring himself another glass. And then, in the heat of the spring afternoon, he froze.

Francesca was there. Staring at him from the middle spread, across the crease in Ciaccio's paper. Ciaccio folded her down the middle as he put the paper aside and looked at Allmen.

"Bandol tomorrow? More rosé? Or on to Italy for the reds and the whites? What will you try to drink yourself under the table with?" He was laughing, but it was a humorless sound.

Allmen reached an index finger toward the paper. "Can you translate that for me?" His voice was a croak as he pointed to the two page article.

"This? Some former tennis star...how do you say it? Too many drugs?"

"Overdose?"

"Just so, my friend. Let me see...ah, former tennis prodigy

Francesca Rimini, daughter of Alberto and Giulia, found unconscious on a holiday retreat in Capri. Investigators are calling it an accidental drug... overdose."

Allmen felt sweat bead on his forehead. He reached again for his glass. It was empty. He poured again.

"Pretty lady," Ciaccio said.

"Very," Allmen sighed and stared upward at the gray sky with an uneasy feeling.

"You know her?"

"Intimately." Allmen didn't feel sorrow per se, instead he felt a deep sense of miscalculation.

"I am sorry my friend."

"Yeah. Me too." He had been wrong about Francesca. Very wrong. He knew for sure it wasn't any drug overdose, not from a woman that was calculating. He felt a deep sense of loss that was not at all foreign to him. He felt the need to drink and to forget.

"John?" Ciaccio was looking at him, a look of mild concern on his face. "Are you okay?"

"I'm fine, Ciaccio. But I don't think I want to keep going tonight. I'm tired. Can we spend the night here?"

"Of course, the hotel is there." He pointed a meaty thumb toward the stone facade behind him. "I'll get the bags and get us rooms."

That night, in an adjoining room, Ciaccio slept in great gasping snores while Allmen sipped at an open bottle of red from the local Rhone vineyards. From the terrace, he could sense the great river rolling by in darkness as it had done for Popes and Emperors and as it did now for John Allmen, cutting through the rolling soggy landscape toward the great sea to the south. He fell asleep upright in a chair facing the open window. In the morning, his socks were wet. The wind had changed direction during the night and let the rain into his room.

❋ ❋ ❋

He knew the dreams had come back that previous night, propped up in the chair with the wind and water blowing in. But now, in the car, racing southwest along the curving roads skirting the mountains and the sea, he couldn't remember them. *Except for her. Except for Francesa.*

He could remember her from the dreams quite vividly. Just her, no setting and no background. He could feel her body again, taut muscles and a grace of movement. He could hear her little moans and soft sounds of pleasure. He could smell her perfume and taste expensive wine with a hint of tobacco on her lips. And finally, he could hear her voice whispering words she never actually said to him: '*Libero Arbitrio.*' The words echoed in his ear. He tried to place where they were in the dream, but somehow knew it wasn't his hotel room on Elba. They were somewhere else. And they were together.

He and Ciaccio wound up making it to Nice that day. Finally, the rain stopped and after a short stroll down the Promenade des Anglais they could look down on the crescent shaped blue Baie des Anges. They sat in a pleasant shady restaurant, the streets steaming as the day heated up. Caiccio ordered Ratatouille with Veal. And he insisted on a shared plate of white asparagus. Allmen had gazed at the menu for a long time and settled on mussels in a cream sauce.

Ciaccio ate heartily, as usual swabbing the plate with giant chunks of fresh baguette and occasionally kissing his fingers and whispering words of appreciation. Between bites he told bits and pieces of personal stories and local history while Allmen stared out to sea.

"Baie des Anges',"Caiccio said, "gets its name because it is supposed to be where Adam and Eve came after they were locked out of paradise. They followed a group of angels who hovered over a lush and beautiful place just like Eden. A good story, no?"

Allmen smiled dutifully and resumed his brooding.

After a while the older man had grown quiet too, sensing his subject's mind was elsewhere. Then he pointed a thick finger at Allmen's glass and said gently, "You want to order some wine?"

Allmen considered for a moment. He shrugged; the gesture contagious. "Not thirsty today." Then he pushed his cold bowl of mussels away, most of it untouched. "And I'm not hungry anymore either."

Caiccio sat back and regarded him with one raised eyebrow.

"I don't think I want to go on."

"Back to Paris tomorrow then?"

"Yes Ciaccio. I think it is time. And you were right about one thing. The damn asparagus was quite good."

* * *

It took a day of nonstop driving to reach Paris. Except for niceties about bathroom breaks and coffee, there was no chatter. Allmen stared at the countryside without a word. Caiccio dropped him at his apartment and they agreed on plans for the next day, Allmen's last in France. Then he slogged his way upstairs and fell asleep with his clothes on.

She was there again. Francesca was there. And Allmen realized in his dream state that he hadn't forgotten the background last time. It was just that there was none. It was only her, and this time she was walking with him, holding his hand. The gesture felt odd, something she had certainly never done with him. And her hand felt cold. But on they walked toward nothing, while she made her little sounds, moans and whispers.

And then suddenly they *were* somewhere. The darkness lifted and they were in an open field. A barren field that looked like it had been cleared by burning. *Maybe napalm.* A helicopter sat motionless in the clearing, a dark hulking shape in a burned out landscape. But its lack of motion, the absence of whirring blades made it seem less sinister than in previous dreams. And so, they walked toward it until Francesca let go of his hand and turned to him, a soft kiss on his cheek.

"What do you Americans say when they don't want to say goodbye?"

"See you around," his unconscious mind murmured.

She nodded. "Yes, see you around my American friend."

And then she walked off and boarded the helicopter and it lifted off in an impossibly quiet hover and then took off across the horizon like a UFO...or, he thought, like an angel.

He realized as he watched it sail illuminated across a dark starless night sky, that she had left something in his hand. It was a napkin from the resort in Elba and he knew in his dreaming mind what it said well before he unfolded it to read 'libero arbitrio' smeared in her blood red lipstick.

Allmen woke up completely sober for the second straight night, some kind of record in recent months. And he stared at the ceiling until morning came. Then he packed and took a walk, ambling aimlessly until the crowd around the Louvre beckoned. He joined it and let the waves of gawking tourists carry him down under the glass pyramids. He paid his admission and rambled room to room with college kids and old ladies taking selfies with the great artistic works of human history.

Eventually he wandered into the antiquities wing and found himself alone, the masses crushed against each other in another wing in front of the Mona Lisa. *Thanks, Dan Brown.* Allmen stood in front of a monolithic slab filled with the scrawl of a dead language. He knew the Code of Hammurabi from a computer game he had played as a child. There, on the pillar in front of him, the magic words "I Hammurabi" had been inscribed 1700 years before Christ. "I Hammurabi" was the preface to the 282 laws inscribed on the polished rock. This was the ancient law of Mesopotamia. And it was cast in stone.

"Once again, I find you in a museum staring at rocks." Ciaccio had shuffled next to him, stealthily for such a big man.

Allmen just nodded. Then he shook his head and said, "Not just a rock. A monument to brevity. All the laws of the land in 44 columns and 28 paragraphs."

Ciaccio considered. "Twenty-eight paragraphs might cover

the EU regulations on bathrooms. Speaking of which, I need one on the way out."

Allmen nodded. "You know there are over 200,000 pages in the United States Code. That is a lot of room for bullshit."

"Sometimes more is better."

"And more often, it is just more."

Ciaccio sighed. "From Babylon to...babble on. Eh? Come on, I need to get you to the airport." For the first time in what seemed like weeks, Allmen smiled. It was a damn good joke for someone speaking their third language.

They strode with purpose toward the nearest lavatory sign, past shards of pottery and statues missing a variety of limbs or heads. Allmen drew away with no need for the facilities.

"Who is that?" he heard one of the American tourist's mutter. Allmen followed a chubby finger pointing to a statue he was familiar with.

"That's Cato the younger," he heard himself say. It was a statue of a middle aged man draped in a toga, a scroll in one hand. Blank looks greeted his answer. *Time to take my historically illiterate countrymen back to school.* "He was a Roman Senator who opposed Julius Caesar at the end of the Republic. He was also a Stoic, refusing to live under the thumb of tyranny. So, when Caesar took power, he slit his own belly with his sword." Allmen pointed to the statues other hand, holding a short sword. "He was found and stitched up by his son and his servants. But when he woke up, he pulled out his own stitches and intestines to finish the job."

"Wow," someone muttered, "he killed himself twice."

"Yes," Allmen said automatically, staring at a point somewhere far away. "He sure did.

"If at first you don't succeed, eh?" some wise ass cracked. There were titters of nervous laughter and the group slowly edged away from the glass eyed man in front of the Roman guy with a death wish.

"John, you okay?" Ciaccio was back, wiping his meaty hands on his pants and grimacing. "No towels. Every artistic work in the history of man… but no bathroom towels."

Allmen came back instantly. "Yeah, fine. Ready to go? I just need to swing through the gift shop."

"A reminder of your new friend Ciaccio to take home?"

Allmen grinned half-heartedly. "Not quite…besides, I've got five pounds to take home with me to remember you by." Allmen patted his belly and set off toward the exit. After a brief perusal and selection process, they were out and into the mottled Parisian sunshine. Allmen glanced at his watch and did a quick calculation. "Two more stops Ciaccio. I think we'll have time."

"If not, at least you will be left behind in Paris, no? Where to?"

"Back to the cemetery. But first, I need a good knife."

✳ ✳ ✳

Ciaccio dropped him off at the curb at the airport and hefted his bags onto the asphalt with a grunt. Then he grabbed him by the shoulders, kissed him twice on the cheek and shook his hand vigorously, up and down like an old water pump. There was real emotion on his face, his eyes dewy. "You'll be alright John. You don't need all that drink to be okay. You just need to keep on living and enjoy your life. Forget the war. Forget politics."

Allmen nodded. "You sound like a stoic."

One last time the man shrugged his trademark shrug. "Find a nice woman and make a life for yourself." He thought of Francesca, then the blonde woman. One made him feel sad, the other gave him some hope. *Out of the darkness and into the light?* Then oddly he thought of his ex-wife. How did she make him feel? That would have to wait.

"Thank you Ciaccio. It has been a pleasure to know you." The big man smiled, let go of his hand and hefted himself into the driver's seat. The lights came on and after a hesitation, the passenger side window came down.

"And John, I am sorry about your friend the tennis player."

Allmen swallowed hard. "Me too. Thank you Ciaccio."

He felt for the knife in his pocket and thought of the miniature statue of Cato that was now resting in Père Lachaise Cemetery. He'd placed it atop a stone shelf at the top of the Monument aux Morts under the relief sculpture of a naked man and woman facing eternity. In his mind, he saw the passing of seasons around his little contribution to the Monument of the Dead, rain, sun, fall leaves and a dusting of snow. Perhaps a tourist might pick it up, or a vagrant might steal it. If they did, they'd find the inscription he'd carved in it while Ciaccio drove. *For Francesca, Libero Arbitrio.*

A blast of the horn brought him back to his senses. Allmen waved at the car then stepped away and put the knife into the garbage by the sliding glass entry doors. He turned back to see the Corsican drive off, the BMW's lights disappearing into the gloom. It had started to rain again.

GREED:

a selfish and excessive desire for more of something, such as money

B ehold the transient farce
  Of goods that are committed unto Fortune,
  For which the human race each other buffet;
For all the gold that is beneath the moon,
Or ever has been, of these weary souls
Could never make a single one repose."

- Dante, Inferno Canto VII

When Allmen ventured out for necessaries in San Francisco, he did so fully aware that he might be recognized, even with the perpetual unshaved look he found himself sporting most days. The 7x7 mile city was often too small to hide in and former clients or colleagues could be lurking anywhere, awkward conversations to ensue. Thus, he usually did his grocery shopping at the Safeway in the Marina District, where the median customer's age was somewhere in the low thirties. Even though the food wasn't as good as the more upscale markets in town.

It was on one of these trips that he noticed he was being followed down the fruits and vegetables aisle while picking out tomatoes for a salad. And, hoping for a decent steak, he was still followed into the meat department.

"Mr. Allmen?"

John fought the urge to vault the meat counter and bolt through the delivery doors. But something about the soft, almost whining tone of voice made him look up at his pursuer. He wore a gray sharkskin suit, well made and well-tailored . And his shoes were a gleaming black any Marine would have shown pride in. Was that where he knew him from? For a few heartbeats he tried and failed to recognize him. He looked him full in the face and thought, *Thai? Chinese? Laotian?* Such thoughts made his belly lurch and he made a mental note to schedule a discreet visit to one of the better Asian restaurants out on Geary Street.

Geary. Gary. "Holy shit," Allmen jerked his head back in recognition. "Gary the Gnome? The Berkeley prodigy? Jesus kid, how the hell are you?"

"Gary the Vice President of Investments now. Thanks to you."

"Yeah, well, when opportunity knocks, make sure you open the door, right?"

"Open it? Mr. Allmen, eight months ago the door *fell in* on me. It was a miracle. And I have you to thank. I've wanted to reach out to you, call or something. But to be honest, I've been afraid you'd change your mind and come back." He shrugged like a hopeful but bashful teenager who had just professed his love.

"No chance of that kid."

Gary eyed his scruffy face and unkempt clothes. "Yeah, I see that now." Allmen realized he was wearing cargo shorts, a Jimmy Buffett concert tee shirt and his Key West flip flops. Still trying to work off some extra pounds from his trip to France, he probably looked more like the Whale of Wall Street than the wolf.

"But Mr. Allmen, things may look good," Gary pointed to his suit as if it had fallen on him from the sky, "but it is getting a lot harder to keep your former clients happy over the last few weeks. You are a hard act to follow. How did you do it? I mean, how did you know when to get out of the market and when to go short? This selloff we've been going through has clients worried and I... Well, I don't know what to tell them. I don't know what to do."

Allmen frowned. He was aware of the most recent market swoon. He'd been paying some attention lately to his own financial affairs after mostly ignoring them for months and the recent statements had gotten his attention. His money needed to last a little over a year or more and at the current rate, it was going to be tight.

"I wish I could tell you Gary."

"I get it, trade secrets, nondisclosure...that sort of thing."

"No, I mean I really wish I could tell you, but I have no idea. You aren't the only one who has had the door fall in on them in their career. Sometimes, like the Beatles said, luck is all you need."

"Pretty sure they said *love* is all you need."

"Did they? What a bunch of saps." Allmen gave a lopsided grin. He saw the joke had fallen flat and softened into a more thoughtful tone: "Gary, find a way to talk to people about what *you* do, not what I did. It's a cold place in my shadow and that is no fault of your own. So, grow out of it, and fast. Choose free will." Allmen grabbed his grass-fed ribeye and made for the checkout trailing awe and confusion in his wake.

Before taking the turn at the end of the bread aisle, he half turned: "And it is okay to call me any time. I'll help if I can. But I'm through kid. Count on that."

✳ ✳ ✳

There was no Virgil and no itinerary that Christmas. Allmen moved his one-man hermit act to the mountains above Lake Tahoe. He'd rented a place there with his wife and daughter years before, memory at once pleasant and painful. He brought snowshoes and took long meandering treks through new fallen flurries, feeling the cold air course through his lungs and working off his puffy bloated look. He read several histories of the American Civil War and then a few stories by Jack London. And when the snow wasn't flying, he'd drive to a lake or stream and drop a line for a few hours trying for trout. Winter trout were like honest business bankers, rare, but they happened. You had to slow down your routine and present a much smaller fly, but the rhythmic movements of casting put him in a trance. Then most of a day would drift by without him much noticing.

He tuned in more often than usual to the idiot box, the lone television in the family room where he'd catch the latest financial news while viewing his portfolio on his laptop. US markets had entered a steep and full-blown correction after the euphoria of Thanksgiving had worn off.

The S&P 500, like Allmen, shaved off a few percent points from its pre-Holiday figure. But unlike him, it persisted in dropping. This continued to be mildly disconcerting to him. He needed money to finish out this journey and if this were a short-term correction, he'd be fine. But if it turned into a steeper, more protracted cyclical downturn he'd be in a bit of a pinch to cover costs in the waning months of the following year. Ultimately, based on the research he gleaned, no one knew what the hell was going on and most had little idea of what they were talking about. So he decided to stop worrying and let it all ride.

The day before Christmas dawned clear and bright and he set off early, clad in a blue Columbia ski jacket and silver snow pants. He wore a light day pack and carried his show shoes, looking forward to a long 'hump' as the Marines called it. He looked back at the house, all towering log facades and picture windows, sure it was valued at north of $5 million. At one time, in very different circumstances, he had thought about buying something nearby.

A few miles out he cut north across an old logging road to make a big looping arc that would take him back to the house. It was a new route, one we had scouted the day before on his local map, highlighting landmarks and writing in bearings from his compass. Allmen had done a number of land navigation exercises in the Marines and he enjoyed ditching the electronics for the day. Leaving your phone and going for a long walk was about all it took to pass for a daredevil these days. *Or a hero.* It was late morning when light flurries started to fall, which were not in the forecast. Typical of the weather guessers, the snow continued and began to intensify as he cut a trail through deepening powder. He was feeling more winded than usual. An evening in the hot tub drinking entirely too much Scotch combined with the high altitude and thin air were to blame. As the day drew on toward late afternoon his mind began to wander.

He often entered a dream state in his days of long marching with the Marines during Officer Candidate School. The rhythm of the footfalls created a dazed state where you could have hazy visions as if you were sleeping. He felt himself going there now and didn't resist.

In Allmen's mind, the falling snow became pennies. *Pennies from heaven? He* thought not. Money didn't grow on trees, Dad had reminded him often, and it didn't drop magically from heaven. You had to earn it. *I did Dad. I earned a lot of it. And now I am spending it. Merry Christmas old man.*

Burl Ives Christmas classic played in his head: *Silver and Gold. Silver and Gold.* He came to a circular clearing where the pennies continued to fall, creating great heaps of change. Men were picking up the coin, filling their pockets. They were pushing and shoving each other back and forth, trying to get more of the money, yelling and screaming obscenities at each other. One of them, faceless in the dream, came toward Allmen and stopped him from approaching.

"Why do you spend all of your money?" The man screamed and Allmen felt wet spittle land on his face.

"Why not? Why hoard it?"

The man didn't respond. But he leaned into Allmen as if to say something quietly, secretly to him. Then, with a start, he extended his arms and pushed Allmen over backwards with a heaving shove. Allmen reached out, caught the man's arm but it only turned him, twisting him as he fell to land on his face.

"Oh shit."

Allmen was fully awake and alert now that his shoe had dipped into a snowbank and caught on a dusted over log. He was falling for real. *Down and down.* And finally, he landed with a thud, splaying out into a snowbank in a heap. He was lightheaded, a bit disoriented, and when he regained his footing, he felt sure he was a bit lost too. He was unsure of how long he'd been marching and hadn't really been paying attention to his course.

Perhaps he had been reading a bit too much of London's To Build a Fire. In the later, darker version of that story the unnamed protagonist takes the never-ending sleep after freezing to death in the wilderness. In the earlier version, which Allmen had read years ago, the protagonist lives to be a wiser, bitterer man after suffering from frostbite. So, which story would it be this time in this man versus nature narrative? Allmen suddenly had a thought about just letting go. He could, he thought, sit right down in the snow and give up. It would be a short, uncomfortable period of cold and then everything would turn warm again as he drifted off. Just like that Jack London story, he could just let the darkness wash over him, killing the helicopter dreams and the guilt. *Tempting, I have to admit.*

He sighed, dusted himself off as he stood again and squared his shoulders against the wind. No, it wouldn't do. It was not part of the plan. He shrugged off the idea altogether and trudged onward, legs feeling their way through thickening powder. His watch told him he'd been at it most of the day and his lower body burned with the exertion, while his hands had gone cold. Losing a few fingers wasn't really in the plan either. It might drastically affect his ability to hold a wine glass. Allmen gritted his teeth. *Fuck Jack London and both his stories.* As the sun started to slant through the trees in the late afternoon, it occurred to him that he may not have a choice. That he might die out here from exposure regardless of his feelings on the matter. *Knock it off. That's panic starting to set in.*

And then, hope dwindling, through the swirl of snow, he saw something that looked like it was written in the sky about a hundred yards ahead. The snow obscured his vision again, and he stood squinting into the wind. The breeze softened for a moment and Allmen saw it clearly. It was a dollar sign. And a cartoon dog. "Save $ On California Attractions. Exit Now." It was a billboard with a knock off of Mickey Mouse's dog Pluto. He remembered the sign from his drive in and he began triangulating his position. He guessed he was less than three miles from the McMansion in the woods. He would make it, though it would be in the dark. *Saved again by the almighty dollar.*

He trudged in the door just before 8PM as a full-blown snowstorm erupted and temperatures plunged into single digits. Allmen warmed himself next to the wood fireplace, drinking eighteen-year-old Scotch still humming to himself: *Silver and Gold. Silver and Gold.*

He had explained to his daughter why he wouldn't be around for Christmas, too many bad memories in San Francisco that time of year. He thought she would be better off if he weren't around. And she seemed to understand. But with the adrenaline wearing off he felt sadness wash over him as he stared into the roaring blaze. He tried music to ward it off the holiday blues. But Christmas music had the opposite effect, making him think more, not less. The television, with stories of rich financiers trying to screw over the famous mortgage lender George Bailey, didn't help either. Finally, he settled on listening to a 1990s channel. *College vibes. Easier times.* The Gin Blossoms and Nirvana strummed power chords as snow continued to swirl outside. He fed more wood onto the growing conflagration in the fire box.

Allmen felt himself going down into the fire, his eyes settling on the hulking burned out husks of the logs he had piled there. They spat fire and cracked. Pop. Bang. Absently, he added another log. He watched it, new and protected by its bark, take the flame, peel back its protective covering and add to the blaze. He recognized the radio change to Social Distortion's cover of Johnny Cash's Ring of Fire.

And it burns, burns, burns...that ring of fire.

Tendrils of smoke rose in spectral traces, leaving smoky suggestions, impressions of faces, shadows. Curling wisps of dark hair seemed to hang there.

I fell for you like a child.

Then the smoke curled upward like a mustache, a thin black mustache. Pop. Bang. And then the fire leapt up again and the smoke dissipated, fading into nothing.

Oh, but the fire went wild.

He watched a piece of ash float above the fire like a wayward snowflake, twisting and turning, riding an updraft away from the flames. Then it hovered, turned and slowly started to descend again. Finally, it was sucked in on a downdraft, disappearing again in the blaze.

And it burns, burns, burns...that ring of fire.

Allmen sat watching the scene like a television where the reception was fading in and out. A swirling, confusion of thick smoke built up, obscuring the fire box for a minute, two, three. Then a violent pop from the embers beneath and all would burn with a new intensity, clearing out the smoke. The cycle repeated: obscuration, confusion, violence, clarity. And then, as he felt his eyes grow heavy, the embers cooled and quieted and the smoke thinned and disappeared. And then the fire, without violence or sound, ceased to be.

When Allmen woke, there was a bell ringing. *An angel? Every time a bell rings, one gets their wings.*

It turned out to be his phone, announcing a series of text messages. Mack Mason had sent three:

"Merry Christmas.
When you come out of hibernation, call me.
It's business."

It was Christmas Day and Allmen decided to go for another walk. A shorter one, keeping the house in sight the entire time.

❊ ❊ ❊

A few months after Christmas, Flight 2405 from San Francisco to Houston reached an eastward cruising altitude of 35,000 feet with John Allmen staring at the mountains from his window seat, 1A. It was spring in San Francisco and the weather was cold and rainy. So, when Virgil had called during an afternoon walk in the Marin Headlands to confirm his departure for the Caribbean, Allmen had felt a surge of excitement. He was a year into this grand sabbatical, something to celebrate with surf and sand.

It was just after beverage service had begun, that Allmen heard a muffled thump from somewhere aft of the first-class cabin. To be fair, most of the airplane was aft of First Class, but that didn't change his immediate perception of something back there going wrong. Engine?

It was not an *oh my God, we are all doomed kind of wrong,* he knew. Nor was it a *you are free to move about the cabin and congregate in front of the lavatory* kind of wrong either. He felt the jet's throttles ease back and the great aluminum tube slowed while beginning a gentle descent. Gradually, the pilot brought it into a curving turn northward as a low murmur of conversation broke out all around.

"Something is wrong. I was listening to the radio traffic and they cut that off," someone was saying louder than necessary from behind the curtained off seats in the front of coach.

"*Down, down down,*" Allmen hummed to himself, "*as the flames went higher.*"

"Uh folks, Captain here, you may have noticed we are in a descent. Had a minor malfunction and are going to have it checked out. Seatbelt sign is on for the duration. We will have more for you when we are on the ground in a few minutes." He might have been ordering a taco at the drive through such was his tone of voice. *Cool under pressure.* Allmen admired that. But Allmen also knew very well from working with pilots in combat that the calmer they usually sounded, the bigger and smellier the shit hitting the proverbial fan. Despite himself, he cinched his lap belt tighter and watched through the window as the desert took form and grew closer. Allmen briefly wondered if it wouldn't have been better to die in a snowstorm than a plane crash. *Certainly more poetic.*

And then it was over. They were on the ground, the plane smoothly touching down as the fire trucks rolled with it. In the distance, Allmen saw the familiar outline of the Eiffel Tower. And then the pyramids at Luxor came into view.

"Uh, ladies and gentlemen, welcome to Las Vegas, where the local time is 1:30 PM. You'll notice the rescue trucks escorting us to the gate, that is merely a precaution and we plan to deplane as usual once we can get to a complete stop at the first available gate. So, stay seated and we will hopefully have some more information for you about connections and rebooking once you are inside the terminal." And just like that, John Allmen had fallen out of the sky and landed in Sin City.

* * *

"Sorry about this Mr. Allmen, I don't see a way to get your out of there and on your way until tomorrow. Unless they can fix the airplane you were in…"

"Virgil, John Allmen does not fly on damaged hardware. Let's just say that I am superstitious like that."

"Okay…"

"Just rebook me and grab me a room here for the night."

"Feeling lucky Mr. Allmen?"

"Something like that I guess." He heard Virgil clattering away at a keyboard.

"Got it. Head on over to the Four Seasons. I've got you in a room there. Quiet. Nice pool."

"Now I'm feeling lucky, Virgil. Thank you."

"Sure thing. Ah, Mr. Allmen? Would you mind putting $100 on the money line for tonight's Warriors game for me?"

"Absolutely Virgil. I may just do a bit of gambling myself."

Allmen was not a Vegas guy. *Far too many people trying too hard to live out an advertising slogan.* It wasn't that he didn't gamble, he loved the thrill of beating odds he knew were stacked against him like any investing guru or combat soldier would. But Vegas after the 1960s was too fabricated. It was a glitter coat tossed over a fat rotting corpse in the desert a hundred miles from nowhere. It was trying too hard. Too many dental assistants and CPAs spewed out of conference halls desperate to do something, hell anything, that was worthy of being left behind in Vegas. Something never to be discussed except in hushed tones with the lights out. *Good luck with that. Have you fools ever heard of social media?*

He made his way, dodging drunks clanging away at slot machines. They wagered and waited for their flights back to wherever their local bank would eventually notice that they were short on the mortgage payment. He caught a cab and threw

114

his overnight bag in it. Virgil had promised to rebook him and take care of the rest of his bags and fishing gear. In a worst-case scenario, Allmen had a swimsuit and could get away with only that for some time in an island setting. He was in the cab, rolling past the MGM Grand and thinking that really he preferred to do his gambling in Reno. *Dirty Vegas is real, no one is trying to live up to a TV commercial or airline magazine ad.* That was because most of them were just trying to live, period, usually gambling away the grandkid's college fund at the low limit blackjack table. And hoping to get a free pass to the buffet. These days Allmen enjoyed his status as white trash, with cash. For a long time, he'd just been the former.

Deposited at the Four Seasons, a secluded side entrance in the shadow of the looming Mandalay Bay, Allmen checked into a quiet lobby. No slots jangled, and no motorized carts carried diabetic pensioners to the 5PM all you can eat. It was an austere, gold trimmed oasis from the riff raff. Allmen loved and loathed it all at once.

Upstairs he dropped his valise, brushed his teeth and gave his pants a dramatic check to see if he had not soiled himself during the day's drama. Satisfied, he took the elevator down one stop before the main lobby where you could enter the gaming area of Mandalay. You could exit here and go slumming, but the slums couldn't come to you. *One-way trip, first class.* Allmen thought, not for the first time, how nice it was to be somewhat rich, even if it was a temporary state.

Virgil had arranged for a line of credit with the hotel, so $10,000 in chips waited for Allmen. He started slowly, playing hands of $25 minimum blackjack, and sipping at a gin and tonic. He gradually increased his bets and took advantage of several potentially dicey opportunities to double down, receiving the gift of a dealer's bust card. He headed to dinner around 7:00 up around $1000. Not a bad start to the end of a weird day. He gorged himself on a steak at Charlie Palmer's, spending about half of his winnings on a meal fit to be the final one of a condemned man. Stuffed on ribeye and red wine, he was back at the tables as they were starting to fill up for the night.

He found himself at a craps table, a lively bunch of balding men, clearly the CPAs, and heavily done up women, the dental assistants. *Chauvinistic much?* He decided to give his conscience a rest about it. Of course, he turned out to be dead wrong anyway. Between rolls he found out that the women were in town for a biotechnology conference. He didn't talk to the men but surmised from most of their banter that someone from Milwaukee had gotten a divorce and this trip was his reward.

John found himself winning again, extended rolls had chips sliding over felt in his direction with a crisp clank and a nod of approval from the female prodigies and the croupier. At one point, Allmen guesstimated that he rolled continuously for half an hour or more, though time was a malleable substance in Vegas. He wore no watch and had zero desire to touch his phone. He crapped out with a seven and there were mild applause and mutterings of congratulations from around him as he stared at a burgeoning, multi-colored stack that he estimated to be around fifty thousand dollars. However, he respected and honored Kenny Rodgers enough not to count his money while he was sitting, or standing, at the table. It was here and now that Allmen's mind began to wander, imagining all the good he could do with the money in front of him added to his travel funds. His current stack would pay for his next fortnight in the Caribbean, or at least close. And if he got it to fifty, that would ease some of the anxiety over his stock market losses in recent weeks. To this highly questionable rationale, he added a martini. Cold and oily it washed away all logic, statistical analysis and reason.

When the dice came around again, Allmen turned to the woman next to him in a peach colored halter top that might have been appropriate for someone half her age.

"Will you blow on these for me?" She looked at the dice in his hand and arched an eyebrow. "For luck?" She blew. He smiled.

"Luck be a lady," he crooned and came out swinging for the fences. He now not only bet backing the point, the six and the eight as was his usual strategy. But he made exotic bets including large ones on hitting the 'hard ways.' This time his roll lasted half a minute. The crowd around the table was quieter now, more subdued. Soon they began to dribble away, replaced by sullen midwestern men in white Nike shoes and jean shorts, their bored wives in loud floral prints. This was a shift change, and that meant it was probably getting late. But with a stack of chips still in front of him, and a second martini on deck, John Allmen did not care. *It's still house money anyway.*

"Coming out!"

* * *

It was morning when he returned to his room and collected his bag, still untouched in the middle of the neatly made bed. He washed up, brushed his teeth and heard the door slam behind him as he headed for the elevator. He left, cashing in the chips remaining in his pocket and the winning sports bet he'd placed for Virgil. He'd given the house back all but $200 of their money and the room, the one he never slept in, had cost more than that. *Fucking Vegas.* He poured himself into a cab for the short ride back to the airport.

The good news was that the level of exhaustion after staying up all night was such that Allmen had no recollection of the flight to Houston, nor much of the connection where he had to be prodded awake by the gate agent and was last to board. And he was again blissfully asleep over the glistening blue Caribbean when the tinny speaker above his head sprung to life and John Allmen's bloodshot eyes creaked open.

"No," he moaned, "not this. Anything but this."

"Ladies and gentlemen, we are happy to have you with us on our flight today to the Cayman Islands and we will be on the ground shortly."

"You bastards."

"To say thank you for joining us today, we are pleased to offer our credit card with fifty-thousand bonus miles..."

"No,' he croaked, "not the goddamn credit card spiel." But no one heard his inaudible cry for mercy above the droning of the fully functioning CFM56 turbofan engines.

"Would you like a credit card application sweetie?" The flight attendant in first class was a matronly woman with frosted hair and tortoise shell glasses.

"Only if you force it on me." He managed a smile that caused a jolt of pain to arc across his forehead. The attendant chuckled.

"Oh, we wouldn't do that to you. Can I bring you a drink? Maybe a Bloody Mary?" He was quite sure that an airline Bloody Mary would finish the job that a snowstorm and disintegrating airplane engine had begun. It would kill him.

"Given a choice between the two, I'd rather have the credit card." She seemed confused by that and retreated to the galley, leaving a form in his seat back pocket. Allmen ignored it.

* * *

He spent the first two days in Grand Cayman recovering, snoozing away on Seven Mile Beach. On the third day he roused himself from slumber and spent the day bonefishing on the other side of the island, letting the sun he had been missing in San Francisco soak into his bones and feeling the water and salt air replenish everything he'd left in Vegas. Everything but the money.

He was staying at the Ritz, another high dollar property, but one where Virgil had gotten him a decent deal. It was a pearl outcropping on a white sandy beach where one could relax, fish, go kayaking and free up some mental space. There was still a lot for Allmen to accomplish and his anniversary of quitting his job was coming up. He had a lot of loose ends to tie up.

After nearly a week he was tanned to a deep brown. And after a day casting into the surf behind the hotel, he returned empty handed to find his in-room phone ringing.

"Hello?"

"Hey, you've been ignoring me since Christmas. What gives?"

"Mack...how the hell..."

"Did I find you? I know you consider Marine Intelligence to be a contradiction in terms, but let's just say I still have connections that know how to find people when they get lost."

"Right, tracking down wayward business owners who get cold feet before they sign the buyout paperwork, that sort of thing. I get it." Silence hung on the end of the phone line and Allmen thought about how long it had been since he'd held a real phone in his hand, not some brick with a mini-computer embedded in it. "Look, I knew what you are going to say Mack and I'm not coming back, so there was very little reason for me to call you."

"Well, how wonderful for you, smart guy. Happy Fucking New Year. But listen, things are getting serious here, you need to come back. People are no longer worried, they are pissed. This guy is losing us money and I'm getting the blowback on it. Little fucker called me the other day saying something about patient, long-term investing and a wait and see attitude."

"Why do you assume I would do any better?"

"Fuck, I don't know. History? A track record? Personal fucking experience? You've got something special. A gift, whatever. In '08 everyone else told me to hold tight, that there was nothing to worry about, the housing market is a small part of the economy...blah blah blah. A lot of the same shit I am hearing now. Meanwhile you go in and sell everything the day before Lehman goes tits up. Not only that but you short them, the market, all of it! It was genius!"

Allmen blinked hard, feeling like he might vomit. But when he went to retch, words came out instead.

"It was a mistake."

"Say again, over?"

He shrugged. "A mistake, Mack, ever make one?"

"Sure. All the time, I just don't talk about them on non-secure phone lines." It was a joke, but Allmen didn't laugh. Something had opened up inside of him and was ready to spill out like guts from an abdominal wound. He thought back to that night, something he had not done in years.

"You remember, Mack I was in a pretty bad way back then. Drinking and the painkillers."

"I remember." Mack had lost the stern edge to his voice.

"Well, I came back to the Gnome Garden after happy hour. Well after. With a few steins of beer and some cheap scotch in my gut. And I was feeling pretty shitty and wanted to stick it to the world. I went in and did the only thing I could think of to say screw all of you, everyone who had put me down or passed me over in corporate America. I sold their shitty companies." Allmen gave a halfhearted barking laugh. "I used to do the same thing with my fantasy baseball team, get drunk and angry and cut all of them late at night."

"I don't under…"

"Well, here is the thing Mack, I passed out after I did it. Didn't remember a thing. Woke up in the morning at my desk still feeling shitty and angry. So, I did it again. Sold everything we owned. Shorting it all, in the parlance of the Street." He'd put in a short position against the banks, the market, all of it. The risk was unfathomable, but the upside was tremendous. He'd been on a bender and it took him days to realize what he had done, after which he quietly unwound the trades over a period of weeks. But people noticed. *Everyone loves a winner.* And suddenly Mack Mason was bringing over the rest of his personal investments and his friends with them. While the financial world was seemingly collapsing around them, John Allmen was moving out of the Gnome Garden and into an office with a window overlooking the Ferry Building.

Mack was quiet for a long time. Then he gave a low whistle and swore, using one of his favorite expressions. "Jesus Christ superstar."

John sighed. "No. John Allmen. Phony financial guru. Still want me back?"

* * *

For the time being the answer had obviously been no. Mason did not want him back. At least that is what Allmen gleaned from the sudden and deafening silence on the other end of the line. Allmen had committed the ultimate sin in the financial and big business world, he had admitted to being lucky. Not skilled, brilliant, gifted, well-trained, intuitive, talented, hard working or able to see what other missed. *Just plain lucky. And drunk and lucky at that.* It had shocked Mason into a silence that starkly contrasted with his normal disposition. Their remaining conversation was jumbled and vague. Awkward pauses then piled upon embarrassed silence resulting in an uncomfortable parting.

It had taken Allmen longer than usual to fall asleep that night, turning over his relationship with Mack, wondering just how much of it was friendship and how much was business. He suspected he would find out the hard way. Which was really the only way to do anything.

When he finally drifted off to sleep with the sounds of the Caribbean Sea beating down in endless waves on Seven Mile Beach, his dream was a somewhat familiar one. It started with the smell of sweat and the taste of gunpowder. And then there was the landing zone, the rhythmic beating of a helicopter's rotors and more faceless kids in camouflage around him. But this time, they were all heaving, straining to pull what looked like military issue green sacks into the clearing.

"ElTee! Sir! We need to get these on that chopper!" The kid had a dark complexion and a faint wisp of what wanted to someday be a mustache.

The bullets began to zing and whine past them, but they all kept at it, pulling bags into the landing zone, oblivious to the danger, the bullets. They ignored the agonizing, or if you were lucky, instant, death.

"What's in the bags?" Allmen asked of no one. And he got no reply.

Then the helicopter floated into view and hovered and Allmen had a dreamy certainty of what he needed to do.

Again, came the voice, "Lieutenant, we need the bags on the chopper!"

"No. Not yet!" Allmen screamed above the whine of rotors and the whipping winds in their downdraft, "I have to know what is in there."

More bullets ripped through the air as if warning him not to approach the assembled cargo, whatever it was. He willed himself forward and struggled, pushing at the bags while someone, faceless, pulled on the other end. He felt something give, and saw the form at the other end of the bag disappear. Green bills of every imaginable denomination spilled out and the money whirled and spun through the air, great spouts and geysers of greenbacks. He moved to the next bag, tore it open and did the same, moving mechanically from one to the next as the incoming fire continued at a frenzied pace. No one said anything now, no one interfered. When he was done, the entire landing zone was awash in American greenbacks. It looked like a parade had gone by and everyone had thrown pictures of dead presidents instead of confetti.

The helicopter hovered and watched, its cockpit black, hatches closed. Then it dipped, came closer and hovered again. The hatch slid back aft of the cockpit and the door gunner swung his weapon around to bear on Allmen as he stood still in a shower of cash. He saw the gunner frown, look at Allmen again and then pull the trigger.

He felt a bullet tear into his body, convulsed and fell. There was no blood, just a pain that seemed to radiate from his chest through his entire body. *Friendly fire.* He was angry. He wanted to yell. *Hey man, friendly fucking fire!* Instead, he awoke to the sound of breakers on the beach and shore birds calling out into the scattering dawn. The hotel phone lay heavy on his chest with the receiver still in the cradle. And the words stayed in his head the rest of the day. *Friendly fire.*

That morning, he walked the entire stretch of Seven Mile Beach from the hotel. Headed south, the birds hunted in the emerald green surf to his right and the sun came up over the low golden haze of the island to his left. He felt the sand under his feet, cool and light in the early morning and stood for a time at the end of the beach where the rocks intruded. There he watched the surf drawing at the shoreline, pulling sand endlessly away from the land and into the depths. Mankind, in all of its overconfidence, was trying to stop the process. Allmen had seen dredging equipment in the marina as the cab had brought him in from the airport. *But for how long can you hold back the ocean? Time marches on. Ashes to ashes and dust to dust. Shit happens. Walk on.*

He reversed course and walked to the other end of the great expanse of the strand. By now, the sun worshippers were beginning to appear, sleek women with hourglass shapes in bright two-piece bikinis. It was a contrast to the beaches in America where a daily contest seemed to be raging for who could look *least* attractive. *The bikini was meant to be a privilege and it had turned into a right.*

It was lunchtime by the time he wandered back to the hotel and he was powerfully hungry after a nearly thirteen-mile walk. He chose to dine on the beach and selected a lobster and Caesar salad and asked for a rosé wine to accompany it. *Whatever they bring it will at least be drinkable. It's that kind of place.*

He was again watching the sand pulled out into the Caribbean and thinking about time, always limited time. *Now more than ever.* He had stopped thinking of Mack on his morning stroll. And he had begun to think about Virgil. It occurred to him he knew very little about the man who had been coordinating his adventures and misadventures for the last year. He'd been handed a card by a mystery woman who he couldn't find and had been working with a mystery man he had never met. He liked Virgil, hell even trusted him, as far as he could trust anyone. But the lack of a face with the name suddenly struck him as odd.

Who are you Virgil?

"A Whispering Angel, sir." The beach boy, a British kid with a bad complexion, but a pleasant sing-song cockney accent set down a gleaming silver ice bucket with rivulets of condensation running down its side.

"Huh?"Allmen never even heard him coming. *Jesus, I'd never survive combat these days.*

"Your wine sir. Chateau Esclans Whispering Angel rosé? From *Cotês de Provence?* You ordered it?"

"Oh, for sure. Thank you." Allmen fought the urge to shiver despite the eighty-degree weather. *A whispering angel?* Was Virgil his version of Clarence from A Wonderful Life? *No such thing. Then again it would be my luck to get a disembodied voice coming from an industrial park as a guardian angel.* Allmen sighed, finished the wine, and fell asleep on the beach.

He woke up groggy in the mid-afternoon and trudged off toward his room to figure out his next move, too late for fishing and too early for dinner. Still bleary and muddled he found himself wandering about in the bowels of the hotel looking for an elevator. There was a wide-open atrium area with plants and a few tables here and there. And several signs pointing to creatively Caribbean themed areas like the Guadeloupe and Jamaica Rooms. And then he saw the enclosed poster board near the entrance, and he shook his head with a rueful smile. In neat block letters on a background of elderly people reviewing bar charts was printed: Welcome First Financial Services: Annual Gold Producer Meeting."

"Oh...no." Allmen had wandered into the viper's den, a meeting of financial salespeople. He'd been to a few of these things in various locals. He'd gotten drunk on someone else's dime, swum with dolphins on someone else's dime and played golf at top courses on someone else's dime. He noted the escalator in the corner and thought to head for it, his fight or flight response biased strongly toward the latter. But another sign caught his attention near what was called the Bahamas Rooom: Growing Your Practice-Getting to Yes.

The door was open, and the capacious room was jammed with men and women between the ages of forty and seventy. *Mostly men, and mostly closer to seventy than forty.* And mostly overweight and sweating in the tropical heat despite the generous air conditioning budget in the five-star hotel. All were paying rapt attention to a PowerPoint presentation given by a balding man who looked like he fell out of his minivan driving to a rotary club meeting.

"Your clients and prospects are going to buy based on two emotional states," the man said. His voice was a great booming baritone. Allmen was shaking his head. This couldn't be happening.

"One is fear..." *I wonder if the other one is luck?* Allmen laughed aloud, knowing that it wasn't.

"And the other is..." Allmen's breath shallowed as he remembered all the meetings like this. All the crap about making connections, becoming a trusted advisor and then...and then...running off to the Cayman Islands to count your money and figure out how to print more. He felt nauseous.

"Excuse me, this is a closed meeting. Should you be in here?" A severe woman in a floral print dress that showed all of her many flaws in tropical detail was peering over her glasses at him. She was whispering in a loud voice that was not at all angelic. Allmen was not exactly blending in. The room of finance guru wannabes was dressed in polo shirts and khaki pants while he was wearing a tee shirt and bathing suit.

Allmen threw her a lopsided grin and shook his head. "No. Absolutely not." He turned an about face on a flip-flopped heel and headed through the doors. He found he could breathe again. And his stomach wasn't threatening to summersault out of his throat. But he didn't stop walking until he reached his room and put a call in to Virgil at Circle Nine Travel Services.

"Yes, Mr. Allmen?"

"Get me out of here."

"Out of Grand Cayman Mr. Allmen?"

"No, just out of the hotel. Wait. Virgil?"

"Yes, sir?"

"Can you call me John?"

"I suppose I could. Why Mr. ...ah, John?"

"Because I've known you for almost a year. And it kind of

weirds me out that you are sticking to the 'Mr. Allmen' thing. Time to move on. Grow. Don't you think so?"

"If you say so...John. Can you tell me why you want to leave the nicest hotel in paradise?"

"There is a conference here. No one I know, it's not that dire, but it is a bunch of financial types and I don't want to be around them right now. Or ever again really."

"I see."

"You do?"

He sighed. "No, not really. But let me see what I can do. I'll call you back in twenty minutes. Maybe you can go down and get a drink while you wait?"

"Not a fucking chance. I'll order room service and wait right here. You never know if there might be some insurance or muni bond salesman trolling the hotel bar."

"Well...John, suit yourself. I'll call you back."

"Hey Virgil?"

"Yes?"

"Thank you."

Good as his word, Virgil rang back before twenty minutes elapsed. That was just after room service had delivered the largest Mojito Allmen could talk them into making. In an hour he was cruising northward with his bags in the back of a small SUV watching the sun start to go down over the emerald green and blue waters. The big hotels disappeared and small farms and neatly fenced ranches popped up. Allmen watched as a skinny kid in blue jeans galloped along a stretch of uninhabited beach on a white horse.

The cab continued up island, past stretches of dark and foreboding mangrove trees until they spit out into an airy cut in the vegetation where a lone sign announced they had arrived at new lodgings. Allmen did the necessaries and the bags were brought around to a spacious two-bedroom condo overlooking a pool. Somewhere in the distance a karaoke machine fired up and the flyer on his refrigerator announced that it was chicken wing night. *Oh Dorothy, we are not in Kansas anymore.*

His phone rang."Hey Virgil."

"Hey, Mr...ah, John. Everything okay in the new accommodations? I'm sorry, there wasn't much available. I hope you understand it was the best I could do."

"It's perfect Virgil. No chance of meeting some hot shot money jockey here. Do you like chicken wings?"

"Sure. Who doesn't?"

"Rich people."

"Sorry John, you lost me."

"Lost myself Virgil. Some time ago. I mean it is nice to get back to my roots. To stop pretending. A palace for white trash with a little cash is exactly what I need. It's a good place to save a little money for the rest of this journey. Anyway, I'm trying to say thanks."

"You know John...now that we are on a first name basis, I may have some questions for you about this whole journey."

Allmen laughed. "I'm sure you will. Good night Virgil." And he hung up.

* * *

In the morning he drank strong coffee and watched the sun come in over the island from his deck. As the day wore on, he noted the pool and swim up bar below begin to fill with people. *Young and old, sober and not so much.* There are two kinds of swim up bars in the world. The classy ones with craft cocktails and chilled champagne and the ones that exist mostly so lazy drinkers don't have to get out and find a bathroom. This was decidedly one of the latter. For once Allmen was grateful for his aquatic phobia and chose a stool on the dry land side of the bar. The blender worked, the bartender was efficient, if not exactly quick and Allmen felt himself settling in, enjoying several rum drinks and soaking in some sun. It slowly arced overhead, the noise at the pool increased along with everyone's blood alcohol level.

The patrons marinated in seemingly endless pools of Patron and Corona. Allmen felt himself drifting off, there but not really. He avoided thoughts and just felt the warmth of the sun on his skin, now tanned like a boy with quarter Italian heritage ought to be. For a while, with the rum and the loud company, he realized it was still possible to feel like the old John Allmen. The one that predated the war, the divorce and the tragedy his life had become. Before he had an expensive car, big house and a lot of zeroes and commas on all of his bills. For him, this was a lark. *Out of the five star hotel and down to slum it at the one barely earning three and a half.* But for the people around him turning crimson in the Caribbean sun, this was their reality. It was their life, their dream vacation. Work the 9-5, send the kids to college, vacation in the islands, retire to The Villages in Florida. *In a different world it might have been me. Maybe it should have been me. Maybe I would have been…happy.*

"*Banzai*," someone bellowed from the pool, "*Kamikaze!*"

Allmen's head spun toward the group of middle aged men with beer guts. Their thick waisted wives were hefting pitchers of amber liquid and pouring them into plastic shot glasses for the group. They took note of him and waived at the bartender. "One for that guy too!"

Allmen had learned from the various tribal cliques in Iraq not to turn down signs of hospitality, no matter how unwelcome. He tipped the small glass back, felt the sweet and then sour taste of the opposing liqueurs and then felt them fall with a thud into his still empty stomach.

"*Kamikaze,*" Allmen murmured.

"It means divine wind," said the bartender cleaning off spilled Triple Sec with a sponge.

Allmen noted a vague Asiatic set to the man's face but couldn't place it. "I know. My grandfather fought in the Pacific during World War II."

"Mine too." Allmen waited, but there was no more. *So, was grandad Japanese? Or one of the numerous Asian cultures overrun by the Rising Sun?* He sighed. *What the hell does it matter?*

Allmen asked for his bill and began weighing his natural generosity on a mental scale against his newfound, but necessary, frugality. He left what he thought was an adequate tip for pouring beer and adding gin to tonic. Then he uneasily stood. The bartender gave him an insincere smile that turned to a fuming frown as he picked up the tray with his check. He was clearly unhappy with the tip.

Everybody expects more for less these days.

Allmen floated upstairs and flicked the light on entering the condo. He turned and headed for the kitchen and grabbed the in-room dining menu. He needed chicken wings, from his stomach to his soul.

✳ ✳ ✳

He took off walking the next day, this time out the main road as the sun rose higher in the hazy blue sky. Frogs were humming from the nearby drainage ditches, but soon fell silent as the heat smothered the island. After two hours of working up a decent lather, Allmen saw a road sign at a crossroads ahead, black block letters on a white background. An arrow at the bottom pointed off into the mangroves. Behind it, in the distance, was a small whitewashed church where the noon bells began softly chiming. As he neared the sign, he read it several times, rubbing his eyes to stop whatever hallucination he was having. But the sign was still there, even when he reached out and touched it. And it still said the same thing and pointed in the same direction. The last gong of the bells echoed out over the island and Allmen turned and followed the direction of the arrow. He looked back one more time at the sign that read, simply:

← HELL

Up the side road he followed were more signs, and the

distinctive hum and hiss of tour buses. A red and yellow billboard with a pitchfork poked out from the palm trees and announced:

Welcome to HELL

(and Hell's only post office).

Tourists from a cruise ship were walking around snapping photos from wooden viewing platforms of volcanic rock formations- short blackened craggy limestone. The expanse stretched over the size of a few tennis courts.

Allmen snorted. *Well, I'm here, I might as well have a look around.*

From the platforms, Hell was a moonscape of crumbling jagged peaks and detritus, scree covered valleys. Life size cutouts of the devil dotted the walkways and observation areas and tourists giggled as they snapped photos of their loved ones accompanied by Hell's most famous inhabitant.

Allmen thought this Hell looked a lot like one he had seen before in grainy photos. His grandfather had been on the Pacific island of Peleliu fighting the Japanese during World War II. It became famous in the Marine Corps as a dystopian island of rock, a larger versions of the hell in front of him, that the Japanese had fought hard to keep it or kill everyone trying to take it. The Marines had suffered cruelly by day, hot work with little water. They struggled up rock escarpments to attack machine gun nests where enemy soldiers had dug deep into the earth. Indeed, they had tunneled beneath it and run an underground supply network that gave the Americans fits. Enemy soldiers could pop up anywhere, including in the rear and start lobbing grenades. And at night, howling mad men would charge forward with samurai swords, screaming "Banzai." They were the flesh and blood kamikazes. *Suicidal killers.*

Of course, he'd learned all of this from history books. His

grandfather never talked about the war and was long gone by the time Allmen had followed his footsteps and joined the Corps. They called it Operation Stalemate. *What kind of idiot names an invasion Operation Stalemate? Some idiot at headquarters in a starched camouflage uniform, for sure. Some prick with an Ivy League degree and zero point zero common sense.*

Despite himself, he thought of Mack. *Banzai, shithead!*

He didn't like giving Mack any mental space just then. So, he turned his attention to someone else, anyone else, in his life. *I owe Virgil a postcard. From Hell.* The thought made him grin wolfishly and he strode with purpose to the red barn that served as the gift shop.

A bell tinkled softly to announce his entrance. *Do angels in hell still get their wings every time a bell rings?*

A matronly woman with long steely gray hair and a hard London accent greeted him from behind the counter. "Welcome to hell." She pronounced it "'ell".

"Thanks. I always suspected I'd get here sooner or later." He gave the wolf grin again.

She waived him away dismissively with a good natured laugh. "Oh, you Yanks. I'm sure you think I've never heard that one before."

He shrugged. "Sorry, short notice. Best I could do."

"Well, look around. I'll be with you as soon as I help this young lady."

The lady was not young. Indeed, she was quite old, busily fussing in her change purse to pay for the trinkets laid out on the counter in front of her. And Allmen needed very little time to look around, selecting an oversized post card from the metal wire revolving display that read: "I've Been to Hell and Back." Finally, the old woman tottered off, trailing a waft of cheap perfume behind her.

He stepped up the counter and the English woman, she was in her late fifties he guessed, lowered her horned rim glasses and sized him up. "You aren't from the cruise ship." It wasn't a question, but a statement of fact.

"No, I'm staying up the road."

"Fancy. Any interesting stories from America? Nothing much exciting happens down here."

"You mean it's boring in hell?"

"Boring *as* hell. What's your name?" She rang up the postcard and Allmen paid her.

"John, and you?"

"Pauline, but people call me Polly or just Pol. John and Pol…if we find George and Ringo, we can start a band, eh?"

"Love is all you need, right? But truthfully, I've always been more of a Stones fan."

"Wicked boy. What brings you to the Caymans?" She put the postcard into a tiny white paper bag, which Allmen thought unnecessary. The bag probably cost more than the card.

"Extended sabbatical."

"Quit your job? Or got fired? Or was there a woman involved?"

She's awfully quick on the uptake. "Quit. Got tired of playing stock jockey and watching everyone get rich while I just got fat and old."

She arched an eyebrow and looked him up and down. "You don't look either one to me dear. Maybe you can help me with my money? Get me fully retired. You know, working here is hell on earth." She smiled. He wished she hadn't. British dental care was notoriously bad and living in the islands didn't improve upon it.

"Thanks, but I gave all that up. I'm retired."

"Must be nice at your age. What are you forty?"

"Forty-five."

She nodded appreciatively. "Not bad, John."

"Well, it wasn't what I set out to do in life, but I guess it was a good run. It's all over now."

"Got you here. Paradise and all. What are you going to do now?"

Allmen shrugged. "Something different."

"Like what?"

132

He sighed. "I can't really tell you."

"Because you don't know?"

"Something like that. I've got a plan for the next year or so, but I'm having to sell most of my stuff to afford my travels. After that..." He trailed off with a shrug.

Well, John, a man's life does not consist in the abundance of possessions." She handed him the little bag with the card tucked inside.

"Did the Beatles say that?"

She paused for a long second and then whispered: "No, John. Jesus did." She smiled wryly without showing her teeth. "Luke 12:15."

Allmen nodded. "Ah, I see. I'm not much of a bible guy."

"I gathered. You don't look the type." Again, she sized him up, like his mother used to before she sent him off to school

"Well, hey, thanks for the postcard."

"My pleasure. Come back and see us in hell, okay?"

"Yeah. Yeah, I'll do that."

* * *

In his room that afternoon Allmen picked up the postcard and turned it over in his fingers. Then he got out a pen from the little desk and began to write in neat, small, block letters. There was a lot to say and he wanted it to be legible.

Virgil,

After a year or so, I guess it is time you begin to know me. We have another year on this contract, and you have a right to know a bit more about who you are dealing with. I think that is only fair.

I was born in Youngstown, Ohio, a remnant of the industrial age striving to pull itself up by the bootstraps and instead decaying into a rusting hulk where politicians go to score cheap points with people feeling left behind during elections. You know, bring our jobs back, that sort of thing. They never use the words Rust Belt in public, but I assure they were thinking it. We all were.

I was lucky. I got out. Went to Ohio State and got a decent education, played tennis while I was there and managed to squeak by and graduate. And then things got weird. I bummed around a bit, wondering what to do with a degree in history and literature. I tended bar, lifeguarded, even did a stint with a tree removal service. And I was about to move back in with my Mom when a bunch of assholes knocked down the twin towers with passenger jets. You may have heard about that.

Like most, I was pretty pissed off. You see, I was raised with a hearty love of America, freedom, rock and roll, hot dogs, apple pie and Bic lighters. I was thoroughly enamored with the idea of the individual rising above the fray to do great things. But my time in college taught me that Americans were a mixed bag. We made some wonderful, brave men and women who wouldn't go down without a fight on 9/11. And we made some real pieces of shit who were back to complaining six weeks later if someone wanted to look through their bags or give their fat asses a pat down. I joined the Marines, like my father and grandfather, supposedly fought for my country, and came back loathing just about everyone.

Allmen paused and looked out the window, past the deck into the pool where the sun was shining and a group was starting to gather again. He had run out of space. And time. In the lower margin he crammed in one more sentence: To Be Continued. Then he went down to the bar to have a drink.

A day later, at twenty-five thousand feet Allmen felt yet another arcing left-hand turn commence and checked his watch. They were clearly circling, drilling a hole in an empty piece of sky, now twenty minutes past their scheduled landing. He hailed a flight attendant who was sitting cross legged in a jump seat playing a game on her phone.

"Drink?" He mouthed while hoisting his empty fist in a universal signal of thirst.

She shook her head, an equally universal signal of denial and pointed to the seatbelt sign which was still illuminated.

He sighed. Showers had rolled in, unusual for this time of year, and were drenching the runway in San Francisco. They'd frozen ground operations and put everyone in holding after a lightning strike in the area. At least, that what was the pilot had divulged in a five-minute laconic soliloquy. Allmen figured a few more minutes of this and they'd be diverting to San Jose or Sacramento. Neither potentiality particularly appealed to him.

As if on cue, the airliner leveled out and started to descend.

"Ah folks, the weather is clearing in San Francisco, and just in time. Call it a divine wind, I guess. So, we are going to head in and see if we can get you to your destination. Sorry for the delay." *It must be a joyless existence as an airline pilot, always having to be sorry for this and that.*

It was a bumpy descent and great plumes of spray erupted from the runway as they touched down. A trickle of water rolled down the taxiway like a river as they lumbered into the gate, Allmen sighing, this time with relief. Spilling into the terminal, he turned right and made the long trudge past the other arriving and departing cattle. He was sun-tanned and happy after his island adventures, at least as happy as he was capable of being these days. He crossed through the one-way portal from the secure to the non-secure airport and there she was. To his left, moving through the same security checkpoint in the opposite direction was a blonde woman with cascading curls hanging down over a smart blue business blazer and cream-colored blouse. *The blonde woman.* She wore matching blue kitten heels and Allmen registered that she hadn't taken them off, which meant she traveled often and was on the TSA pre-check list, as was he. Why did this woman make his brain think in varying degrees of gibberish?

"Hey," Allmen said, moving toward the security line. And then louder, "Hey!" Yelling in an airport in the post 9/11 world is a wonderful way to get attention. And sure enough the TSA agents manning each side of the checkpoint froze to take in what could be an imminent threat. She looked at him then, and Allmen felt sure he saw a flicker of recognition pass over her lovely angular face as she pursed her pink lips in concern. Then she turned on a heel, gathered her bag from the x-ray conveyor and strode off toward the boarding area.

"Hey...wait!" Now radios were crackling, and someone yelled something about a restricted area as Allmen attempted to retrace his steps and cut her off near the hub of the B Gates. It was a mistake, but that would only register for him later when his head cleared of nonsense and stray electrical voltage. Instead, an older black man with salt a pepper hair loomed in his path, white button-down shirt and blue pants. *Probably security.*

The command to "Freeze!" confirmed it. The man moved like a former cop, probably former military, unholstering a weapon from his right hip in a smooth, professional motion.

"Oh, shit," Allmen said, trying to stop but catching his foot on his rollaboard bag and tumbling forward in a sprawl. He felt the muscles in his neck ripple, a cramp spreading between his shoulder blades that turned to a burning spasm. And then his body seized as he rolled and convulsed on the floor. The guard, nearly knocked over by the idiot who had tried to run through the security barrier, switched off the voltage running to his Taser and Allmen's body relaxed. Now Allmen felt nothing. He closed his eyes. And thought of her. *I was so damn close.*

WRATH:

strong vengeful anger or indignation, a retributory punishment for an offense or a crime

Forget your fear, no one can hinder our passage;
One so great has granted it.
But you wait here for me, and feed and comfort
your tired spirit with good hope,
For I will not abandon you in this low world.

-Dante, Inferno, Canto VIII

They apparently allowed more than one phone call from an airport holding cell also known as airport jail. Indeed, the security guard who had Tased him said he had ten minutes to use the landline. Allmen registered his odd name, Officer Phlegyas embroidered on his short sleeve shirt, while he stood by and supervised. In desperation, Allmen tried Mack's phone but immediately went to voicemail. He left no message. He did leave a message for his lawyer, who probably wouldn't get it until the morning, but would start billing the instant the message was time stamped. Finding himself with time to spare and feeling a gnawing need to talk to someone, he dialed Virgil.

"Circle Nine, this is..."

"Virgil, It's John. John Allmen, on a landline."

"Hey Mr....sorry, hey John," came the usual chipper greeting. "Did you just get back?"

"I did. But I've had a, ah, complication." Allmen glanced at his guard who rolled his eyes.

"Okay. What's up?" Allmen told him. Virgil let out a low whistle that crackled into the beat-up receiver. *This phone has probably been handling airport perp calls since Bill Walsh was coaching the 'Niners.* "So, why call me John? What can I do? Call a lawyer?"

"Nah, I have that covered Virgil. I just...well, I just wanted you to know. That's all. I might need to travel domestically for a while if you know what I'm saying."

"Yeah, maybe a stay-cation is in order. Maybe wine tasting in Napa and a nice hotel and spa downtown."

"I knew you would understand." Allmen paused thinking of a hotel in downtown San Francisco where he'd become smitten with the woman who had just gotten him put on a terrorist watch list. It was, after all, she who had given him Virgil's number.

"Wait a minute...Virgil, do you remember who referred me to you? Last year around this time, someone gave me your card."

"No. We never discussed it."

"Let's discuss it now, because it was the same femme fatal who earned me forty thousand volts of..."

"Fifty thousand," said the guard, hulking in the doorway and checking his watch.

"...earned me fifty thousand volts of electricity and a few legal entanglements."

"Describe her," Virgil said in a clipped voice.

"Blonde, beautiful, legs that go on forever, curves that would make a priest swear off altar boys. Come to think of it, not only did she give me your card, she flat out insisted I call."

Virgil sighed and then answered in a quiet, measured tone. "Sorry John. You aren't exactly my only client and, honestly, that could describe a lot of the women in Greater San Francisco and Marin County. Besides, I have confidentiality agreements. You signed one, remember?"

"Not particularly."

"Well, you did. Along with the privacy policy you ignored. The point is, even if I did know *exactly* who you are talking about," he emphasized the word exactly by pronouncing all three syllables equally, "I couldn't give you any information about her." He finished in an almost pleading tone, "I just couldn't."

"Maybe I'll just have to drive up there and beat it out of you." The line was quiet for a long minute. "Jesus Virgil, I'm just kidding." He heard the other man's sigh of relief.

"Okay tough guy," growled the guard patting his Taser. "Ten minutes are up."

"Gotta go Virgil. Good talk."

They couldn't hold him overnight at the airport, so he was transferred to the Federal Courthouse downtown in a police cruiser. Cuffed with his hand behind him, he sat uncomfortably, rain slanting in sideways from the Pacific and hitting the cruiser in staccato bursts. He wriggled in the backseat as they cruised unhurriedly up The 101.

When they stopped, he was manhandled out the door and stepped into a running river of sludge and filth at the curb. It was just that kind of day. And it didn't get any better when the sun went down and the lights came up in the City By The Bay. He spent a restless night on a rock-hard bed in a small cell with a sink and toilet, studiously avoiding using either. It was around 10AM when he was shown to a small conference room and found his lawyer waiting for him while tapping out a message on his iPhone.

"Morning Phil." Phil Argento had slicked back black hair and an Italian suit that probably cost as much as Allmen's vacation. He was notoriously showy in a city that was known for excess in many things. But Allmen knew it was mostly an act. The guy barely made his bills every month except for an inheritance that Allmen had managed for him up until a year ago.

"You made bail," he said without prelude. "I pulled a few strings, mentioned your military service. I think I can make this thing go away with a slap on the wrist. But you will need to sign up for counseling. Get mental help."

"Okay. Is that the court's opinion or yours?"

"That is the opinion of the justice system. I have no opinion. That's not my job"

"Well, thanks. I appreciate you coming down. Give me a ride home?"

"Not a chance. And John, do me a favor?"

"Sure."

"Lose my number. You aren't my advisor anymore and I'm not your lawyer. Deal?"

Allmen looked him hard in the eye. "Yeah, sure. Deal."

He trudged behind the lawyer as they both made their way out of the building. Then he stood for a minute under the eave watching the rain pour down as Phil turned right and headed toward the parking lot to retrieve his Mercedes. Argento's knee buckled as he slid on the filth that was cascading down the sidewalk and he went down awkwardly, saved from a full face plant by extending his arm and having his briefcase cushion the fall. Allmen was twenty yards away and had to work hard not to laugh hard enough for his former lawyer to hear.

"Serves you right asshole," he said under his breath as he hailed a yellow cab.

He burst through the front door of his house and set about packing a bag with athletic shirts, shorts and comfortable clothes for the late summer. He gassed up the BMW at the Shell Station off of Van Ness. There was a colony of homeless people across the street, shuffling and grumbling, then pointing at him.

"Prick in a "Beamer!" Someone called. Allmen smiled and waved.

What he was about to do was questionable, he knew, with a case pending in California Superior Court. But he couldn't stay here. He needed fresh air and couldn't sit idly by while the wheels of justice clanged forward at a rusty crawl.

He drove north across the Golden Gate, traffic flowing easily in the mid-morning and then east along the 580 for an hour before he stopped at a Big 5 sporting goods store. He bought a small one-person tent, a sleeping bag, small grill and a single burner propane stove. At the Albertsons next door he stocked a small cooler and spent several minutes in the parking lot arranging and then rearranging the trunk and backseat until he was fully satisfied. Then he motored eastward, picking up Highway 99 and heading south.

He dialed Circle Nine and Virgil answered on the first ring. "Hey Virgil. I want to climb a mountain."

"Literally or figuratively?"

"Literally. I'm on 99 south, can you get me a permit to hike Mount Whitney? I always wanted to do that."

Virgil exhaled and said, "I can try. Tricky during summer months. Call you back."

In twenty minutes, he did. "I texted you everything you need. Be careful, though, John. It's not the easiest hike in the world, people have had problems up there with the altitude. Hikers have died, though best I can tell it's usually during the winter. Tell me something? What made you want to climb a mountain? Today of all days?"

"Because it's there Virgil." He fidgeted uneasily in his seat. "Because it's there." *And because I need to go somewhere else and am finding excuses not to.*

He hung up as the sun arced slowly through the sky. He hammered southward past Fresno until his nostrils filled with the unmistakable smell of mass industrial farming. A huge cattle ranch loomed out of the nothingness where the animals stood nuts to butts staring at the freeway, seemingly begging to be put out of the misery. Many were. And they were served up steaming hot at the hotel and restaurant just off the exit. Allmen stopped, not for the steak, which somehow made him squeamish just now, but for the beef jerky. And as he stood in line to pay, he added a postcard from another wire revolving rack of nearby attractions.

He kept driving on 99S past Bakersfield until the green farms gave way to a dusty plain that started to rise toward the horizon. The BMW hummed slowly along a single lane road toward Death Valley, great rocky cuts and gorges dropping away on either side bathed in a pink sunset. After half an hour he found his camp site in the dark and set up the tent and stove by the lights from the car. He cooked a pork chop, his taste for red meat lessened a bit for the time being. And he drank a couple of beers and curled into his new sleeping bag.

After a few minutes staring upward into the darkness he reached out for his backpack and extracted his headlamp, a pen and the slightly bent postcard. Allmen looked at into, turning it over in the soft beam of light projecting from his forehead. It showed a scrubby green and brown hill overlooking a salt flat. Flowing script said Greetings form Death Valley. On the back, in fine print, it said "The lowest dry point in North America as seen from Dante's View in the Black Mountains." He began to write:

I'm not sure why I came back from combat hating the world, I just did. Before combat I figured it was the Pareto Principle. You know, where eighty percent of an effect usually comes from twenty percent of the cause? I thought that eighty percent of the world's misery was brought about by twenty percent of the population. That a minority of assholes were really fucking it all up for the rest of us. But combat has a way of clarifying many things. Something about the simplicity of combat, the binary nature of it, win or lose, live or die, frees the mind for other pursuits.

Anyway, after Iraq I didn't think that way anymore. It was more like, one hundred percent of us are miserable shits and making life intolerable for each other. I know, the math isn't crystal clear, but I was a liberal arts guy in college. Anyway, they told me the therapy helped. I suppose they are right. Who am I to tell the experts their business? Maybe it was the difference between making and not. Well, I made it. I survived.

I think about the helicopter in Fallujah. We got ambushed on a routine patrol. As if there was such a thing as a routine patrol in a place where everyone not wearing camouflage wanted to cut your head off and hang your entrails from their front window. I was the senior officer, trying my best to rally our kids and get them to the landing zone. We were shooting back, a running fire fight until we got to the clearing and then the fire slackened enough for the chopper to touch down. I got everyone on board, like you are supposed to do. Take care of your men first. You don't eat until they eat, you don't evac until they are already aboard, that kind of shit. Well, I was laying down fire until the last of them were aboard and then I took off at a dead sprint to catch up. Twenty yards away an RPG, that's a rocket propelled grenade, went right into the cockpit. The whole thing erupted in a ball of flame in front of me. I saw Gomez, the immigrant's kid with a ridiculous attempt at a mustache get blown through the gunner's door and pieces of him started landing all around me. I don't remember anything after that. I woke up in a hospital in Italy. The rest of them...they never woke up.

Allmen stared for a long time at the card, now covered in fine neat script. He tried for a long time to sort out what he was feeling, to label whatever was nagging at the edges of his consciousness. In the end, the only feeling he could pinpoint was fatigue. *I am very, very tired.* He put the paper, headlamp and pen back in his pack and went to sleep.

He woke in the predawn darkness, his breath making a plume of visible steam in the cool of the morning mountain air. Somewhere nearby a stream was gurgling, and he could hear the rush of a small waterfall tumbling over the rocks. He brewed instant coffee, terrible, but not undrinkable on the portable stove. He threw a couple of thousand calories of bread, cheese, nuts and beef jerky into a small daypack, laced up his hiking boots and drove over to the small town of Lone Pine. There he parked and joined the trail heading to the highest peak in the lower forty-eight states.

Allmen set off at a brisk pace, awakening the body and mind to the task ahead. He'd been called a sadist in Officer Candidate School for loving just this sort of thing, a long walk with nothing to do but put one foot in front of the other, simple, primal, something modern man and all of his conveniences couldn't manage to muck up. Just a walk in the woods.

Three hours in he passed the tree line and he came to a grassy meadow where he could stop and pay attention to the hints coming from his stomach. He ate a meal of bread and cheese and drank as much water as he could, knowing what was to come. He refilled his water, took a piss behind a boulder and stepped off again, winding his way up the mountain path that took him past twelve thousand feet of elevation. He felt the sting of a headache around the periphery of his skull that told him altitude was beginning to be a factor. He backed off his pace, focused on his breathing and was rewarded as the flaring pain subsided to a dull ache.

Halfway in distance to the summit, and crossing 12,000 feet, he reached Trail Camp. This was a boulder strewn clearing where a few tents flapped in the wind and gear for those summiting lay in neat piles. He filled his water again and pushed on up a long series of switchbacks that seemed to last for eternity, finally cresting a large rocky bowl that still had fingers of snow reaching down the crags and crevices. His headache returned and he knew he was stuck with it until he came down. He set a plodding rhythm and narrowed his consciousness to the path, no more than six or eight feet in front of him. The Sierras, forests of pine and the desert all unfolded below him, and he was dimly aware of the intense beauty. But there would be time to enjoy it on the way back. For now, he climbed into fields of granite, scrambling over sheer rock and occasionally feeling the slide of ice underfoot despite the summer. The last stretch leveled out, but he was above thirteen thousand feet and his head and heart were pounding out a rhythm twice the speed of his feet. He hugged the side of a cliff, looking down thousands of feet to the valley below. One slip, he thought, one missed step on the rocks or ice and thus would end the occasionally tragic tale of one John Allmen. *Nah, not just yet.*

It was early afternoon when he reached a small clearing, really just a widening of the path before the final push to the summit. Backpacks and miscellaneous gear were stacked haphazardly along the cliff wall as hikers had shed unnecessary weight before heading to the top. Allmen saw one of the backpacks move and then groan, realizing it was man, hunched over with his head in his hands. He was muscular, veins outlining biceps and triceps accentuated by a sleeveless red Columbia performance tee shirt.

"Hey, you okay?"

The man, in reality a kid probably in his mid-twenties or early thirties, looked up at him, eyes slowly focusing. "I'm fine." He said irritably.

"You sure?"

"Yeah, I'm fucking sure." The kid tried to stand and wobbled, dizzily.

"Is the altitude getting to you? We're pretty high up. Why don't you let me take your pulse?" The kid seemed ready to comply, reaching out a hand with swollen fingers, then suddenly recoiling from Allmen, the testy look returning to his red face.

"Don't touch me, bro. I don't know you. I don't need your

fucking help. If I did, I would have asked for it..." He trailed off, retching and heaving but nothing coming up.

"Are you up here alone?"

"No asshole, I'm here with you. Unfortunately."

Allmen eyed him. The kid was in bad shape, altitude sickness was potentially critical if he kept pushing for the top and wasn't able to get down and regain his senses in time. But Allmen had a mental filing system for a reason, and this kid was pissing him off. *Not My Problem. Done. Filed.* He walked on.

He passed a series of jagged pieces of rock known as The Needles and navigated a few switchbacks before arriving at a stone hut on a promontory at 14,508 feet. He walked a little way up the stone path from the hut and he was at the top of Mount Whitney. To his surprise, his phone vibrated in his pocket.

"Congratulations," read the text from Virgil. "I was able to track you for the last hour." Allmen smiled, snapped selfies overlooking Death Valley and Kings Canyon, sent them off to Virgil and headed back down the way he had come. When he rounded the bend below The Needles, he noted that the kid was gone. Allmen shrugged and trekked back to his campsite, this time soaking in the expansive views as his head began to clear.

He heard the helicopter long before he saw it, that unmistakable *whup, whup, whup* sound of rotor blades lashing at the air in order to stay aloft. Allmen felt beads of cold sweat trickle down his neck. And then the craft broke out over the treetops, Allmen fighting the urge hit the dirt, subconsciously reaching for a weapon he hadn't carried in years. This helicopter was orange with a black cross painted on it above the block letters: Tulare County Search & Rescue. Allmen watched it go overhead, breathing again, his eyes following it over the horizon. Was the hiker he had left on the mountain being searched for? Or rescued? He had no way of knowing. *What else could I do?*

He walked. And to take his mind off of wayward hikers, he thought about what to do next. He would not make the drive back to the Bay Area just yet. There was more to do. Indeed, as the desert landscape rolled out beneath him, he admitted what he had known from the minute he left San Francisco. But he had been hoping that something back there would reel him back in from a trip he didn't want to make. *No such luck. Go east young man.*

✳ ✳ ✳

He was sore the next morning, progressing from camping to cramping as he eased back onto the mountain roads and was happy to link up with Interstate 40 where he could relax a bit and stretch his legs with the cruise control engaged.

"Circle Nine...oh, hey John. How was the summit?"

"Wonderful Virgil. Nice to tick it off the bucket list, you know?"

"Sure, what is next? Are you on the road?"

"Listen Virgil. I need to do something, and you can't be a part of it. Okay? I need to fire you for a few days. I need to be off the grid."

"Are you leaving the state?"

"Damn it Virgil, I was trying to keep you from being an accomplice or an accessory or whatever."

Oh, please, John. I think we are past all that. I'll do whatever you need me to do even if that means being an accessory to you jumping bail."

"Wow, you make it sound like I'm a hardened criminal dodging the man."

"Hardened, yes. You just climbed the highest peak in the contiguous United States on a whim. But you aren't a criminal in my mind. At least until due process has run its course." He exhaled a small nasally laugh. "Are you planning on being back for that to happen?"

"Yes Virgil. This is a short getaway to clear my head. When my shit head lawyer needs me back, I'll be back."

"Great, so there is no problem I can see. Is there anything I can do for you?"

"Not right now. I am going to need you again, but this is something I need to do myself."

"Fair enough. Call me when you need me. I'm always around."

"Yeah, I know. Thanks."

Allmen hung up, turned off the phone and drove on across the Colorado River into Arizona, officially crossing a state line with his case pending and violating the terms of his bail. He drove on through the desert for another hour, ate dinner at an In-N-Out Burger and drove on to Flagstaff. There he stretched his aching legs and watched the night come to the desert. He thought briefly about a hotel, but figured he'd rather not spend the money just yet. Sleeping on the ground was good for the soul and it would serve him just fine for a while.

By midnight he was perched over a great gaping hole in the earth, though in the dark it all looked much the same, up or down...heaven or hell? He finished the last of his beef jerky, stretched aching muscles out on his sleeping bag. And he fell asleep to the braying of coyotes somewhere out in the darkness that loomed over and in the Grand Canyon.

The following day he spent in camp, recovering and rehydrating, which for him meant drinking on the wide veranda of the lodge above the Bright Angel Trail. Parks serving the great mass of tourists from sea to shining sea weren't known for their wine lists, so he made do with Jack Daniels. It made him feel rugged, like a cowboy who had ridden in on his German sports car. He watched the hikers coming up off the trail with dour sunburned faces. Exhausted by the journey up from the river below, they shuffled, heads down, legs burning. Tomorrow he might look and feel the same. But looking at the flimsy gear, and the flabby midsections one man Allmen thought probably not. *One of those guys was wearing flip flops. I'm smarter and in better shape.*

He was mostly right. The eighteen-mile round trip just days after logging twenty-one up the side of a mountain was an extra bit of stress on the leg muscles. But in the early going, downhill, he clipped off the miles at a jaunty pace. Or as jaunty as one can be the night after drinking brown liquor. The switchbacks on the way down became less and less crowded as the day wore on, though he did have to give way to a group of sullen mules carrying their touristy loads to the campground below. At the bottom, crows circled overhead as he crossed the suspension bridge over the Colorado and cruised into Phantom Ranch just in time for lunch.

Then he turned around and retraced his steps at about half the pace going up as coming down. Late in the day, with an eerie red light bathing the surrounding desert, he emerged from the underworld and smiled up at the veranda he had watched from the night before. No one was there. He took a pay shower, changed and made his way back to the lodge, again drinking cowboy liquor and watching the sun set in a fiery red ball that seemed to be swallowed by a great gaping maw carved out of the earth. And when the sun had just about set in the west, Allmen turned his gaze toward the deep purple blackness in the east. Phil hadn't called. It was time to go.

The next day he was on the road again, turning on his phone for directions as he entered Utah. He half expected the phone to erupt in a series of messages and phone calls, but it was quiet. As quiet as the road stretching out in front of him. He briefly toyed with a side trip to Las Vegas, it wasn't far. But unlike most people he was smart enough to learn from his last trip there and instead he steered east toward Zion and found a campground in between its majestic ravine and Bryce Canyon. It had showers and a laundromat, and Allmen cut an eccentric figure pulling up his BMW among the 4x4 trucks and RVs. But no one called him a prick, they just tended their fires, cooked their meats, spent time with their families and left him alone to go about his business. He spent a day washing clothes and provisioning, then the following five descending to the depths of another gaping hole in the ground and sloshing through The Narrows, a watery path between the rocks and boulders deposited along the Colorado Plateau. Then he was off again to Moab, taking a morning stroll for five or six miles out to Delicate Arch, a postcard picture that symbolized the untamed west. Then he stopped in town for pizza and beer.

By now the exercise and limited diet were making room in his clothes and he stopped at a Walmart as he crossed into Colorado at Grand Junction, buying a couple pairs of shorts with a 32-inch waist. *Lean. Mean. Marine.* He'd forgotten how good it could feel to be this trim and ship shape. Though he had never developed the industry wide malady known as 'broker butt' from sitting on his assets all day, he had nevertheless seen his fitness level dip a bit after his time as a Jarhead.

Outside of Grand Junction he stayed in his first hotel, a modest affair meant for business travelers featuring amenities like a hot tub, a kitchenette and happy hour. Allmen had a long soak to loosen up his aching muscles, then took a cold shower and went down to the bar.

This was middle management territory. Men and women in business casual wear, unwinding after a day of corporate drudgery away from their families. *Blessing or curse?* He supposed it depended on the individual and the timing. He had liked traveling for work when he first got the chance, finding the time away exhilarating when there were deals to be made and clients to bring on board. But eventually it wore him down. He ordered a drink.

"On me," said the bartender, her name tag said her name was Hope, offering the first glass of merlot gratis and indicating that the bottle had been open "a while." After tasting it, Allmen thought 'a while' might have been the last ice age. But he was in no mood to play the wine snob that night and polished it off and ordered another. This one was fresh, cheap and marginally better than the last. So, the evening was looking up.

He thought it might be pleasant to spend a night in civilization. But civilization had a problem that might have predated the ice age, Allmen wasn't much of a pre-historian. The problem was tribalism. Ever since the days of the Utes and the Navajo one tribe had cast a wary eye on the other, questioning their motives and wondering how to make them assimilate or just go away.

There were several televisions dominating the lobby and bar area, all tuned to a television news channels. It being 21st century America, the Natives were long gone, working the casinos and selling dream catchers on E-Bay. Instead, tribal lines were clearly marked between the two main American political parties, neither of which particularly appealed to the man at the bar drinking cheap red wine and nursing a deep ache in his sun-tanned legs. Red versus blue, your guy versus my gal, played out amidst the flickering light of fifty-inch televisions and John Allmen did his best to ignore it. But the conversation grew louder, the initial hour over and the happiness draining away. It was all replaced by brooding murmurs about Supreme Court rulings and the Federal Reserve. Whatever was masquerading as 'Breaking News' at that moment. He figured it must have been economic in nature, at least tangentially, as a gray-haired middle-aged man wearing a green polo shirt with his embroidered company logo was liberally using the C word.

"You're a communist! Not even a socialist a full on, dyed in the wool communist." He waggled a finger at his bespectacled co-worker. They wore the same logo wear Allmen noticed, thinking this would make for good banter around the water cooler. The Commie, as he had been labeled, was younger, and fuming with all the barely suppressed rage of a Berkeley radical.

"And you are a Social Darwinist..." he spluttered, found traction "and a fucking fascist." Allmen sighed and walked out the automatic doors to grab some air. The night was cold in the high desert and a full bright moon shone over the strip malls and hotels lining the exit to the interstate. He wondered what Old Ciaccio, the man without a country, would think of what America was becoming.

He ambled back into the bar and attempted to collect his drink and make a retreat to his room. But Hope was a tad slow to bring the check and he was subjected to more political theatre from the morons from Accelerated Transportation Service, or whatever their shirts said.

"What a country." Allmen shook his head.

"Yeah, well some people are born stupid. You a Republican or a Democrat?"

A heavily made up woman in a cowboy hat sat across the bar eyeing him. He could tell she felt left out of the initial altercation and wanted one of her own. He did his best not to oblige.

"Neither."

She gave a derisive snort. "Neither? Then who did you vote for?"

"No one."

"You had to vote for someone honey."

He frowned into his drink. "Not if I didn't vote."

Her look of mock horror would have made him laugh if he wasn't so disgusted by the spectacle around him. "That's terrible. My son is in the Air Force, you know. He is fighting for people like you, so you enjoy the freedom to do your patriotic duty."

Allmen eyed her hard. Adrenaline surged in his veins. "Air Force, huh? What does your precious boy do in the Air Force?"

"I...well, I don't know. Something with satellites. Very secret and very important, I'm sure."

"Satellites." Allmen threw up his hands. "Fucking satellites. Did he deploy?"

"Deploy?"

"Did your precious little prince go away from home?"

"Of course he did. All the time... out to the desert."

"You mean the desert...around here?" Allmen waived expansively, warming to the task before him.

"Yeah, or in California."

"So, your son was protecting my democratic virtue in California with satellites. Thank him for his service, please, I'm sure if aliens invade, he'll be on the front lines. Did he ever fight any bad guys?"

"Bad guys?"

"Terrorists? People with guns and evil intentions? Bad guys."

"Well, no."

Allmen polished off what must have been his sixth or seventh glass of cheap Merlot with relish and signed his check. "Well, I did. In the Marines. So that pretty much means I don't *have* to do shit." Allmen got on the elevator scowling at her the entire way across the lobby.

He didn't notice that he'd gotten on the elevator with the finger wagging fascist, who was sweaty and smelled of sour beer. "Hey, I heard what you said to that lady. And I wanted to thank you for your service."

The elevator doors opened and Allmen held them for an extra second as he slowly turned to the man and scowled at him.

"I didn't do it for you." Then he stepped off, let the doors close and went back to his room to finish his drink.

He sat at the desk, the curtains open and the moonlight slanting in over another postcard, this one from the hotel lobby.

You see Virgil, I don't really care about these people. I thought I did, but it turns out I can't stand them. I love the ideals of America, the hope and promise of the Spirit of '76, you know? The idea that your rights come from you, that you are born with them, not given them by some suit with a narcissism complex.

But it turns out I can't stand Americans, my countrymen. They've forgotten who they are. Sold their soul for fast food dinners and low brow entertainment. And then tried to export it overseas. I fought for a culture that doesn't exist anymore. I saw people killed for that mythical ideal. And it really pisses me off. Or maybe I've just had too much to drink.

He put the pen down and stared at the paragraph, reading it twice before stripping naked in the moonlight and crawling into the moderately priced, but luxurious king-sized bed.

✻ ✻ ✻

The next day he just drove. He went heading down out of the mountains around Denver and into the prairie. His mind, as it had on the hiking trails, narrowed to the road immediately in front, interrupted only by gas, coffee and the bathroom. By nightfall he was out of the endless rows of corn and crossing the Mississippi, pointed eastward like a missile. Gas, coffee, drive, repeat. He was really in no hurry, no one expected him anywhere. Indeed, as far as planet earth was concerned, he was a chastised hermit, reading books in his house while the legal system pondered his fate. That said, he didn't drive fast, obeying the limits to avoid an uncomfortable conversation with a state police cruiser. But he kept driving. On and on through the night, past Chicago around midnight, probably his last chance to stop and get some rest. Adrenalized, he pushed on. Eastbound he continued into the small hours of the morning and finally saw the glimmer of light on the horizon and the sun coming up in his face.

Deep into Ohio he left the highway and drove into a town of brick buildings and corner bars, bowling alleys and abandoned warehouses. Sullen faces watched from porch steps instead of getting ready for work, as his foreign sports car wound its way through the dilapidated streets sprouting weeds from the cracks. Allmen thought that if he had a craving for meth instead of coffee he was in the right place. *But I don't. Which is nice.*

Past the hulking empty buildings downtown and the rising red spires of abandoned smokestacks, he turned off of a side road and found his way past the high school. There was only one now, and some genius had scrawled graffiti on the brick wall around the football field, "Fix Dis Town" it read in irregularly spray-painted letters. He turned left onto a long asphalt driveway with overgrown grass on either side. He coasted up to the squat brick house with a broken screen door that was flapping in the freshening breeze. He stood for a long moment as the door banged and the floorboards in the porch beneath him groaned, all the caffeine and adrenaline draining away. Why had he come back here? Or was the question *why not sooner?*

The interior door creaked and an old woman in a nightgown, gray hair piled atop her head and pinned back with her reading glasses, stood blocking the light from inside. A cigarette burned in her left hand and Allmen smelled burnt coffee and cats.

He gave a lopsided grin, unsure what to say. He put his hands in his pockets fidgeting nervously and settled on, "Hi Mom."

✳ ✳ ✳

She kept him waiting on the porch while she changed her clothes and fed the cats. With a sigh, she emerged again, a fresh cigarette in hand and said, "Okay, let's go." She continued to smoke in the car, cracking a window after noting with disdain that there was no ashtray.

"What kind of fancy European car doesn't have an ashtray?" She flicked the ashes out the window managing to get about half into the wind and half into the back seat. John Allmen said nothing. *What does it matter now?*

"So, big shot, what brings you back here?" They sat in a downtown diner, a thoroughly depressing greasy spoon filled with the wheezing elderly toting supplemental oxygen on a trolley. His mother had slid into a booth and was greeted by name by their waitress.

"I wanted to see Dad." It was cruel, he knew, to intentionally hurt her like that, but their relationship had long devolved into a series of barbs and accusations. She had played the foil to his father's festive, world be damned attitude, and seen her son follow in his footsteps. He still felt a perverse pleasure in getting a rise of the woman he had often referred to as "WB", short for "the wet blanket".

"A bit late isn't it? For you to show up here?" She was brooding into her coffee cup while absently stabbing at a stack of pancakes slathered in butter and blueberry syrup.

He sipped at his scalding cheap black coffee, making a conscious effort not to touch anything he didn't have to.

"I wanted to see you too Mom."

"Well, gosh, thanks so much Mr. Hot Shot for thinking about your dear old Mother. You could have called. I would have saved you the trip."

"I enjoyed the trip."

"I am so glad to hear it." If his *joie de vivre* came from his father, his sarcasm clearly descended from his mother's side. Allmen frowned at his coffee. *This is not going well. N*ot that he had expected otherwise. Too much left unsaid over the years. Too much morose anger bubbling just under the surface.

"Look Mom, I'm sorry."

"For what?"

"For all of it. The times I was absent, the times I was here physically but checked out mentally. For the drugs. For almost dying. Maybe for not dying, I don't know."

She watched him carefully, laconically rolling her deep-set eyes as he finished. "When you were growing up, you were such a sweet boy. And then..." She pushed her plate back and glanced at her deeply wrinkled hands and their pink chipped nails. "I need to wash my hands." She shuffled off toward the restrooms and he glared after her.

"John?" He snapped his head up and looked, for the first time, at the waitress who had taken their orders. Her face, gentle and doe eyed, framed by a boyish blonde haircut, had probably once been pretty. Now she used too much makeup to cover over years of hard times, hard use. She smiled a thin smile and he saw years melt away and suddenly he was thinking of a teenage girl in a baseball field dugout after the sun had gone down. And he was a teenage boy clumsily attacking the mystery of her bra strap. Even then, nearly thirty years ago, he was reduced to giggles by the irony of her name.

"Chastity?" She frowned and shifted her weight from one foot to another. "Yeah...but I don't ...well, no one calls me that anymore." She pointed to her name tag that said Marie. "My middle name," she explained."

"Yeah, I knew that." He hadn't really, but it seemed the polite thing to say.

"I mean I have four kids, ya know. So, I'm not exactly, well, you know...It's a little bit too..."

"Ironic?"

She put her hands on her hips to contemplate that and he noticed a sleeve of green and black ink reaching down her right arm. *How many diner paychecks had gone to the tattoo artist?* "Yeah, ironic." She smiled sadly. "How have you been?"

"Oh wonderful. And terrible. The usual. I spent some time in jail recently."

"Huh, you sound like my second husband. Though, truth be told, he is still there and won't be getting out...well, ever."

"Yeah, I guess I'm quite the renegade." Allmen was nodding and he felt the conversation sliding down a winding path toward awkwardness. "Can we have the check?"

He paid, tipping her twice what the meager breakfast had cost and stood as his mother returned. His mother beamed, the ragged expression softening into something like a matronly smile at Chastity. From stone, she had turned animated, like Medusa in reverse. He hadn't known she was still capable of warmth.

"It was good to see you again honey."

"You too Mrs. A. See you, John."

Allmen nodded absently. "Yeah, see ya...Marie"

"Plan on dropping in again unannounced?" His mother was smoking in the passenger seat again, this time all the windows were down, a freshening breeze cooling off the coming heat of the morning.

"Not in this lifetime." There was no question of sticking around 'Dis City.' She said nothing and was out of the car and halfway up the front steps to the house when he stuck his head out of the window.

"Hey Mom? I meant it. I am sorry for all of it. I thought you should know that. Okay?"

"Okay."

"One more thing?" She raised heavy eyebrows, wary,

guarded. "I want to go see Dad."

"Yeah? So, who is stopping you?"

Allmen looked away, drumming his fingers on the leather steering wheel. "I don't know where he is."

✲ ✲ ✲

He drove for ten minutes east of town, the unused smokestacks receding in the rearview mirror, out past the old volunteer fire department. A dilapidated fire engine sat in the parking lot and Allmen noted that the roof had caved in on the garage where it should have been parked. Snow, time and a declining tax base had done their work. A left at the flashing yellow light took him onto a tree lined lane where he pulled to the side and parked. He gulped fresh air and walked for a bit to stretch his legs, attempts at wakefulness that were only partially successful.

Well, this is why you drove three quarters of the way across the country. He mounted a few cracked concrete steps and went through an automatic door into a large reception area. The room made a half assed attempt at cheerfulness with colorful art prints in flimsy plastic frames and floral arrangements, also plastic. He smirked. Pops was a lot of things, but picky about his decor? Not so much.

He checked in with the desk and they sent him on his way up two floors and down a long dimly lit hallway. The sound of overly loud television, news programs from either of the party propaganda channels mostly, gave way to an electronic hum. He knocked at his Dad's room, though the door was open. His father lay breathing quietly on the bed tucked in the corner. He walked to it and put a hand on the old man's shoulder. His father was warm and smelled faintly of antiseptic. Or was it the room?

"Hi Dad," he said. Nothing happened. *Well, what did you expect?* The senior Allmen continued to breathe quietly, an occasional snort the only change in meter. For all intents, he could have been sleeping off a binge, or blissfully napping in the middle of the day like old people were supposed to do. But he wasn't.

All of the remaining energy seeped out of the younger man. He sat down in a metal chair next to the bed and became aware of the soft hum of machinery. "I came to say I'm sorry." He stopped, thought for a minute trying to capture exactly what it was he was sorry for. *Why did I come? He's not really even here.*

"I came to say I'm sorry for not being here. Not coming home more often, or...." and here his voice caught, "to see you in the hospital."

"I thought I was doing something important when you had your stroke. And after that, well, I was pretty messed up. It's no excuse." He laughed. "I know how you hated excuses." He assumed his father's mock lecturing pose, hands on hips and looking down over his reading glasses and mimicked his deep baritone voice: "Excuses are like ass holes, everyone seems to have one and they all stink." Allmen smiled, shaking his head. The old man always had some nonsense like that to simultaneously teach a lesson and make you snort with laughter.

"Anyway, Mom won't forgive me. And I don't really blame her. I never told her what Iraq did to me. She wouldn't understand. Hell, I don't understand it most days. I'll make it right for her, I think. Soon." He let out a deep sigh. "Anyway, I wanted to say goodbye. I won't be coming back this way if I can help it. I think this part of me..." he gave an expansive wave at the nearby town, "it died."

"And the rest of me..." Allmen's phone began to vibrate. He was glad for the interruption, but his pleasure didn't last long. The caller ID said it was Phil Argento.

"Hello Phil."

"Friday at ten at the courthouse you are going in front of a judge to plead no contest. You'll get a slap on the wrist to include counseling and community service. Be there."

"Okay."

"See you then. After that our deal stands and you find yourself a new lawyer."

"Sure. Thanks. Wait, Phil?"

"Yeah?"

"What day is today?"

"Huh?"

"You said to be there Friday and I will, I just don't know what today is."

Argento sighed with annoyance. "Tuesday."

The line went dead. Allmen put the phone back in his pocket and stared at his father's emaciated body, the machines keeping him what passed for alive.

"Shit." It was going to be a long couple of days. He turned and headed for the car.

* * *

He made it just past Chicago when exhaustion finally caught up with him and he decided to grab a few hours of sleep at a rest stop. He fidgeted for a few minutes, reclining the bucket seat and closing dry eyes expecting to fall away from the exhaustion. Instead, he pulled out his pen and a post card from the drug store around the corner from his father's facility: Greetings From Youngstown, with a clean and tidy view of downtown airbrushed to look like it had circa 1950. Or maybe the photo was that old. It was hard to say. He wrote Virgil's address at Circle Nine on the card and paused. Then he began to write.

My father was an alcoholic. Not the violent, angry kind, but the happy, devil may care sort. The kind of guy who would come home from the corner bar late after work with a bag of candy and wake me up to tell me how the Browns had come this close to winning but had fumbled it away in the fourth quarter. He worked two jobs, one at the factory in town turning big metal slabs into smaller metal parts for cars. And the other as a janitor at the church where he kept things neat and tidy and, I suspect, had access to the sacramental wine.

He was my hero. As nuts as that sounds, to a midwestern kid who didn't know the first thing about the world past the Pennsylvania border, seeing your Dad work his ass off and do it with a smile is a pretty powerful potion. And did I mention the candy? He always had it. Brown paper bags stuffed full of sugary treats to share with his son. My Mom figured it was pure bribery. She was frustrated, locked into a marriage with a happy go lucky spendthrift who could make a bit of extra money and blow it that night betting one of his buddies on the Monday Night Football game. It was not a happy marriage despite him being a happy guy. Go figure.

One day after I had gotten out of here, he just didn't come home. They tell me he collapsed inside of Jimmy's Tavern in the middle of a story about the AFC Championship game, one of the ones we lost to Denver. He went into what they later determined was a diabetic coma and never came out. Of course, he had no will and no medical directives, so they hooked him up to a machine to breathe for him and one to feed him and another collect his waste and there he sits. I know he wouldn't want it that way. So, I've treated it like he died that day. I mean, he should have, you know?

I could have gotten leave to come back when it happened, but I didn't want to leave my Marines. I owed it to them. I figured Dad would understand and that I'd be able to get back and have my own private talk with him. But things kept coming up. I never made it back until yesterday. That's pretty much unforgivable.

Allmen stared out the windshield. "Unforgivable," he said to the car humming idly around him. Closing his eyes, the renegade John Allmen drifted into an uneasy sleep.

HERESY:

adherence to opinions contrary to dogma, dissent or deviation from a dominant theory, opinion, or practice

O f every malice that earns hate in Heaven,
   injustice is the end; and each such end
   by force or fraud brings harm to other men.
However, fraud is man's peculiar vice."

-Dante, Inferno, Canto XI

Allmen swung the BMW into a parking garage in downtown San Francisco, aware that he was sure to pay an exorbitant amount for the privilege of a mid-morning space. He hadn't much time to spare though, having driven since the early morning from outside of Reno. Sure enough, after appearing before the black cloaked judge with wispy white eyebrows, entering his plea in a low voice and grabbing a sorely needed cup of coffee at the courthouse sundry shop, he paid thirty-five dollars to the parking attendant. Then he rolled through mid-morning traffic going up the hill on Broadway. The fog was lurching in off the bay and the whole city felt heavy and slow. In a few minutes he was pulling into the driveway of the house, collecting food wrappers and empty coffee cups and unloading his camping gear from the trunk. As he thought about getting the mail, he noticed someone was sitting on his front steps, legs akimbo and head propped on one curled fist.

"Can I help you?"

The man, or boy, Allmen wasn't sure because he kept his eyes firmly locked on the ground, rose slowly, dusting off his faded denim jeans and adjusting his Cal sweatshirt.

Recognition dawned. "Gary?" The kid nodded, still not meeting Allmen's gaze.

"Hello Mr. Allmen. I've been looking for you." He said it in an uneven, croaky voice.

"I've been away on business." The kid just nodded, taking the little white lie for gospel truth.

"Well, I've been coming by here every day for a week, I think. On my lunch hour... to see if I could find you."

"Bob Strong lets you have lunch? You've really made it to the big time Gary." Allmen knew that Vice Presidents didn't dress in jeans and college logo wear to lunch any more than Google coders wore three-piece suits.

Sure enough, the kid slumped his shoulders and made a sort of mewing noise as he stared hard at the cracks in the sidewalk. Then he finally looked up at Allmen with glassy eyes and said, "I don't work there anymore." He pointed vaguely in the direction of the financial district. "I'm interning with a startup with a little office over on Polk Street." He frowned and said again, "I don't work there anymore."

Allmen set down the daypack and tent he had pulled from the trunk, dropping them with a thud on the driveway. Gary flinched and finally his eyes seemed to focus. "Why not?" Allmen asked.

"Client retention," the kid sighed.

"Say again?"

"Client retention. Or lack thereof." Gary fidgeted with something in his left hand, the one that hadn't been cradling his head, clasping the object like it was a wounded animal. Allmen looked hard sensing something potentially foreboding, perhaps dangerous? Then he saw that it was the nameplate from an office door, black laminate with the words Vice President of Investment in neat block letters. "I tried to do what you said. I chose free will, made it my own, told people what I was going to do. Tried to make them forget you."

"Kid, I..."

"And they fired me. All of them, well not exactly all, but most of them. And all of those that really mattered. Then Mr. Strong fired me too." He shrugged sadly. "It was really shitty advice Mr. Allmen."

Allmen stood still, felt the verbal slap but didn't flinch. *Bad advice with a smile...my specialty.* He said nothing.

"I just thought you should know." Gary the Gnome, Cal Bear and failed investment guru slunk up the walkway, letting the office door plate slip from his fingers. He didn't look back as it clanged to the ground. Nor did he look back as Allmen retrieved it, watching the kid move like a ghost down the hill toward the city.

"Shit," Allmen whispered. The name plate had been broken neatly in half. He hoped the kid had kept the part with his name on it and only left the part with the title as trash on a San Francisco street. Two words from his Marine Corps days rang in his ears as he turned the plate over in his fingers and stared out at the bay: collateral damage. *Or was it, friendly fire?*

"Shit," he said again, and turned to get his mail.

* * *

Allmen thumbed through junk mail for a few seconds, noting the end of summer sales and two for one pizza deals with half his mind still on Gary. Gary the intern, né Gary the Vice President, né Gary the Gnome. *Gary the guys life I made... and then ruined within the space of eighteen months.* He stopped on a cream-colored envelope with a neatly typewritten address and no return information. There was also no postage. Some messenger service had delivered the envelope and, since it was on top of all the other mail, had likely done so today. "Sonofabitch," he swore to himself.

He'd gotten a lot of official mail in his life. Discharge papers, court custody orders, divorce papers. They had all come in similarly neat and tidy packages, only to go off like an explosive once the sealed tripwire was opened. Dreading the outcome, he opened it anyway, sitting on the hood the of BMW with a sense of foreboding boiling up in his stomach. He read the letter, once. Then again. Then, despite the tension of the moment, he laughed.

"No fucking way," he said to the universe.

He called Virgil.

"Virgil, where can I go two weeks from now where no one will find me?"

"Can I ask why?"

"You can ask anything you want. I'm a big believer in free will. And, as far as I know, it's still a free country."

"Okay, I'll bite. Why?"

"I've been asked to give a deposition. My former clients are demanding an arbitration hearing accusing me of fraud, misrepresentation, etcetera, etcetera, so on and so forth. I'd like to not be around for a while before, during and after that."

Virgil thought for a moment. "Believe it or not, you aren't the first client to take a short notice sabbatical in the middle of a legal proceeding."

"How about something coastal with decent fishing and an ocean of alcoholic beverages? And spotty cell service if you know what I mean."

"John, this is going to be a while out of the country during high season. What is your budget?"

"Unlimited Virgil. Do your worst." That would take some adjustments, but there was little choice.

"Call you back in fifteen."

He hung up still feeling angry and betrayed by the offensive piece of paper in his right hand. "Fuckers," he murmured. Then he dialed a number from memory.

"Gladys," he said to the cat loving receptionist on the 30th floor of the high rise on California Street after her company approved answering script was complete, "it's John Allmen."

"I'll put you right through," she said breathlessly. So, they were expecting him. Pieces fell into place.

"Bob Strong," came the Muppet voice.

"Hello Bob. It's John Allmen. But you already knew that. Anyway, I got your letter and I wanted to RSVP yes to your party. We all have reputations to protect, right? Let's get on the same team and fight this. "Allmen stood and walked to the trunk of the car, fiddling with his camping kit and extracting his lighter.

"Great John, I'm glad you are on board with the team on this one."

"You bet Bob, and again, thanks for sending me this letter. I really appreciate it." He let loose a geyser of flame from the lighter and the letter crumpled into black carbon, smoking and spitting fire. He dropped the note onto the pavement and watched it disappear. "See you in a couple of days Bob."

"You bet John. You bet." Had John Allmen owned one of those old school phones like he'd had in his room in Grand Cayman he would have slammed it down in equal parts disgust and triumph. He had to admire the stagecraft of it all, he really did. It was clear to him now why Phil Argento had been so adamant that he was no longer representing Allmen. He couldn't be both the defendant's council and the aggrieved party in any action against him. *Legal ethics. A triumph of contradictory terminology.* Thus, likely moments after watching him cop a deal in Superior Court, his messenger had delivered his summons to appear at a deposition for the Securities and Exchange Commission. There, Bob Strong and his puppet masters would nod their heads, take a slap on the hand for their lack of oversight and pin all the recent losses of his former clients on their advisor who had assured them they were protected from losses just as they were during the last downturn. Whether Allmen had ever said such a thing was irrelevant. What he had said, to a former client no less, was that he had been lucky. It was financial sacrilege, a desecration of the Wall Street ethos. And they were aiming to make him pay for it.

Instead of slamming his phone into a thousand pieces, he stashed his gear and headed for the bar down the block. He was thirsty and didn't want the neighbors to hear the next call he had to make.

"Cavalcanti and Uberti Realty, this is Mr. Cavalcante."

"Guido? Hey, it's John Allmen. Remember me?" Guido Cavalcante was an old school real estate agent pushing seventy. An elderly Italian gentleman who wore ascots and managed to not look silly, said things like "at your service" without sounding servile. He seemed to Allmen to be one of those septuagenarians who worked late in life because he wanted to, not because he needed to. That was one reason Allmen liked him and felt like he could be trusted.

"Yeah, sure John. Of course, I remember you. What can I do for you? I am…at your service."

"I'd like to sell my house and have the closing done in less than ten days. Is that possible? Some tech millionaire with cash to spend or a shadowy Chinese conglomerate, I don't really care. I just want the money and to be out of this house. Sooner rather than later. Doable?"

There was a moment of silence and Allmen could feel the older man turning over the prospects in his mind. It had a vague tang of something fishy. *But wasn't that the specialty of Italian businessmen the world over?* "Probably. Let me poke around. There are a lot of cash deals going down now on short contracts. Though...I have to say...I mean, I can't predict the future or anything you understand. But I think you probably would get a better offer if you waited until the summer, or at least allowed some competing offers to percolate."

"I understand."

"And John, I know most of the details about the house, it is my business after all, but there is a question..."

"Go on."

"The pool area..."

Allmen cut him short. "I filled it in. Is that a problem?"

"Not really. For a certain buyer a pool is nice, for others it is an encumbrance."

"Great, let's find one of the latter. I'm interested in unloading it as soon as I can. I'll accept less than market. Let's just get it sold. I'll accept the long-term consequences."

✲ ✲ ✲

"I can get you into a resort in Mexico," Allmen was listening while sipping at a draft beer. He'd brought his backpack with him and was absently rummaging through his paperback version of The Sun Also Rises as he listened.

"I just need out and just about anywhere will do."

"Okay, well, there is also a very limited extradition treaty with Mexico, in case things get more, uh, complicated."

Allmen shrugged. "I don't think it will come to all that Virgil. He quoted from the page in front of him: "'Secret of my success? Never been daunted.'"

"Right. Okay. Let me get to work."

He hung up and continued to read for a while about bullfights, fly fishing and war wounds. Not all wounds were physical. Jake Barnes had both the physical and emotional scars of war, just as Allmen did. And he too had engaged in a long country to country bender, only to find that there was no getting away from yourself by moving from place to place. *If I can't get away from myself, at least I can get away from Bob Strong.* Allmen read through the scene where Jake Barnes wanders into a church to begin to pray. It starts well, but soon he proves to be a lousy Catholic, praying for money, a good fiesta and a good bullfight. Allmen could relate to a less than zealous practice of religion. Finishing his beer, he flipped the book closed, then peeled back the last page as he noticed his own handwriting there. It was old, graying ink in what he recognized as his teen-age cursive script. He still had the habit of taking notes in his books, and it made him smile for a moment. And then he read what he had written over two decades ago:

Hemingway: "All stories, if continued far enough, end in death."

His smile faded. There were a lot of stories out there. And a lot of death. He'd seen his fair share. *And then some.* An empty feeling washed over him and he began to sweat, great beads running from his forehead. He threw cash on the bar and walked as calmly as he could to the door.

"Hey... You left your book." The bartender with pink hair and a nose ring was wiping down the pock marked bar and holding it in her hand with the money.

Allmen suddenly felt daunted. Very daunted indeed. "Keep it," he mumbled.

"What am I supposed to do with a book?" She called as he pushed through the door and out into the street.

* * *

Virgil sent him to Baja. Sunshine and blue water would do him well, a failsafe prescription. And for a while they did. He found himself ensconced in an all-inclusive resort high on a hill with a view of the sea crashing over rocks and crags below. The food was only decent, but the drinks had no bottom. And, predictably, that worked for him.

He had a small apartment with a sitting area, king bed, small kitchen and a stocked bar. The college kids who worked there made sure that the basics were on hand. They were also more than happy to drop by with special cocktails late in the day or provide a tequila upgrade from behind their lobby desks. The apartment also led out onto the beach where the Pacific, anything but peaceful, frothed and crashed on volcanic rock before rolling lazily onto the brown sandy beach. It was a perfect place for irresponsible drinking, followed by long naps in the conveniently placed hammock strung between two trees outside his sliding door.

On his second day in Mexico, with Mack Mason becoming a hazy drunken memory, he'd awoken from an afternoon snooze face down, tasting sand.

"Shit!" he said, scrambling behind a nearby tree. Where was he? The hot sand stung his face and mouth and he knew he had to be back in the desert. He'd hit the deck hard and was gasping for air. *Had they been hit? Was the convoy hit? Where was the air cover?* He looked skyward and saw nothing but azure blue and white thin clouds.

Eyes wide and panic building, he looked to his left and stared, his breath coming in short gasps. He smelled bananas. And he saw a rope hammock swinging and twisting in the wind. It was the same rope hammock he had fallen asleep in. And then fell out of. Instead of his platoon in battle dress, one of the resort college kids stood a respectful distance away, unsure whether to

170

be terrified or amused. *No rest for the weary. Or the wicked.*

Allmen took a deep breath and stood erect. He waived.

"Hola señor! Margarita? Special today!"

"Yeah, sure. Gracias."

After that Allmen avoided the hammock and opted to take his afternoon snooze at the main pool in a very stable wicker chair. The pool was also an area that, given the wet bikinis and techno music, would never be mistaken for Iraq. And it was there, making his way to a dip before the bar, that he had an awkward right of way dance with a tall angular woman with a pretty face overshadowed by a wide brimmed beach hat. She was hustling a young girl toward the sign with an arrow pointing to "Kids Camp."

"Excuse us," said the woman in a clipped, very American voice exuding stress and exasperation. She looked up just in time to catch Allmen staring at her cleavage.

"No problem," he smiled and watched them move off, tugging and pulling each other in the way that parents and children do when neither is really getting what they want.

He was a couple of beers in at the bar, half watching a Mexican league soccer game with the sound turned down, when the mother removed her hat with a flourish and sat beside him.

"Hullo again," she said conspiratorially.

"Hi," said Allmen, using the moment where she looked down and adjusted her bar stool to size her up. She was athletic in a yoga-mom, Lululemon sort of way. Maybe a dancer earlier in life. She smelled of coconut oil and without a wedding ring, everything about her screamed divorcée.

"Is there a bartender working?" She was impatiently trying to flag down one of the brown men in starched white uniforms.

Allmen inclined his chin and said "Amigo," to the nearest one, who instantly appeared flashing a toothy smile. "For the señora," he nodded at her next to him. It helped that Allmen was already known to tip well.

"Thank you," she said after ordering her daiquiri. She sighed, settling in. "It is so nice to have some time to myself, you know."

Allmen frowned into his beer. "You daughter. She is about the same age as mine."

"Well, you are lucky to get some time away to yourself too."

"Yeah," Allmen mumbled, " I guess so." She chattered away for a few moments. She was down from LA to get away from it all, blah blah blah. Allmen began to realize that she wasn't going away and with some effort he began to listen to her, or at least pretend to. Her name was Anna, short for Anastasia. She was really quite a good looking woman, a MILF in the crass parlance of his Marine Corps days. Long legs with a modest floral sarong to cover them, and, of course, the fake chest he'd been mesmerized by at the pool. Allmen got the feeling that wasn't the only work she'd had done in her life. There was just something so unnatural about her, like she was out of Southern California central casting. And this was her getaway tryst in a foreign land. And yet, no one could ever say that John Allmen would not do his duty. He concluded the usual ritual by buying drinks, nodding his head at the right times and asking her if she'd like to have a drink back at his place before the childcare center closed. To the shock of no one around them, including the two bemused bartenders, she did.

They had cocktails out on the beach, Allmen giving the hammock a wide berth as they passed. He loosened up a bit, coming near to enjoying the conversation, the great flirtatious game, once again. No, his heart wasn't into it, but his heart wasn't what she was after. She excused herself, her long, elegant strides taking her indoors. She came back with a devious smile on her perfect pink lips.

"Well," she said, "that is all settled."

"What is?"

"I've got a babysitter through the resort. No need to rush. I thought we might order dinner. Room service okay with you?" Allmen felt a wave of revulsion cross over him. I am taking a mother away from her child. He didn't let himself follow the thought with: *Again.*

* * *

She snored. The surgically altered queen of SoCal snored in great breezy gasps, lolling about in his bed. He had to admit her surgeons knew their stuff. Indeed, the work was immaculate. But it had given him more guilt than pleasure, and he found himself awake, looking over her with something like self-loathing as the hour approached 2AM. He quietly crossed into the sitting room and flipped on the television, more out of habit than any hope of finding something to watch in English. He poured a scotch and settled in on the couch, trying to read a magazine by the flickering light of the television.

It turned out to be tourist information masquerading as a magazine, lots of "stories" about amazing day trips and fishing excursions sandwiched in between quarter and half page ads. One of the ads featured a gaudily dressed man facing down a wall of muscle and horns. A little money and a good bullfight. A bullfight suddenly seemed like exactly the thing he needed. He'd never seen one. *No time like the present.*

Allmen put the scotch down and turned off the television. The Queen was still sawing away in his bedroom as he crept around assembling some toiletries and clothes. He wrote a brief note on the resort stationary:

"I had to go."

He hoped, that like Hemingway's writing, brevity told its own story. He crept out of his room like a thief.

There was a young Mexican girl working the concierge desk and she cheerfully greeted him despite the unusual hour.

"You need drinks?" The seniorita sure knew her business and her clientele.

Allmen smiled. "Not this time. Where can I go to see a bullfight?"

* * *

Anna's smell of coconut oil was still on him as he pulled out of the resort in a rental car. It was eight hours to Mexico City and he watched the sun come up on the road in front of him as the ocean disappeared behind. Though the ocean air smelled fresh and tasted salty, the closer he got to Mexico City, the danker the air became. He drove, following signs mindlessly toward the international airport and found himself on the northeast side of town when he turned on his phone and checked the map. He found a parking garage as the sun was high overhead, wondering if he'd be able to find it again later. He marked the spot on the map application and headed off walking at a brisk clip. Mexico City was no place for a car.

The afternoon was warm, and a consistent torrent of sweat began running down the inside of his collar. He bought a cold beer from a roadside stand, drank it in three long swallows and bowed to the applause of the ancient man who'd sold it to him. Allmen thought he looked like one of the old cigar store Indians come to life, square features and smiling eyes. He pressed on, continuing to pick his way through food stalls, tasting grilled meats and cold beer.

Mexico City was a hodgepodge of neighborhoods built on top of one another. The result was flashy elegance and overwhelming poverty cohabiting within a city block of each other. From ground level, Allmen was dizzied by the constantly shifting landscape. Or maybe it was the heat. Regardless, by the time he spilled out into the wide arcade of the Plaza de la Constitución in front of two cream colored bell towers in the middle of a sea of steaming concrete, he figured a church was a good place to rest and regroup.

There were few tourists out in the heat and he found himself alone. The air smelled musty as he hefted open the immense wooden door and involuntarily cringed away from the echoing clang of the ancient iron door handles.

"Fuck," he murmured, then realized he was standing inside of a church and waited resolutely for lightning to strike him down. He waited a long time. But nothing happened. He shrugged.

Noted.

His eyes adjusted slowly to the darkness, but his nostrils immediately picked up on the smell of old incense and mildewed plaster. He stood in the narthex, the wide gaping entrance, and noticed the wall behind him was peeling. The building had seen better days and seemed to be under renovation. Scaffolding was scattered throughout the nave. *Man's ever present battle against time.* He noticed that small chips had fluttered down to land in the font of holy water. His footfalls echoed as he wandered in. Ahead in the gloom was a chandelier casting shadows across the wide stone floor. On the far wall was a tall altar of gold that reached skyward and ended in a giant arch.

A small plaque read: Altar del perdón. Allmen typed *perdón* into his phone for translation.

Perdón = Forgiveness

The olden wooden pew creaked and groaned as he sat at the Alter of Forgiveness. He sighed. An old sinner comes to church. To repent? Or was he just seeking a cool place out of the fiery sun that was tormenting the few souls in the arcade outside? *The latter, but while I'm here, why not cover all the bases?*

Allmen's mind wandered, thinking about the topic that had popped up after his visit home: forgiveness. Yes, he had a lot to ask forgiveness for, and a limited time to do it. Wasn't that true of everyone? Allmen recalled the words of a famous economist. There was no better way to impress clients, to sound pithy and yet smart, than quoting John Maynard Keynes.

"In the long run we are all dead."

Allmen was certainly no exception. He thought of Jake Barnes, Hemingway's lousy Catholic, praying for a good bullfight. Allmen closed his eyes.

"God, if you can hear me…"

Allmen stared at the altar, his thoughts scattering between his platoon, his ex-wife, his daughter, his Dad. He wanted to cry. Really, nothing would have given him more pleasure than to release everything he held inside of him. He wanted to wail and confess his sins and beg for forgiveness. He would weep until some Mexican priest in flowing robes put his arms around him and told him in a language he couldn't understand that 'my son, all is well, you are loved my son.' He closed his eyes, felt the cool air and smelled the musty, but not unpleasant smells.

"My son?"

Allmen's heart raced. Had he imagined it? The touch on his sleeve? The syrupy voice of English spoken by a Spanish speaker.

"You are here for seeing the tombs?"

Allmen opened his eyes. An old priest stood before him in jeans and a high collared black shirt.

"The tombs?"

"Yes, the tour of the crypt? Where the Archbishops are laid to rest awaiting the coming of the glory."

"Yes, of course father. Yes, the tombs." Allmen imagined the subterranean crypt and shuddered. Little light, cramped space, no breeze. *It would be blazing there. On fire. Worse than being outside.* It was time to make another discreet exit. Allmen lingered a moment, taking in the altar once more.

"God, if you can hear me..." he smiled to himself, "grant me a good bullfight." John Allmen stood up, turned his back on the altar and walked back into the sweat sodden sunshine of Mexico City. He didn't want to be late .

He covered the nine kilometers to the Plaza Del Toros in just under an hour and a half. The physical exertion, though mild compared to his usual routine, took its toll due to the altitude. But it served its purpose, pushing conscious thought to the background as he ground his way toward the arena.

The neighborhoods were dense on the route, the parks and museums away to the north. This was the part of the city where people lived and died, worked and whiled away the hours. The onlookers were sullen, the traffic congested. A low fog hung over many of the intersections he crossed. There was little breeze to wipe the landscape clean.

He was crossing the great thoroughfare across from a green

square and starting down Avenue Augusto Rodin when the great cylinder of the Plaza came into view. The largest bullring in the world sat blotting out the smudgy horizon in the middle of the urban sprawl. It was draped on all sides by banners and buntings. Stone statues surrounded the grounds featuring famous matadors, and their decidedly less famous competitors. Pockets of tourists and locals stood idly in the arcade, some staring up at the stadium. The hulking, brutalist bowl sat eerily quiet.

Allmen stared for a while disbelieving.

"Where is the goddamn corrida?!" He said to himself.

"You are looking for the bullfight Señor?" A dirty kid selling bottled water raised an eyebrow at him.

"Yes, the corrida! The bullfight, is it not today?"

"Si, señor. It was today."

"Well, did I miss it?"

"We all missed it, señor. No bullfight. No money for me." The grimy kid frowned and Allmen rolled his eyes. He knew a sales pitch when it floated past him.

"Give me two of those," Allmen and paid him twice what he was asking, "and tell me what happened."

"Take a look for yourself." The kid hooked his thumb over toward the far corner of the empty lot where a drainage ditch cut at an angle to the stadium. Allmen walked that way.

"Be careful señor." The kid cautioned, stuffing dollar bills into his frayed jeans.

Allmen saw what looked to be an ambulance. There was a small crowd gathered. All around were people in white-white smocks, white rubber gloves, white surgical masks. They were pulling and tugging with some effort at several white body bags.

The stench hit him. *Decaying flesh.* It overpowered his nostrils and sent his mind racing. He whirled away from the nasal assault, looking up into the blazing sun. For a minute, it was a desert sun and the smell of death was from his platoon. He retched, putting his hands to his knees, feeling his breathing come in hard gasps. But looking down he saw concrete blocks and pigeon shit instead of sand. And he heard beat up cars and taxis instead of Humvees.

Allmen tried to gather himself, shuffling back toward the boy with his shirt over his face.

What the hell happened?" He asked.

The boy shrugged, as if to say it was a common enough thing. "The Cartels man. Couple of hours ago they came, found some guys they were looking for, lined them up over there and shot them. And they did other things...."

"Jesus, in broad daylight?"

The boy looked exasperated. "Hey, Yankee, it's the Cartels, man. Any time. Anywhere."

Death in the afternoon. An attack. Allmen had missed it while in the church praying for a good bullfight. "I get it. The Mexican Cartels: when you absolutely positively need someone whacked overnight."

The kid looked at him askance. "Whatever man. No corrida today." He walked off, hoping the weird foreign guy wouldn't follow. Instead, the weird foreign guy walked briskly away in the direction he had come, dialing his cell phone.

"Virgil, I am a twenty minute cab ride from Mexico City International. Can you get me on a plane to Spain? I want to see a goddamn bullfight. And so far, my prayers have not been answered."

VIOLENCE:

the use of physical force so as to injure, abuse, damage, or destroy

Behold the monster with the pointed tail,
Who cleaves the hills, and breaks walls and weapons,
Behold him who infects all the world.

-Dante, Inferno, Canto XVII

Allmen was falling. Dark walls of sharp black rocks shot past him as he plummeted downward, gaining speed until he felt as if the flesh on his face would be torn off and scattered on the wind. The rock of the walls changed, growing darker and sharper. Then it changed again, like black ice, dark and yet translucent.

His stomach lurched and gyrated and a sweaty nausea permeated the building terror. He wondered if he would throw up or hit the ground first? He was falling into some sort of pit. *A pit with different strata of rock.* He counted nine of them when the wind in his ears gradually dissipated, though he wasn't falling any more slowly. He began to make out sounds coming from somewhere below. *The bottom?* He didn't know.

A mewing, wailing toddler screaming one two syllable word: "Daddy!" Over and over, and Allmen could feel the bile rising in his throat. "Daddy! Daddy!"

He tried to say her name, but he choked on the acid in his mouth.

He wondered if he would fall forever, or if the torment would end in a bone shattering death somewhere down below. And then he floated above the bottom of a narrow opening. It wasn't a tube or a pit he fell through, he decided, but a funnel. And at the bottom, like the fan in an air-condition shaft, whirred the giant, disembodied, blades of a helicopter.

As insane as it was, he began to flap his arms, trying to fly away from the whirring, chopping blades beneath. He floated for a minute, then felt himself descending again, slowly downward. Other voices flowed upward from below.

"El-tee! We gotta go!"

"Daddy! Daddy!"

"El-tee, this way!"

"Plan on dropping in again unannounced?"

"Jesus Christ superstar."

"Daddy! Daddy!"

"Name it to tame it."

"My friend Virgil is exactly what you need."

"Well, you are lucky to get some time away to yourself."

"I went to Cal. Sorry Mr. Allmen."

"I'm sorry sir, there was nothing we could do."

He was staring at the blades, close enough now for him to see the rivets, the smooth curve of an aerodynamic shape. Instinctively he brought his knees to his chest to keep his toes from being lopped off. But it was no use.

I'm sorry too. I'm so very sorry.

Gradually, he touched the blades, and he felt pain in the toes of his right foot. He recoiled from it and opened his eyes. Her brown eyes, soft and sad, were looking into his. He felt his heart lurch. Then, the airline attendant, an attractive young girl with the face of an Aztec princess grinned sheepishly at him.

"I'm sorry sir, I stepped on your foot while I was trying to wake you." Allmen smelled coffee and he felt the plane lurching, but not through the air. They had landed, and he was in Spain.

* * *

There was a festival in Spain. There was always a festival for either the Catalans or the Basques. This one, for the former, was a religious festival in Valencia honoring Saint Joseph. He'd checked in amid the building revelry of a late night. Disregard for the clock was the way of all Spaniards, and despite his military mind, Allmen appreciated that. *Free will, right?*

It was not yet eight in the morning when the pop-pop-pop of small caliber rounds came echoing down the narrow alleys and spilling out onto the beach. Allmen's eyes came wide open from a deep dark sleep and he screamed:

"Take cover!"

He threw himself to the floor and belly crawled to the wall

near the sliding doors leading out to a small patio. He was looking down from the fifth floor. *A good ambush position if insurgents came this way.*

He'd done this in Fallujah, taking an apartment building with a cracked stone stairwell outside and, for once, ambushing the bad guys instead of being on the receiving end. He waited, forced his breath to slow, then looked down to make sure his combat kit was ready to go. He saw he was wearing boxer briefs and was wrapped in a floral bedsheet. Kids were running through the streets below. He heard laughter. Inching up over the cement wall, he could see them scattering firecrackers along the streets. He swore to himself. *I'm getting worse. Going ape shit over firecrackers.*

He learned at breakfast that it was called La Despertà, the wakeup call. This was the traditional rousing for the Festival of Las Fallas. One was expected to be up late and at it early again the next day. The festivities, which included the usual street markets, live music and children's carousels were set to run for five days. They included a nightly procession of bulls through the streets from the corral to the amphitheater. The Plaza de Toros de Valencia was built to look like a Roman coliseum, following the old road lined with broken rocks. It was, he imagined, like a miniature version of Pamplona, with fewer thrill seeking idiots in the streets.

Allmen stood near the stadium and ordered yet another beer while he watched the rippling masses of muscle and razor-sharp horns careen through town from behind the safety of a wire fence. It reminded him of being a child, lined up along the streets of downtown, watching the Saint Patrick's Day parade go by. Shriners in funny cars, the high school band and then new convertibles from the local Ford dealership with pretty high school girls in too much makeup. After the parade, Dad usually went to the corner bar while Mom went home and made corned beef and cabbage. He estimated that the old man made it home for that dinner less than half the time.

"Ten cuidado con eso." Allmen's reverie was interrupted by

an ancient and impossibly thin Spaniard with a shock of white hair on a deeply tanned face who was eyeing one of the bulls as it ran through the street.

"I'm sorry?" The bull, solid black and menacing, came on in a measured trot, not out of control and careening like the other savages. It was almost as if it was looking or searching for something or someone.

"Ah... you speak English?"

"No, but I speak American." The old joke was probably as old as the man he told it too. *Maybe older.* The Spaniard just arched an eyebrow and nodded.

"I said, 'be careful of that one.' He is a beast, yes. A brute, yes. But he is also intelligent. You swear looking into his eyes, he is half human. He was raised on a farm near my town."

"That so?"

"Indeed, he lives up to his name. Chiron, the centaur. Half man, half bull. Good, no?"

"Good." Allmen raised his beer bottle in a toast to all things literary. The skinny geezer grinned and produced a wine bottle, pulling the cork with his teeth and spitting it unceremoniously into his hand. Then he took a long pull. They toasted each other, toasted the bulls and wished each other a happy festival. The interaction left Allmen feeling light and happy. He liked this festival. He looked forward to a good bullfight. *Amen.*

Allmen wandered about the streets once the bulls were gone, watching kids on the carousel while he drank more beer and pondered the plight of the bull. *A noble death? Certainly.* These animals were celebrated, revered and even occasionally spared and put to stud if they proved worthy enough. *Talk about motivation.* But most were put to the sword in front of the crowd after being weakened by jabs and cuts from the matador's posse. Which was much less noble. The thought threatened to depress him. He chose a mental subfile of the folder Shit I Don't Worry About and chucked thoughts about the plight of bulls there. He titled it: Shit I Don't Worry About_ Lest It Depress Me. He wandered back to his hotel near the center of town and fell asleep seeing the bull Chiron's eyes whenever he closed his. *Human eyes. A hunter's eyes.*

In the morning it rained, and the soggy fireworks didn't wake him. Instead of battling the teenage insurgents at zero dark thirty, he slept peacefully until after nine and awoke refreshed, ready to take in his first bullfight. But plump raindrops were bespattering the Nissans and Dacias that were already queuing up along motorways and main arteries into town. Allmen was just hours away from completing his quest, viewing the ritualistic killing of a bull, six or more of them actually, for the first time. And it was raining. It would be rather cruel if this foray was a washout too. Exactly no one inside the city limits, swelling with humanity by the minute, shared his fears. Instead, they were parking haphazardly, as Europeans in a hurry are wont to do, beginning a few kilometers outside of town. Great soggy masses, they rushed forward toward town clogging the cafes to talk about the bulls, the rain, football.

Allmen did the same, sitting at the bar in his hotel, drinking pink Rioja and eating green olives and a fish paste on toasted baguettes. It was around four o'clock when the rain lifted and turned to a moderate mist. He chose to go in early and enjoy the spectacle from inside the old stone walls. Grabbing a beer, he would read the program in his halting Spanish and get some sense of the *toreros*, those defying death by goring. He had paid little attention to the sheets when he first saw them the night before, figuring that he wouldn't know any of the names anyway. But to his surprise, he did recognize one. Fighting the third and sixth bull was Cayetano of Madrid. Cayetano who at age six has seen his father Paquirri gored to death. Cayetano the grandson of Antonio Ordonez who Hemingway thought of as a friend and profiled in his book The Dangerous Summer. Cayetano, the great-grandson of Ordonez, who had been the model for Hemingway's young fighter in The Sun Also Rises. Cayetano, who had his torero's suit of lights designed by Armani. Okay, that last should have dampened Allmen's enthusiasm a bit. But he was drunk on Hemingway nostalgia, though not even mildly buzzed off of the microscopic draft beer served in the amphitheater.

He went charging for his seat as the 5:00 start time neared, which was also sobering. How skinny the patrons must have been when the arena was built in the 1800s. Allmen found himself wedged between a petite middle-aged woman and an old man smoking a cigarette. Below, the matadors and their entourages paraded, tipped their hats and bowed to the President's box. Being right behind it, he could easily imagine that it was all for him. His own private ritualistic sacrifice. Or semi- private, given that he was crammed into a row of ten patrons that would comfortably sit eight. *Or six Americans from Houston.*

The crowd gave encouraging shouts and lusty applause as brutish naked fury charged into the sand, rippling its neck muscle and snorting anger. Rarito, was the bulls name, listed in the program at 515kg the biggest beast of the evening. But he was also slow, and the matador worked methodically, ending one series of passes with an impassioned stamp of his foot while he raised his right hand. It was an emphatic gesture of dominance and control. The crowd loved it, seemed to turn in favor of the young man and "*ole*" rang out across the enclosed oval.

Then he linked several passes with his large cape, and this was enough to get the crowd fully behind him. He worked close enough to streak his white pants with blood, the bull streaming pink and red down its flanks. The white suit was a brilliant move to accent how close to the bull you worked. *But it's murder on your launderer.* The kid showed flair but kept a respectful distance. When it came time for the kill, it wasn't until the third try with the long sword that the bull died, crumpling into a muscled mass and bleeding out on the sand. The crowd, ready to be wowed was mostly silent. They expected their killing to be much more efficient. And they seemed to turn again, now against the youngster.

The president of the fight, whose role was filled by some

local dignitary, would allow the matador to cut the ear from the vanquished in the case of a well fought bull. The kid had fought well, but he hadn't killed well. *And wasn't that the real test?* Thus, no ear was granted for his efforts. The kid saluted the president's box and seemed to slump a bit, before turning to leave. And then all hell broke loose.

From the far side of the arena a bare-chested man in jeans jumped onto the sand, carrying a sign that Allmen couldn't read. He was certain it was one of the animal rights folks who'd been trolling about town all day with semi-organized protests of the festivities. This one ironically charged like a bull, running flat out at the matador who looked at him dumbly with his long cape in one hand. Allmen wondered if he would shout "ole" and sidestep Mr. Greenpeace with a whirl of his cape. Instead, as the clouds parted and the setting sun illuminated the stadium in a warm glow, the security guards tackled the interloper at a dead run. Kicks and punches rained down as more security swarmed in. The bare-chested man was hauled up to a sitting position while security banded his hands behind his back. His face was streaming blood. The crowd went wild cheering the guards, jeering the protestors. *The Christians in the coliseum.*

When the arena floor was finally cleared, the second matador strode to center stage in a pink suit that made the woman next to Allmen feign a swoon. He met a lean black charger that leapt on all fours and careened and crashed about, crunching into a horse and almost toppling the picador, who took his revenge, stabbing the beast between the shoulders. Señor Pink linked a series of six forehand and backhand approaches with the cape, beginning to pull the crowd to his cause. Then his long cape caught on the razor-sharp horns and fluttered to the ground as the crowd groaned.

The disappointment was palpable. He switched to the smaller cape, turned inside a fast charge and then decided it was time for the kill. But the bull wasn't done yet. Three times Señor Pink sighted down his sword, intending to puncture the bull's struggling heart. Each time the beast pawed the sand as if to charge and he had to stand down. He waited as the heart pumped its remaining life out onto the sand in little spurts and dribbles. The matador finally tried to ram the sword home but missed and continued past the struggling mass of muscle to sight and try again. On the second try the beast collapsed in a heap. This time Allmen watched in fascination as the ear was severed, flesh parting in fatty lumps while blood dribbled to the sand. Some of the crowd whistled and hooted, raining seat cushions down in an obvious sign of disapproval.

Allmen sat quietly. *I thought I was ready for this.* He'd read the books, watched videos on YouTube and had a decent idea of what bullfighting was all about. He knew about the ritual of the ear. In his novel, Hemingway's Jake tells Lady Brett to look away from the ghastly spectacle. But she doesn't. *And neither did I.* Instead, he thought about Van Gogh. He had cut his own ear off and gave it to a chambermaid at the local brothel after watching a bullfight up in Arles. Apparently, you could find it fascinating or have it drive you toward madness. Watching the dark ear cut from the head, seeing the blood, it brought something back, something that gnawed at him. Then he knew. He remembered the explosion of the helicopter. How body parts had rained down on him, including an ear. A charred black ear.

He'd forgotten that, pushed it down so far it couldn't resurface. Until now. *God, if you can hear me...grant me a good bullfight. Oh, and take away all these flashbacks.*

The musicians started again with the lull in between bulls, momentarily pulling Allmen from the depths of his memory.

"Shit," he whispered gasping for air.

The trumpeter rang in with brassy but soft lead... *ta ta de de de dum dum, ta ta de dum dum ta de dum.* It was a low, haunting melody that Allmen recognized as an old Simon and Garfunkel ballad. Despite the energy and thirst for blood in the arena, the crowd recognized it too, and went still. The trumpet sang out again and Allmen heard the words go through his mind to match it, verse for verse.

Hello darkness my old friend.
I've come to talk with you again...

The trumpeter was a famous South American virtuoso and he suddenly held the entire stadium in a trance. No one moved except for some of the workers grading the sand for the next fight. And even they held their heads up periodically to look at the entire stadium holding their breath.

In restless dreams I walked alone
Narrow streets of cobblestone

Allmen was mouthing the words now, mindless of the spectacle that had gone on, the blood that had spilled. Tears threatened to well in his eyes.

That split the night
And touched the sound of silence

And then ten thousand people, maybe more, disturbed the sound of silence, roaring approval as the great musician bowed low from his seat high above. Allmen stood stunned, perhaps the last patron to sit down as the final torero entered and more traditional Spanish *pasodobles* launched from the seats above him. He watched the action, but little of it registered. Indeed, he remembered little of the next fight or the encore of three more bulls, one for each matador. He had a vague impression of Cayetano, the old master going through the motions like a man who knew his work but took no pleasure in it. Like a great impressionist forced to work with a kid's watercolor set. The crowd, so encouraging and expectant, slowly turned against him. Greeting him with little more than that mystical sound of silence when his first bull died.

In the end, Señor Pink had rallied, fought his second bull from his knees, cut two ears and been carried off on the shoulders of his crew. Allmen saw it all through a haze, a swirl of light and sound. Saw the capes waiving and the crowd cheering and jeering, but none of it registered in the normal way. Instead, he felt like he had entered a Van Gogh painting. Every color and object amplified, unnatural, every sound like a hammer in his ears.

When it was over and the crowd spilled out of the arena, he walked in the same trance back to his hotel and squeezed into the last seat at the bar. He ordered a beer, suddenly feeling very sober. It arrived in front of him bubbling up and over the rim of his glass. The bartender was a lovely Spanish girl. Her lustrous black hair fell to the waist of her long white skirt, as she wiped up beer with a dirty rag. Allmen stared at the glass in front of him.

"You are lost *amigo.*"

Allmen's started in his seat. "Pardon?"

She smiled an embarrassed smile. "I said, you are lost in thought *amigo.* Sorry to bother you."

"No, no it's no bother." Allmen felt the world suddenly shift, clarify, focus and he was back to his normal self. "I was just trying to figure out where I can get some dinner before they set the whole city on fire?"

Following the Spanish girls' directions, he walked a block or so away from the hotel and sat down to eat Esgarraet and drink Albariño, watching the waves come in from the Mediterranean. The raging party had already laid a few revelers low. Allmen could make out several forms, supine on the beach, oblivious to the small bits of paper and charred and blackened ash, floating down from the starless night sky. Tradition held that on the last night of the festival, the giant twenty-foot-high paper *ninots*, works of art that were paraded through the streets for the festival, would be burned in a communal bonfire. Hundreds of them, spitting flames and turning to ash. They had started burning the children's paper statues at around ten that night. The conflagration for big boys and girls erupted once the party was really going, well after midnight. So, he had time to eat his meal while the world burned.

189

The wine was light and floral, the dish of salt cod and sweet red peppers was the Catalan version of comfort food. It was not what a condemned man would want for his last dish, but it was a soothing mixture of salty and sweet. And it helped calm him. The hazy, punch-drunk feeling of the afternoon was replaced by a dull ache behind his eyes. He paid his bill and joined the throng heading toward the city center.

It was not all happiness and religious fever on the roads during the festival. Beggars and street people lined the passages into town. Harpies with ancient faces and bony, grasping hands begging for some mercy while their partners deftly picked your pocket. Allmen saw a roving packs of dogs, terrified by the noise and smoke, racing amongst the thorny tree lined alleys. Snarling and snapping, they scattered revelers in their wake. He hurried on into the night, following a smog-like cloud that hung about the street.

He emerged, pressed along with the building crowd into a wide plaza. The middle of the square was barricaded and filled with the paper statues that had been displayed all over town. There was a theme to them, supposedly, but Allmen had never bothered to ask what it was. They were whimsical, many using famous people in satirical poses. Donald Trump, two stories tall and dressed like a Musketeer, fought a duel using missiles with Kim Jong-Un. They were both ablaze, fire eating away their arms and heads. And the crowd was cheering wildly. Firecrackers barked a staccato beat in time with the crackling of the blaze. And somewhere in the square a band played. Allmen could feel the bass drum in his chest.

He felt the heat of the fire, flames reaching higher into the blackness of the night. And then darkness. The crowd cheered again. Bottles were passed around. Another fire erupted and spilled smoke high into the night. Allmen was not there. He was in Iraq on a day when he learned what war was about. *What death was, and how quickly it came, dropping on you like some unseen winged monster.*

The helicopter exploding. The small arms fire. The heat on

face as the fireball erupted, flared and then abruptly went dark. The ear. Gomez's ear he figured. *He'd been the one sitting in the gunner's door.* He couldn't be sure about that. But something deep inside him told him it was true. *That kid's ear had landed on me. The rest of him probably never landed at all.*

He stood for hours, pressed close by the swarms of humanity drinking, yelling, kissing, fighting. But he wasn't with them. He wasn't one of them. They cheered the burning. They loved the noise of firecrackers. They would likely never know what a truly violent world they lived in. Allmen knew. And he realized that night in the middle of a religious festival, just how much he had come to hate it.

He was walking back to the hotel, the crowds starting to break up and traffic starting to run again as people made their way home. A van, a white rental with a dented fender and bald tires, was slowly motoring down the other side of the street. It paused, idled. He saw the driver look right and left. He had a dark face and a thick neck, and the motion of his head reminded Allmen of one of the bulls, hooking left and right with its deadly horns.

And then he charged, the van accelerating and bouncing on the cobblestones as it picked up speed. Time slowed to a crawl as Allmen's brain registered the malice, the ferocity. The van veered sharply, plowing into the crowd that lined the street in front of the bodegas and little restaurants and clubs. *This is real.* The sidewalk was crowded with revelers and he saw bodies flip and flail. A woman screamed, and he saw the old Spaniard who he had sat next to as the bulls had come through the streets. *This is not a dream.* That man was thrown into the air as if gored, falling on his back. *This is not a flashback.* Allmen watched from fifty yards away as the old man slowly got to a seated position and then stood, dusting himself off like the torero had earlier in the ring. It was miraculous. The old man should have been dead. He couldn't make that part up and it was the last reassurance his mind needed that this was really happening.

Something was still not right.

Now Allmen was running, screaming, combat instincts involuntarily awakened. "Get down!" He was zig zagging across the street, dodging potential gunfire when the van just disappeared. Glancing up he saw it, hovering, frozen in the streetlights, surfing on a cloud of smoke and flame. Then the concussion hit him, knocking him to the cobblestones as the explosion reverberated off the low buildings surrounding the square. The van cartwheeled and fell back on the spot where it had exploded. And for a moment, all was quiet.

Allmen gasped, pulled himself up to a seated position on his elbows and took in a deep breath of burning gasoline and putrid smoke. Then the screaming started. It was a high pitch keening that was fully human, fully heartbreaking and blended effortlessly with the European police sirens snapping to life all over the small town all at once. Allmen ran through a quick combat checklist and found that he was still alive. He bled from his hands where they had scraped the pavement, his lip where he had bitten it and his ear which was ringing with the shock of the concussion. He also felt like vomiting, but that was likely jus the noxious fumes and the adrenaline. He was still alive. *For now.*

"Fuck me."

He looked toward the smoking wreckage of the van and saw the old man was down again. His body lay crumpled on the curb, surrounded by burning bits of metal and plastic, blood running in a river out of him. This time he had no head. A river of blood and fire. That was enough for Allmen. He emptied his dinner and drinks onto the cobblestones in three violent heaves and then stumbled away from the heat of the flaming wreck. *Well, they know about the violence now, don't they?*

❉ ❉ ❉

Allmen burst into his hotel room and headed straight for the mini bar. He drank a tall glass of water and then another of scotch to calm his nerves. *What the fuck was that?*

Terrorism. *Random fucking acts of violence.* That kind of attack had been *en vogue* for a few years, mowing down innocents and killing anyone who came to their aid in the following carnage. It could have been Islamic, ISIS or Al Qaeda. Or it could have been domestic. Spain was a deeply divided and poor country, a toxic brew for malcontents. Basques and Catalans had periodically fought for independence with terror tactics. *Thank you, professor, but right now who really cares?*

He had another Scotch and felt the adrenaline draining away. He felt drunk and drowsy. He turned on the TV and flipped past the news channels. They already had the story and Allmen had no desire to relive the last few hours. He found the Travel channel. Travel, adventure, escape. *A two year splurge with a periodic change in scenery.*

The host was Anthony Bourdain, chef, author, *bon vivant.* It was one of his older shows, where he focused on eating and drinking, and not politics. *Perfect.*

Allmen turned up the volume and was pouring himself his third drink when he heard the host say: "When death is coming your way anyway, drinking too much is not something you need to feel guilty about." He had Allmen's full attention. Indeed, it was as if the host had been talking to John Allmen through the television. *Weird, yes, but it had been an epically weird day.* And it was no mean feat given that the celebrity chef was dead and gone to the great bistro in the sky.

The episode went on. "A dark, dank, suicidal time of year for most people, for Icelanders is anything but..." Bourdain and his shock of silvery hair was sitting in a lagoon, steam rising from a natural hot spring in an eerie green light while he sipped at a beer. Allmen watched the scene for another few minutes until the episode ended. When the credits rolled, he noted the title: Iceland, Hello Darkness My Old Friend.

He felt his jaw go slack.

And the vision
That was planted in my brain

Still remains
Within the sound...
Of silence

His phone rang. It was Virgil.

"John, you okay? I just saw the news. Were you there? I was trying to figure out where you were, but the signal wasn't great..."

"Yeah, thanks Virgil. I'm okay. I saw it all happen."

"Oh..."

"You know Virgil," he said thickly, "this had been on my bucket list for quite some time. I always wanted to see a bullfight and now I have. And man, when you mess with the bull, you are liable to get the horns, you know?

"Yeah...John, are you sure you are okay?"

"Yeah Virgil," Allmen said dreamily, "I saw an old man die today. And several bulls. Ya know what I realized?"

"Go ahead, John."

"We're all dying Virgil, some faster than others."

"Yeah, I know." Virgil sounded sad. "And some without really living at all, John."

"Yeah. Yeah, that is right. But not me..."

"No, clearly. You are living about the best life I can imagine for the past, what? Almost two years now?"

"Almost two years exactly. Two years next month in fact. But hey, who is counting?"

"So, anything I can do for you? It's been a pretty weird couple of days. Are you ready to come home?"

"Get me out of here. But not home yet."

"Okay, where to?"

Sitting in a hotel room without electricity, he tasted blood from his lip and heard the wail of sirens still blaring off into the distance. "Darkness, my old friend." He explained a bit, hung up and fell hard asleep. And in the morning, he flew two hours to Iceland hoping to find some light in the midst of the gloom.

194

FRAUD:

an intentional perversion of truth through an act of deceiving or misrepresenting. A person who is not what he or she pretends to be

I once heard about the devil's many vices –
they said he was a liar and father of lies.

-Dante, Inferno, Canto XXIII

Allmen looked out the window at the landscape below. Mossy green and brown, an island rose from the cold waters in a dramatic upheaval. Pock marked and steaming, the rocky expanses gave way to plots of snow and ice to the north. To the south, virescent fields fell into the sea or ended at the villages and towns. It was a magnificent amphitheater of stone, forged from the sea by fire. He yawned and thumbed his worn paperback, The Tragedies of William Shakespeare, alternating reading with futile attempts at sleep. He'd replaced his lost copy of The Sun Also Rises before leaving for Mexico opting for classics by The Bard. He'd breezed through The Scottish Play with its pandering underlings and psychotic usurper, the treachery and seduction of the scheming subordinate, Iago, and the flattering and cunning daughters of Lear.

As the final descent began, he turned to Hamlet. The Prince of Danes would have ruled Iceland too, at least during most of the Middle Ages, so it seemed logical. Not that logic was guiding his decisions anymore. *People that take travel orders from their televisions late at night lost all claim to logic. If not sanity.*

The first-class attendant was a giant of a man with close cropped red hair, a full beard and a ruddy complexion. His hairy arms gave way to hints of gaudy tattoos beneath his sleeves when he came to collect the empty drinks before landing. His name tag said Geryon. *First name or last? Doesn't matter.*

"Good book?" The big man smiled.

Allmen nodded. "A classic. Actually, several of them."

Geryon or Mr. Geyron, nodded then turned away. As he did, the masks of civility and servility both fell away and Allmen caught the smile vanishing to a blank stare as he carried the trash back to the galley.

Landing gear extended, the great winged monster settled on

the runway as the Prince of Danes was suffering the slings and arrows of outrageous fortune and devolving into a brooding mess. Allmen could relate. Hamlet was professing his love to Ophelia.

"Doubt that the sun doth move; Doubt truth to be a liar..."

Ophelia. Abruptly Allmen put down the slim paperback and felt sweat beading on the back of his neck. Ophelia had died. It had been years since he'd read or seen the play. Probably since Mel Gibson starred in the movie. *Not bad actually.* But Ophelia, he now remembered, hadn't just died. *Ophelia had gone in the water.* He thought back to what it was like to fall from the boat into the warm waters of the Gulf of Mexico near Key West. It seemed like a lifetime ago. But the terror of being in the water was still close at hand.

Ophelia had gone in the water...and she had drowned herself. Had she seen the darkness zeroing in? The tunnel vision? The white light at the end? The panic began to build inside him. *No, not now.* He felt sweaty and nauseous. *Get a grip, she's a fictional character. She's not even real, John.* Nevertheless, when the jetway opened he lurched to his feet and headed for the door, a bit unsteadily.

"Sir, you forgot your book." The big man stood near John's vacated seat holding the paperback between two massive hands. His fake smile was back. Apparently, he had punched back in to work on his mental clock.

The crush of passengers from behind was already building and John looked back. "Keep it."

The masks melted again, the look now vaguely reptilian, sneering. "What am I supposed to do with a book?" That was the second time someone had asked him that stupid question. *Fucking read it! It's a book. What was wrong with the world?* He shrugged helplessly and was pushed onward by the surge behind.

He fled through the gate and was in Reykjavik. *What the hell am I doing here?* All along the terminal passengers were disgorged into a maelstrom of mankind. It was a clean but crowded airport, and he dodged pockets of tourists speaking a variety of guttural languages.

He had a miserable hangover. The four- and half-hour flight and two-hour time change didn't help. Nor did the Scotch the night before piled on top of adrenaline, fear and a failure to sleep. He stopped at a small sundries shop, paid a ridiculous amount for ibuprofen and a beer to go. Airports were great places to grab an early afternoon beverage. No one could judge if they didn't know what time zone you were coming from. He didn't think the Nordic stock of this island would have cared much anyway. They had been raping, pillaging, feasting and drinking since the Little Ice Age. *What self-respecting Viking sipped at an Evian and waited for happy hour?*

A van picked him up. A white van with a long streak of something reddish brown along the passenger door. Blood? His mind flashed to bull horns, flailing limbs of innocents abroad, exploding metal riding a pillar of flame, and an old man's head rolling in the gutter. It turned out to be rust on the door. No one's fault. How could they have known? Different van, different country. *A new day for John Allmen. Right?*

He coaxed himself inside and slammed the door shut mere seconds before the driver became annoyed. It was a mercifully short ride from the airport to his first stop in the town of Grindavik, where he stowed his luggage, got a locker and a bath robe and began retracing Tony Bourdain's steps.

He emerged from the locker room into a slate gray sky with hints of snow in it. The air smelled like something rotting and took him back to the streets of Iraq and burning bodies after a daylong firefight. He realized though that this smell was earthier. And then his mind placed it: sulfur. Beneath him, fiery lava churned away in a never-ending flow to the center of the earth. It superheated the local waters and provided convenient electrical power. And after it had served its greater good it was ejected into a man-made lagoon in order to bring in the tourists.

I need a Bloody Mary. He stood, for a long moment, shivering in the cold in his thin, recycled robe. And he realized that the tourists were cued up at a large full-service bar separated from him by twenty yards of four-foot-deep lagoon. Steam rose in tendrils above him, ensconced in a pocket of warmth despite the flurries drifting off the sea and floating on the wind. A great, superheated bathtub and a rescue beverage awaited. *Ophelia had drowned in the water.*

It was mercifully not crowded. The water was clean and the high silica content of the mud was supposedly good for skin ailments. Allmen did not care a wit. His skin was the least of his worries. It was his soul that was irritated and inflamed. *Bloody bull ears and decapitated old men can do that.*

He dipped a tentative toe into the water, felt warmth shoot through his toe, his ankle and then radiate up through his body. *C'mon, you can do this.*

"Silica mask?"

A beefy blonde girl with gleaming white teeth beckoned him.

"Say again?"

She showed more teeth. "A silica mask. Good for the pores. Refreshing too. You look like you could use some refreshment. Long flight?"

"Uh huh." Allmen toed the steaming water.

"So…silica mask?"

He looked at the bucket of ooze in her hand and shook his head. "No, thank you."

She moved on with a small shrug, pandering to the next tourist. People wore masks for many reasons. To be someone else, or to get away with something and not be recognized. Or to be healed, at least for a while. *The healing powers of the earth? How about the healing powers of a drink?* Allmen stared across the twenty-yard expanse of water toward the bar. *Ophelia had…fuck!*

He looked away, saw the blonde fawning over another fair-haired man with a shoulder length mane. He patted her arm and she looked doe eyed at him. He spoke and she nodded earnestly. He wore the uniform of khaki pants and a white polo shirt. He abandoned her to do whatever job was his and came within hailing distance. His name tag said Jason, something Allmen could pronounce with confidence.

"Excuse, me Jason, is there a bar...inside?"

"Of course, sir, just after the locker rooms. You can have lunch and a refreshment after you swim."

"Thanks, but I'm going to pass on the swim today. Maybe another time."

Jason cocked his head curiously but thought better of asking. "Of course, sir, let me show you inside."

✳ ✳ ✳

His hotel was small, a few rooms clustered around a breakfast hall that doubled as a self-service honor bar during the day. Allmen checked in, helped himself to a few half bottles of white and red wine and headed to the room. He maneuvered in with his bags and allowed the door to slam shut with a bang behind him. He flinched, then scanned the room. Light wood bed frame and dresser. A desk along the wall and a large, framed mirror that faced the bathroom to his right.

He paused. His tired, recessed eyes gazed back from atop three days growth of stubble. He touched his gaunt, sallow face. It was pale despite the sunny climates he had visited, the result of SPF 30, late nights and sleeping through prime tanning hours. At least the skin was smooth if a bit taut. *Who needs a silica mask?*

He smiled and it felt like his face would crack. This was not the face of someone who had been compared to a movie star in recent years unless the part was of someone like Yorick, the skull Hamlet pulls out of the graveyard.

Allmen stared at himself again in the mirror.

"Alas poor John...I knew him...a man of infinite jest."

He sighed, drew away from the increasingly foreign form in the glass and unpacked. Then he opened a bottle of wine, red and murky, poured it into the provided glassware and toasted himself in the mirror.

"What a piece of work is a man."

He drank and slept, long and dreamless. And when he woke there was rain splatted on the windows and he could hear the wind gusting off the sea. He asked himself again: *Why? Why come here? Why had the random coincidence of a song lyric and television show title brought him to this place?* He didn't know. But he was here and if darkness was an old friend he had come to see, at least there was plenty of it.

* * *

He walked most of the day. Through steaming stone landscapes, he plodded over cracks and trenches in the earth's surface. There was a crevasse deep in the black soil where continental plates had collided and there were geysers of erupting water. He crept across glaciers and fields of sulfur mud and finally back through town and to the hotel. He ached. And while he signed for a few more bottles of wine, he noticed that his was the only name on the list multiple times. He shrugged. *First time I've been on an honor list in quite a while.*

In his room he shed his bulky jacket and twisted open the first bottle of wine. His bladder demanded attention. As he hustled toward the bathroom, he stopped abruptly at the mirror.

There was a face staring back at him he didn't recognize. Familiar, yes. But only in the way you might recognize a distant cousin at a family reunion who had been in prison for a stretch.

That is not my face. It sure as shit wasn't the ruddy face of kid playing outdoors through a Youngstown winter. He'd spent hours in the yard, building tunnels out of the snow that piled up as the hulking plows pushed it up off the street. There he could find shelter, peace, quiet. No absent father, no fun sponge for a mother. That was the face of a boy who got spoiled at Christmas and mostly ignored the rest of the year. This was the face of a man. A man who had seen the world for what it was and couldn't hide from it in a snow cave. It had been better to be the boy, ignorant and full of promise.

Nor was it the face of the summertime camps at the YMCA or the sunburnt afternoons spent at the tennis and basketball courts. It wasn't the face of a young boy taking his first communion and grinning from ear to ear to be let in on the mysteries of the faith. No, it was the face of man who had seen his religion melt away with age. Who had stopped putting coins in the offering basket and trying to buy his way into Catholic heaven. Who had recognized names of priests exposed as pedophiles and been glad that it was no longer his money supporting the scam.

It was the face of a man who was about to piss his pants if he didn't stop staring at himself in the mirror.

Afterward, he sat in a gloomy darkening room and heard the wind pick up outside. He had nothing left to read and he dared not sleep. Not yet. He hoped the television might bring some relief. Sky News was in English, but it surely wasn't going to restore anyone's hope in humanity. The handful of stories that he caught involved a civil war in Africa, a judge being impeached in the United States and the trial of a man accused of killing his brother in Wales. *Were we really meant to live our lives a brutes?* Finally, there was a story of Sunni and Shiite violence on the border between Iran and Iraq. *That may be "news" but it certainly isn't new.* Someone had been beheaded. John had a mental image of large man in a turban, black beard flowing as he swung an immense bloody sword in a deadly arc. He changed the station.

He watched a movie for a while with English subtitles about a kid who grows up to learn how to pass bad checks and impersonates an airline pilot. DiCaprio was good in it, even in another language. During a commercial he flipped again, opened another bottle of wine and watched an extended clip from the US Senate chambers where they were play-acting at debate. Given the choices between the dealers of discord, imposters, counterfeiters or hypocrites he chose darkness and turned off the television. *Hello my old friend.*

He slept.

He dreamt about the mirror. His mind focused on the bulky light wood and smooth glass. He was standing in front of the bed and looking toward the framed surface when it shifted to become more than one mirror. His reflection, dark and gaunt, seemed to repeat over and over, receding to the horizon and stretching out toward eternity. It was called an infinity mirror, parallel mirrors creating a series of smaller reflections that seem to be endless. But unlike the standard illusion, in his dream, the individual reflections began to change. Slowly, like a pebble dropped in a still pond they rippled and resolved into snapshots from his life.

He could see in the distance his face as a child on the first day of school with terribly angled bangs accenting a horrific "bowl cut." *Thanks Mom.* And he could see another in Pop Warner football gear, a lopsided grin on his face. He'd gotten injured that day and never played again. No mother nicknamed the Wet Blanket was going to let her son play that dangerous sport. She'd considered swimming, worried about him drowning and chosen tennis for him instead. *Swimming, oh the irony.*

One mirror showed his senior prom, where he wore a horribly fitting tuxedo and plaid bow tie and cummerbund. Chastity was in a blue gown and big bangs. Then came college graduation. And Officer Candidate School. With Trisha when she was pregnant. With his baby daughter. Some of the mirrors were darker after that, harder to see. He didn't try. Instead, he let his glance move steadily forward until the mirrors showed scenes from his recent adventures.

Key West. Florence. Paris. Las Vegas. Mount Whitney. Mexico City. A bullring in Spain. A frozen landscape with a waterfall plunging into a wide gorge. And then one more mirror with nothing in it. No reflection, no scenery. Translucent and glassy yet totally dark. He heard a familiar sound of walking on ice, something he'd been doing a lot of lately. Then a crunching, grinding snap as the final mirror cracked at the bottom. A spiderweb of glass shot up toward the top of the frame. Then the glass fell away without a sound. And behind it was a door. *People in horror movies and dreams do the dumbest things.* He reached out and pushed on the door.

It opened with a groaning creak and he could hear his dreamy footsteps marching down a long barren hallway. At the end of the hall, it forked into two passages. From the right he heard screaming, rotor blades churning, bullets whining and explosions ripping the air. He walked away from the noise and angled left, where he came to another mirror. It was just like the one that had shattered and led him in here, though this one was intact.

He stared at himself for a long time. *That's not my face.* He pulled back his hand and arced a right cross at his reflected chin. He expected to see tentacles of glass spread out from his fist as the glass again shattered. But nothing happened. His reflection didn't change. The mirror stayed in one piece.

He tried again, this time with a straight right that left a long smudge on his reflection, but the mirror didn't break. Instead, it began to talk. His reflection, but not his voice. Other voices, one after another came from his reflected lips.

"El-tee! We gotta go!"

"Daddy! Daddy!"

"El-tee, this way!"

"Plan on dropping in again unannounced?"

"Jesus Christ superstar."

"Daddy! Daddy!"

"Name it to tame it."

"My friend Virgil is exactly what you need."

"Well, you are lucky to get some time away to yourself."

"I went to Cal. Sorry Mr. Allmen."

"I'm sorry sir, there was nothing we could do."

Then there was a scream that came not from his reflection, but from his own mouth. He woke in a tangle of sheets, sweating and noted that the pillow next to him had a dent where he had been pummeling it. He felt feverish and strange. It was still dark out.

❋ ❋ ❋

In the morning Allmen trudged again through a pock marked landscape that could have been the moon or the netherworld if not for the snow falling in light, translucent flakes. Like a zombie he lurched across the harsh landscape alternating between a shuffling hike and a haphazard scramble across scree filled slopes. He was tired, bone weary in a way he had not felt since the sleep deprived, physically demanding days at war. His hangover was a more frequent phenomenon, something he'd learned to live with, and it had therefore faded into the background.

Scuttling up a bolder field and down the other side he crossed a charcoal black slope with occasional darker patches of smaller rock. On he moved through the paradoxical landscape of steaming earth and falling snow. *Hamlet would have liked it here. Or would he have? Hamlet was, after all, a weakling.* Three hours of hand wringing about his uncle was a couple hours too many in Allmen's mind. *Just put a dagger in the fat bastard and move on with life. Or put it in yourself and let everyone move on and adjust.* Ah, but the everlasting canon against self- slaughter. Hamlet, who was living in hell, was afraid to take action for fear of going to hell. *And, that friends, is the exact antithesis of free will.* He suddenly thought maybe he'd been a bit harsh on the young Prince of Danes.

At the edge of a large chasm, steep granite walls fell away in a vertical crevasse to a floor of oozing mud. He stopped and peered down.

"Ah, 'tis bitter cold and I am sick at heart," he quoted from memory into the freshening breeze. He smelled the salt on the wind and knew it was picking up from the sea. And then it reached for him with a gust that filled his jacket like a sail, lifting him, shoving him forward and down. Grasping, flailing, John

205

Allmen lost his balance completely and tumbled into the abyss.

He fell, like in his dreams. But there were no screams, except he thought for his own. He couldn't be sure. Was that his screaming? Or was it the wind in his ears? It was not the long, endless fall into the darkness of his dreams, but a short one that ended on a shallow creek bed. His breath exploded out of his lungs as he impacted the water and then the muddy ground beneath it with a thud and a splash. He felt cold water creep under his collar and a sharp pain deep in his chest. And then he slipped from the world of the conscious and into one darker and deeper down.

❊ ❊ ❊

Bright light, a great corona of white and yellow, hit him full in the face and he was awake. Cheap sheets, a clanky iron cot, a smell of antiseptic and cold air on his bare ass where the robe he wore was open at the back. *Hospital.* The occasional whiff of decay proved it beyond doubt.

A nurse, he instantly wanted to call her Gretel for her stocky Nordic build and golden braids, was bustling about his steel framed bed. He watched her for a while, adjusting computer screens, writing on a clipboard, opening various packages and placing the contents on a tray.

Sensing his eyes on her, she turned and smiled. She said something unintelligible, short and guttural. A command? In her beefy white hand were a series of small white pills.

Allmen pushed himself away from her, recoiling into his pillow. She frowned, confused. "No drugs," he gasped, feeling like his lungs had burst open with the effort.

The frown deepened. Uncomprehending, she took a step forward. He recoiled again and his torso became electric with pain.

"No drugs," he managed again through gritted teeth. She shook her head, blonde pigtails flying left and right. In his delirium he half thought they left trails through the air around her head. He sighed and it made him want to cry from pain and frustration. Then he snapped a finger in sudden inspiration. Allmen put held out two hands, palms up to stop her.

"No."

Continuing his mime show, he held a thumb to his forehead and his pinky to his mouth in the international sign for a telephone. Understanding dawned. Nodding, she moved to a closet nearby and rummaged through what he recognized as his sodden, mud-stained clothes. Finally, she extracted his little magical brick and gave it to him with a patient smile. It was powered on still and he hit the menu button pulling up the translator app.

"No drugs," he said again into the device. "I'm an addict."

Something unintelligible came out of the device, and then out of the nurse. But she nodded, gave him a knowing, perhaps patronizing smile, and left him alone.

He looked at the phone in his hand and felt the air return to his lungs. He dialed Virgil.

"John? That you?"

"Yes, it's me," despite himself a groan escaped.

"I've been calling the hospital for hours trying to find out about you. But between the language barrier, which is not insignificant, and not being related, I couldn't get anything from them. You okay?"

"I can honestly say that I've been worse. I took a tumble but nothing I'm not used to. Cracked a couple of ribs, I think. Listen, I need to get home. I will find out when they will let me go, but it shouldn't be more than a day. Can you manage it?"

"Sure. Should be able to get you out on the first flight the day after tomorrow."

"That will work. And that will be my last flight. Thanks again Virgil. For everything. It's been a hell of a journey."

"That is an understatement. John, do you know any Latin?"

The non-sequitur barely registered as Allmen began drifting toward sleep. "Catholic upbringing, liberal arts education...I know a little. But I've forgotten most of it. Why?"

"I read something recently that made me think of you. *Forsan et haec olim meminisse juvabit.*"

"Catchy. And, may I say, wonderful pronunciation. What the hell does it mean?"

"Perhaps someday it will bring pleasure to remember even these things. It's from the Aeneid. Hard times come and hard times go and maybe someday we can appreciate the things that seemed so hard at the time. I got your postcards. I wanted you to know that."

"That's good Virgil. Then you understand."

"John, I …" But the connection was gone. Allmen hung up and promptly fell asleep.

He took a cab home that night with instructions to rest and avoid any strenuous activity. The doctors weren't thrilled that he planned to fly home and urged him to see his physician when he got back. *Not likely. No need to waste anyone's time.* He spent the dark hours tossing and turning to get comfortable on his ribs. Then, just as dawn was breaking over the sea, he drifted off into an uneasy sleep. He woke to the room phone trilling, a loud, grating sound that brought him surging out from the blackness and out of his bed, his ribs and instant reminder of where he had been yesterday.

"Hullo?"

"Listen very carefully," said a husky female voice with a decidedly European lilt. "There is an envelope under your door. Go pick it up. Right now."

"What? Who is this?"

"My name is Clement, Mr. Allmen. But that isn't important right now. What is important is that you pick up the envelope that was just delivered."

Allmen looked, and indeed there was a large white envelope under the door.

"Okay. Hold on." Too tired and worn down, he dutifully padded over to the door and picked up the thin, legal sized parcel, and came back to the phone.

"What is this?" He winced as he sat heavily on the bed holding the mysterious envelope.

"You've been served," she said matter-of-factly. And the line went dead.

There was a seal on the envelope, branded, and the law firm was familiar. Allmen, suddenly fully awake, tore it open as if it might contain live vipers. He sighed. *Fucking Mack.* He set down the silent receiver in his hand and retrieved his cell phone. He dialed Mack Mason, and to his surprise, the son of a bitch answered.

"Why are you doing this?" Allmen gasped wearily, not really wanting to hear the answer.

"Because you made a fool out of me. Cost me money. A fair amount of it."

"You can't sue me. We had an arbitration agreement through the firm."

"John, I have money and lawyers. I can do what I like and make it very painful for you in the process. Besides, you skipped the arbitration hearing and haven't been heard from in weeks."

"How did you find me?"

"Again John, I have resources for finding people. Especially people who cross certain lines. And you crossed the line my friend."

"I'm not your friend Mack. And I'm not a subordinate anymore. You can't push me around to make yourself feel like the big man. This isn't Iraq."

"No, but the rules still apply John. Rule number one? You don't fuck your buddy. And you fucked me. You made yourself out to be something you are not. And now, last time I checked, it has cost me more than I want to count. Not to mention the relationships with your former clients. People who I referred to you. Those relationships are now in ashes."

Ashes. Ashes to ashes and dust to dust. Allmen seethed. "I'm not the only one who made himself out to be something he wasn't. See you around...buddy." He lathered the last word with as much sarcasm and derision as he could and killed the call. There was a faint crack as he hurled the phone toward the wall.

He turned on the room light and saw the smartphone glowing intact on the floor. Above it was the mirror. A series of fissures radiated out from the middle of the glass and Allmen stood and maneuvered himself so the impact point was over his reflected face. *Seven years bad luck. Wonder if that is retroactive?*

One final time, he looked in the mirror. Through the cracks was the face of a soldier, hard eyed and sleep deprived. The one who took his orders and carried out the plan of the day. Even though the orders trickled down from morons, political hacks who looked at polling data and campaign contributions instead of intelligence reports or simple fucking maps. The inevitable result was that even the intelligence reports became bastardized, politicized. The further from the field, the more exaggerated the claims and the ability to understand the tactical situation and predict the future. They had taken to calling the senior intelligence guys, "the sorcerers." It wasn't a compliment. The fuckers could conjure meaning from the meaningless. *Not a bad skill, really. I could sure use a little meaning.* Some had thrived in that environment. Guys like Mack Mason. And Allmen had followed him upward. That now felt like an embarrassing admission.

He sighed heavily and collapsed with a wince onto the bed. It didn't really matter, any of it. He didn't really care. He forced himself to slow his breathing, fighting for self-control. After a minute, he had it. Or close enough. Then he laughed. It was a wild, cackling sound. A belly laugh would have been too painful. This was, after all, a minor annoyance. He had a plan to evade this lawsuit and any other. The time was drawing near. He started to pack.

TREACHERY:

A betrayal of trust or actions of a deceptive nature. A violation of allegiance or of faith and confidence.

O h, *reader, do not ask of me how I*
grew faint and frozen then – I cannot write it:
all words would fall far short of what it was.
I did not die, and I was not alive;
think for yourself, if you have any wit,
what I became, deprived of life and death.

-Dante, Inferno, Canto XXXIV

llmen landed back in San Francisco, for the first time considering the fact that, like the panhandlers outside his old office, he was homeless. But, thanks to the tidy sum from the sale of said home, he had resources. Which meant he could check in to a hotel for a few days while he figured out what to do next.

He grabbed a cab from the airport noting the gradual descent into gloom, the clouds rolling in the closer he got to the cold waters that surrounded the city. When he spilled out onto the sidewalk it was at least twenty degrees cooler than at the airport and an occasional band of fog blew in from the Bay. Shoppers, tourists and civic employees were scattered across the wide plaza going about their business and dodging the ever-expanding population of the homeless and psychologically imbalanced. He saw something that drew his attention and illegally crossed the street, horns blaring as he stepped into traffic, which he casually ignored. *Can't hurt me now.*

On the far sidewalk was one of the street people. He was dressed in filthy khaki pants, a knit sweater with holes in the elbows and what appeared to be a brand-new pair of New Balance running shoes. His hair was slicked back in a greasy blonde swirl and his gaunt face showed deep wrinkles and a line of white scar tissue across his forehead. He was the Florida Man of the west, with no trailer to go home to and an endless supply of clean needles and human services. He held a sign, black marker on the side of a cardboard box:

THE END IS NEAR.

A chill wind gusted up off San Francisco Bay. Allmen felt a shiver go through him. He stepped up to the man, looking him in the face, smelling his earthly smells and trying to catch his eyes, which shifted continually between points on the sidewalk. Allmen pointed at the sign.

"Really?"

The man raised bushy eyebrows in question but stayed mute.

"Is the end really near?"

"I uh, I uh…." The man's voice was a high nasal whine. "I don't know."

"You don't know?"

"No, man. I don't know." He drew out the last syllable in a high squeal of annoyance.

"You don't know? How can you not know? You're standing out here with a sign indicating the end of the fucking world! I assume you have some intel that led you to turn yourself out on a city street and announce Armageddon! Or did you just wake up in the shelter with a cardboard sign in your hand?"

"I don't go to no shelter man. Those places are scary."

"Nevertheless, wherever you woke up this morning, did a cardboard sign indicating the apocalypse miraculously appear?"

"Uh…"

"Did it?" Allmen was yelling and several pedestrians slowed their walks to take in the show. California Man finally met his eye. He gave Allmen a look that one assumed a homeless man with a marginal grasp on sanity had seen many times himself. A mirror unto his own world as it were. The look said in no uncertain terms: *You are a fucking nut job.*

"Look man, a couple of the bible beaters, a guy and his wife, they give me some money to stand out here with the sign. Occasionally some loot too. He pointed a grubby finger at his incongruently new shoes. "I guess they want to scare people into…"

"Into what?"

California Man scratched himself and thought about it. "Repenting is what they said. Yeah, that's it. Repenting."

"Repenting." Allmen repeated the word as if it were new to him. "Repenting." Allmen shuffled away muttering to himself, making the word a question. "Repenting?"

He was still repeating the word, silently shaking his head as he checked in and sent his bags to his room. And by the time he sat down at the bar inside the hotel the word was on heavy rotation in his inner monologue. It circled the file bin where he stored the strange and nonsensical oddities of life. It was by far his largest file. Exhausted by the mental effort, he set to the one way he had fallen back on to force his mind away from thinking. He ordered his first of what he planned to be several martinis. The bartender set it in front of him ice chips running down the glass, on a branded napkin with the restaurant's name: Central Well.

He raised the glass to toast himself in the big mirror behind the bar.

"To repenting," he said aloud.

He froze there, glass held high and a sudden bead of sweat popping from the skin below his hairline. Behind him, in a booth with plush lining and an intimate table for two, was a blonde woman. *The* blonde woman. He lowered his glass to the bar and hunched inward, stealing occasional glances to confirm that it was her. She wore a black sweater and leggings, dressed for a casual meeting. And she was not alone. Across from her, smiling, was a middle-aged man, extremely tall and fit. He too wore casual but tailored slacks and a sweater whose cost would feed and clothe the homeless man across the street for a week. He was laughing, gesturing. Allmen hated this Nimrod immediately. She laughed too. Seeing her here having fun, literally behind his back was not the craziest thing that had happened to him recently. But it was close. The world was tilting. And now it had run off its tracks.

Another martini. More cloak and dagger observation of the reflection in the mirror. He asked for and signed his bill and strode nonchalantly to the restroom. They were still there making happy noises when he exited the men's room, walking with a purpose toward the door, passing her on his left. And then he executed a smart left face and deposited himself next to the natty gentleman, catching the scent of designer cologne and good scotch.

"Hi, remember me?" He spoke to her, ignoring the momentarily shocked man. He was even taller than Allmen had realized, a giant of a man with newly manicured hands.

She blanched, face as pale as her cascading blonde hair. And then her color returned in a blotchy red that rose up her throat perfectly timed with the words that tumbled out.

"Yes, hello John. Nice to see you again." The sound of his name lit up receptors in his brain that he'd thought long dormant. But there was no warmth in her, there was.... what? *Embarassment? Anger?*

"Will you give me a second?" She was standing and talking to the other man, who was now frowning and beginning to assess the threat on his left. It was, no doubt, a serious one. John had seen his own, bruised and sallow complexion in the mirror too. The man gave a wary nod. She put a hand on Allmen's arm, guiding him upward in a pressure-less grip that was somehow unavoidable and unbreakable.

She led him outside, the cold slapping at him and the dull light punching at his martini fuddled eyeballs. There was an alley to the right of the hotel entrance. And it struck him as odd that she'd want to rekindle anything next to a dumpster smelling like yesterday's fish special.

"Hey, I have a room..."

And then she hit him. A dull thud to his solar plexus that bent him double and threatened to launch half consumed olives and dry gin onto the pavement. His ribs screamed and for a moment his vision went black. Then it came back in a starry blur like a Van Gogh painting. He tasted blood. He breathed hard and smelled the garbage. But he also smelled her, that soapy clean floral scent he remembered.

"Listen to me asshole," she growled. "Just what the hell do you think you are doing?"

"I've been looking for you," he groaned, finally managing to stand upright without lurching in any direction. His stomach held, though it was a near thing.

"Oh yeah, I noticed. Chasing me through the park like a stalker and then that stunt you pulled in the airport. Please, stop looking for me. I work long hours and don't get much time off, so if you see me again don't say hi. Got it?"

"But we…. I was…who are you?"

She softened slightly, moving from outward hostility to mere annoyance in her body language. She put her hands on her hips.

"Haven't figured that out yet? Huh, I thought you were smarter than that."

"Clue me in."

"Remember that life insurance policy you took out?"

"The what?" He spat the words in befuddlement.

"C'mon I don't have time for this shit. The insurance policy you took out. Just before we met?"

"Yeah, sure, I guess so."

"I'm an insurance investigator John. I do some freelance work for companies and individuals who think they may be defrauded. I charmed you, got to know you, figured out what you were up to. And I filed my report and that was that. Except you kept turning up in the wrong places." She sighed. "I guess it is a small town."

"But we…" he left the statement hanging in the brisk air and she brushed it away with a flick of her slender hand.

"Slept together? Hardly. You were so drunk I had to carry you to your room. Awkward that, too many security cameras. Hell, I was worried you'd swallow a bunch of pills that night and that would be hard for me to explain. So, I watched over you, made sure you were breathing and didn't fall off the balcony. And when you came to, I left. But we did not…"

Allmen's jaw snapped shut. He had nothing to say. He'd been getting things wrong in his life for so long it didn't surprise him that he'd gotten so much wrong that particular night. "Not personal…just business." He tried to say this in his best Godfather impersonation, but mimicking Marlon Brando was more difficult than he'd imagined after four cocktails and a punch in the gut.

"Sure, business, whatever. I felt bad for you until you started popping up in my life unannounced. The helicopter in Iraq, your divorce...the accident..."

He held up a hand. "How the hell did you know all that?"

"Jesus John, I knew all that about you five minutes after I first heard your name. It's called Google. Listen. Get some help, okay. Do it. And do it soon. I'd guess you are coming up on two years since you took out that policy. With that exclusion for, well, you know...the end is near. But your plan won't work. They can prove you did all of this on purpose, with forethought, and that will void your policy. No money for whoever you were leaving it to."

He just stared at her, feeling the way he did in Iraq when perfectly good plans got shredded by IEDs or automatic weapons fire. *Or just plain stupidity.*

She frowned, hesitated and then strode away, heels clipping at the pavement. As she rounded the corner of the alley she looked back and said, "I'm sorry. I was doing a job. It was a favor." And then, "Go get that help, okay?"

He just glared at her. And then she was gone again. As she disappeared, he noticed California man was standing across from the alley watching, grinning a half mad smile. He held his cardboard sign out again and pointed at it: The End is Near.

Allmen waved with one hand while he massaged his stomach with the other. "I know," he said. "I know."

* * *

Upstairs he sat at the desk in the spacious hotel room looking out the window at the Bay Bridge in the distance smudged by fog. The temperature was plummeting and, oddly for the Bay Area, approaching freezing. Small icicles were forming on the soundproof panes. On the bridge, traffic was at standstill. It was as if, from his perch high above, he was staring down on a land frozen in place, immovable. He felt his head clear, while the fog out the window out over Oakland got darker. He couldn't just sit here. Not today. He had things to do. *The end was near.*

He caught the elevator down, descending to the lobby and caught a cab, giving the driver an address. The middle-aged hippie with long gray hair and a Grateful Dead tie-dyed shirt mercifully stayed silent.

Allmen watched the city creep by, feeling a longing to be near his little girl. Since he'd landed this time, it had become a physical sensation, like a hunger that gnawed at him from deep inside.

He recognized the car they pulled in behind at the curb and was mildly surprised. Her mom wasn't usually around when he visited. Carefully they had arranged to avoid each other in a city that seemed to be getting smaller all the time.

His ex-wife met him at the gate, tall and erect, her piercing blue eyes coolly sizing him up. She wore jeans and a cable knit sweater that fell below her waist. A scarf was knotted around her neck to keep out the cold. *Or is it to keep it in?* Trim, formal, analytical. *She hadn't changed a bit.*

"Hello John."

"Hello Trisha. What are you doing here?"

"What do you think I am doing here?"

"I think you are doing the thing where you ask questions about questions... like a therapist."

She shrugged. "Guilty."

The word made him flinch. "Then I should call you by your full professional name, right Beatrice?" When they had first met, he'd called her Doc. Eventually that had given way to calling her Beatrice. And by the time they were dating she was Trisha.

"Whatever you like. Listen, after you see her, I think we should talk. Okay?"

"Yeah, sure. Free extended therapy?"

She managed a sad smile. "Nothing is ever free with you John."

No argument there. He just nodded and stepped through the gate. He entered quietly, not wanting to upset the tranquility.

"Hey kiddo," he whispered.

Silence.

Allmen put on a mock face of amusement. "Just ran into you Mom. Got the frost burn to prove it."

He sat down next to her and ran through the few good memories of their times together. Work trips and his constant battles with his inner demons meant he didn't really have that many. Then he spent a few minutes telling her about his recent trips, leaving out the incident in Spain and anything having to do with sex or drinking. Again, there wasn't much left to talk about. He grew serious. "I want to ask you something. I've done some bad things in my life. And not being around for you is really one of the worst I can think of. You deserved better. Your mom deserved better. I should have been there for you. And I am sorry."

Again, the silence. "I came here to tell you something. I came to tell you that I am trying to make this right. Trying to make up for all the damage and the hurt I've done. I'm trying to make it so that you and I can be together, and I can work on getting you to forgive me." John Allmen reached out a bony hand and touched the cold stone of the grave marker. It had a fine sheen of ice over it and holding his hand there made his entire body cold. It felt somehow colder than the ground beneath it. Colder to him than anything in the world.

Florence "Flora" Allmen
Beloved Daughter
December 25th, 2008- April 17th, 2015

"I came to tell you I'm going to be with you soon. Maybe then people can start to forgive me. What do you think about that?" A bird called overhead and flapped by in the icy wind. And somewhere in the sprawling city around him, a car horn blared. But other than that, the silence stretched on.

"I'll talk to you again soon." Allmen stood and walked away feeling icy tears forming at the corner of his eyes that he brushed away with a clammy hand. *No time for that.*

Beatrice was leaning against her car at the curb outside the cemetery gate, a questioning eyebrow arched high on her forehead.

"You okay?" she asked.

"Dandy as usual. How did you know I was here?"

"I worked out the timeline and I figured you'd be here eventually. C'mon. I'll give you a ride back to your hotel." He noted that she didn't ask if he wanted a ride. At the Gold Producers meeting in Grand Cayman, they would have called it the presumptive close.

From the leather passenger seat of her silver Audi Q7 SUV he stared straight ahead as she lurched out into traffic. "What did you mean about my timeline?"

"Two years."

"What?"

"Two years today since you quit your job and took out the life insurance policy on yourself. Its Good Friday."

"And..."

"Aren't I the one who asks all the annoying questions?"

"You used to call that therapy."

"I used to say a lot of things."

He sighed. "And I never listened."

"Oh, I wouldn't say that. You were actually a better patient than you were a husband."

"Or father."

"You tried John. I know you did. But there is just too much tumbling around loose in that head of yours. So, let me make this clear John Allmen, that I don't want the money. Money isn't going to fix anything."

"Good. Because there isn't going to be any. They will fight the settlement because I planned all this. And it wasn't all for you. Some was for my Mom."

She offered him a wry smile. "Yeah, I figured. John, I would have killed you myself years ago if I needed money. She would have too."

He snorted a laugh. "I wanted to do something to make

things right. To show remorse. To…repent."

"Noted. I forgive you. And I mean that. So now there is no reason to go through with it. Right?"

"Ah, sure. I'll just forget about watching my platoon get blown up while my father was having a stroke a few thousand miles away. And I'll forget about passing out in a lawn chair while our daughter drowned in the pool at my feet. And I'll forget about suicidal tennis players and old men with their heads rolling in the gutter. I'll file all that away and get on with my life. Except I don't have a life. I've spent most of my money. I don't have a home or a job. You see Beatrice, one way or another, the end is near."

She jammed on the brakes harder than necessary at the next light. The unyielding seat belt sent a flashing pain through his torso. Beatrice turned to face him. "The dead old man and Francesca were not your fault."

Allmen sighed. He felt himself physically deflating like a deployed airbag after it had taken an impact. "My black cloud followed me, you know? People keep dying around me, because that is my punishment, I guess. Don't you think it's unfair for me to continue subjecting people around me to that kind of risk?"

"I blamed you for a long time, you know. I hated you for what happened."

"Yes, that was made fairly clear during the divorce proceedings."

"But I was wrong John. I didn't hate you. I hated that I couldn't fix you. That I couldn't make you see that post-traumatic stress isn't an absolute. Not every combat veteran comes back that way. You know, a lot of patients actually grow stronger from those kinds of horrible experiences."

"I know." *I used to be friends with one of them.* "So why am I so special?"

She put the car in gear again and they inched forward on a green light. "You aren't special at all. That's the point. You don't get to choose what happens to you in life, no one does. But you do get to choose how you react to it. The point is that you

221

are not a victim of circumstance John. You can choose. You can transcend all this, move on."

"Transcend? Move on? Even after killing your own daughter?"

"You didn't kill her." She said it flatly.

"I didn't save her either. When she needed me most, I wasn't there."

"You weren't yourself John. You were an addict. And sacrificing yourself won't in any way make that right."

"I don't know Beatrice. Maybe I'm just tired."

"Tired?

"Yeah, tired of everything I do blowing up on me, sometimes figuratively and sometimes quite literally."

"Ever heard of William James?"

He thought for a moment. "Yeah, I have. 'My first act of free will shall be to believe in free will.'" He shrugged. "I know the quote but not the man. Blame the public schools."

"He's basically the father of modern psychology."

"Your type of guy."

"Apparently yours too or you wouldn't remember that quote." Allmen was silent. "But before he was a psychologist, he was a depressed, suicidal failure. And then one day he decided that he'd stop feeling like a victim, like the world was against him. He vowed to take full responsibility for everything in his life for one year. And if, at that end of that year, he was indeed truly powerless and hadn't improved his life he'd end it. Sound familiar?"

"Sort of..."

"Spoiler alert, he didn't kill himself. You've had two years to attempt to take control and see that not everything is your fault. That there is plenty of good in the world. Plenty worth living for."

"If that was the game plan, it didn't go so great Beatrice."

They reached the hotel, pulling into loading zone and to his surprise, she parked illegally and turned off the ignition. Seeing his questioning look, she said, "I need to use your bathroom."

Again, the assumptive close.

He shrugged. "Sure, the more the merrier." But his voice was as cold and dull as the marble marker on Flora's grave.

They walked quietly through the capacious lobby, the clicking of heels echoing off of cleaned and polished tile. Something was tugging at Allmen's unconscious mind. Something in a file box that was incorrectly tagged. Some bit of information that didn't make sense.

"You know," Beatrice said conversationally as the elevator doors closed around them, "I can't step foot in this hotel without thinking of that Sean Connery movie they filmed here. The one about Alcatraz."

Alllmen nodded and something tumbled out of a mental file landing face up in a bright beam of light. He thought of Connery in another movie, one he'd watched in subtitles in another country just before…

"Wait a damn minute." They'd arrived at his floor but he reached to the panel and held the doors shut. "How did you know her name?"

"What? Who?" Beatrice was genuinely confused.

"Francesca. In the car, I mentioned a tennis player. But I never said her name. How would you know her name?"

Beatrice sighed. "It's a long story. Let me freshen up and I'll tell you." She put a light hand on his and removed it from the panel of steel buttons. The doors opened. Allmen followed her to his room. He noted that she knew exactly which one.

He sat on the bed and waited, trying to run various explanations through his fuddled brain. But the file boxes seemed to have spilled all over the space in his mind and he was having trouble putting them back in the right order.

"So, how would I have known you'd be at the cemetery today?" Beatrice asked, emerging through the bathroom door.

Allmen stared out the window and sighed. "Beatrice, enough weird shit has happened to me lately that I never gave it a second thought. But I assume some of the coincidences aren't really coincidences and that the insurance investigator with a wicked uppercut has something to do with...you?"

"The insurance company called me when you took out the policy and made me the beneficiary. I thought it smelled fishy. I called my cousin Lucy. She's in the industry and she offered to check on it for me. Things sort of snowballed from there."

It explained why the blonde woman, now that he could admit it, reminded him so much of his wife. Well, his ex-wife. He smiled ruefully. "So, you knew."

"Yeah, I figured it out. And I hoped that two years of blowing off steam in foreign locales would help you to cope. I kept track of you."

"Through Virgil." It wasn't a question.

"Lucy has worked with him before. At first, he didn't know what was going on. But he figured it out..."

Allmen glanced at his phone and Virgil's tracking device. "Why that little Judas!"

Beatrice held out two hands to stop him before he got going on a verbal tirade. "No, John. He's a friend. Probably the best one you've had for most of the past two years. But not the only one." She smiled. "And we are all worried about you."

Allmen gazed quietly down at the street for some time. Then he said tonelessly: "You should be worried about your car. It's getting towed."

"What the hell?" She brushed past him and gazed down at the street below. AAA Towing's beat up red monster truck had pulled up next to Beatrice's car and there was a silent mime show playing out between its driver and one of the hotel bellmen. "Shit. Listen, John, I'll be back. You aren't going to...well, you know? You'll be okay for a few minutes? Can we talk some more when I get back?"

"Talk? Sure." He watched her stride with a purpose out the door. He had loved her once, or at least thought he had. The truth was he didn't really know. He had been so damaged by years of anguish and then addiction and that he didn't know her as a person. It had all been about him, fixing him, healing him. It was, he realized, all rather selfish.

The door clicked shut behind her. It was like the tumbler on a safe sliding into place. Open now were all the dark spaces inside. Filing boxes of varying sizes and states of repair exposed to the light of day. He looked out over the sprawling little city to the cold waters of the bay. How horrible it must be to drown. The very first thing you are given at birth, breathe, taken away. Your vision narrowing, brain screaming for air until the darkness folds over you and then…nothing. No pain. Just a brief moment of recognition before you are gone. It was how Flora had gone. His baby girl had gone in the water and she had never come out.

It made Allmen feel…what exactly? *Sad.* Just sad? *No wonder Beatrice couldn't fix you. You suck at this.* There was more, certainly. Name it to tame it she had said. That was when she was merely his therapist and not yet his wife. *Name it to tame it.*

"Sad," he said aloud to the empty room. "Adrift, lonely…. guilty." He thought about the path he'd decided on years ago when he'd bought the insurance policy and quit his job. It was the path Hamlet and George Bailey had sought and that Ophelia found. The path of Dido and Cleopatra, and the lead singers for the Gin Blossoms and Nirvana. The way Bourdain and Hemingway had taken, and Cato opted for twice. The route of Van Gogh and Francesca. He'd wanted to leave some money behind, to make things right. But that probably wasn't going to happen. Other people would decide that. But Allmen could still take action. Couldn't he?

He stumbled in a trance to the bathroom, turning a light on the white tile of the bathroom. The tile was cold on his bare feet and he saw his reflection in the chrome handles of the cabinets, the faucets. And another reflection in the mirror over the sink. He was everywhere. He couldn't avoid his likeness. *Likeness maybe, but that is not my face.*

He realized staring into it that the cabinet mirror wasn't flush with the wall. It was open ever so slightly, a dim light shining inside and leaking out into the room. It was a stupid place to put the pills and he knew before he tugged it fully open that the shelves were empty.

"Beatrice," he whispered realizing she hadn't really come up here with a full bladder.

He closed the glass cabinet door gently with a soft sound. Click. A fat teardrop welled in the corner of his eye. It fell, streaming down his angular, once handsome face. *Name it to tame it.*

I am....lost, adrift, displaced, guilty.

Francesca had gotten it all wrong. She wasn't some plaything of fate. How many times had he heard her say 'what could I do?' She could have taken control, stopped being a toy and controlled her own destiny. But she didn't. He'd thought he respected her decision to walk out. Now the thought made him wince. Allmen had thought all along that he understood free will, that choosing to take his own life was the ultimate expression of it. *My first act of free will shall be to believe in free will. Well, I believed. I just didn't know what it really meant. Until now.*

But that isn't free will. It is the opposite.

Tears were streaming, some falling on the sink and the tile floor. He looked at his phone and thought of Virgil. Someone helping him, guiding him on a passage through dark times over two years. Someone he barely knew, but who cared enough about him to try and save him. And Beatrice. Beatrice had forgiven him. She was coming back for him. *I am not alone. I can handle the burden.*

He laughed then, despite the tears still dripping from his cheeks and chin. It was a croaking sound, equal parts anguish and relief. Beatrice had taken the pills away, wanting to save him. *I mean, come on Beatrice, I could have just thrown myself out the window.* But he knew now that he wouldn't do that. That he never really wanted to do any of it. He wouldn't give up. He'd been through hell. But he needed to keep going.

The end was near. *Hell, it gets nearer for all of us, every day.* But for John Allmen, the end wasn't today.

Libero arbitrio.

EPILOGUE:

D o not be afraid; our fate
Cannot be taken from us; it is a gift.

-Dante, Inferno Canto XV

T he office was in a business zoned cul-de-sac set back far enough from Highway 101 that most of the traffic noise was a mere buzz. Gary the Gnome's two year old Tesla wound its way silently through the parking lot and pulled to a stop at the spot near the front door. A man got out slowly from the passenger side, taking in the scene around him, smelling the slight hint of salt on the air from the marina a few blocks away. It was a glorious day full of sunshine in Northern California.

He approached the glass door with block lettering announcing the business headquarters of Circle Nine Travel and knocked softly before entering, the tinkling of a bell overhead announcing his presence.

A small man with dark, aquiline features and a friendly smile stood and emerged from behind a desk. It was a large metal framed desk, crowded with blinking monitors and small photos. *No, not photos....postcards.* The locales were familiar. *My postcards.*

"Virgil?"

The man nodded, his eyes widening and a pleasurable smile spreading.

"I'm John Allmen. Listen, I can't buy you a drink. I'm on the wagon. You know...rehab is for quitters. So, how about lunch?"

* * *

AUTHOR'S NOTE:

L ife Insurance benefits under Term Life Insurance coverage will not be paid if the Insured's death is a result of intentionally self-inflicted injuries, suicide or attempted suicide, while sane or insane, unless the insurance was continuously in effect for two years immediately before the death.

-Typical suicide clause of an insurance contract.

I t took me over eight years to finish this novel, and in that time, we lost over 50,000 military veterans to suicide. That is an average of 17.2 per day according to the Veterans Administrations' National Veteran Suicide Prevention Annual Report. The report notes that, when adjusted for age and sex, adult suicide rates were 52.3% higher for veterans than non-veterans. Despite an estimated $2.5 billion donated annually to more than 40,000 military related charities in the United States, the problem isn't going away.

To my friends on "the green team" I apologize for culturally appropriating a Marine ground pounder. As a former Naval Flight Officer who trained in Close Air Support at Camp Lejeune,

NC, I have nothing but respect and admiration for the job you (and the fictional John Allmen) were called to do. For a generation, we've waged continuous war in far off lands, reaping a harvest of mental illness, addiction, homelessness and suicide. I've used the names and circumstances of many famous people in this book (borrowing the technique from Dante Alighieri, I admit) to highlight the problem. I hope they can forgive me. As for the veterans of foreign conflicts, these aren't famous people. They are your neighbors, friends, perhaps your family. Their stories should be told too. I've tried, in my own way, to do that.

Suicide, which for unknown reasons rises in the springtime, can be stopped. Researchers believe that interventions can be effective, that stopping a single attempt can obviate the desire for self-harm in the long term. But, like the fictional Virgil and Beatrice, someone has to notice. Someone has to care. Someone has to say something so that those going through hell...can keep going.

-Patrick Huey
November 2022

ABOUT THE AUTHOR

Patrick Huey

Patrick Huey is a native of Pennsylvania, now splitting time with his wife and son between the Gulf Coast of Florida and the Pacific Northwest. He is a United States Navy veteran with over 1,400 hours in various types of aircraft including the F-14 Tomcat and F-18F Super Hornet. While on active duty he earned the Strike Fighter Air Medal flying combat support missions during two overseas deployments in Iraq and Afghanistan. He is the author of History Lessons for the Modern Investor and The Seven Pillars of (Financial) Wisdom. This is his first novel.

Made in the USA
Monee, IL
28 November 2022

18813730R00134